DON'T RUSH ME

NORA JACOBS
BOOK ONE

JACKIE MAY

Edition 2.0

Edited by Jennifer Henkes (www.literallyjen.com)

Cover art by Joshua Oram

For Kelly. I wrote this one just for you!

CHAPTER ONE

It always starts with a tingling sensation on the back of my neck that runs down my arms, leaving a trail of goose bumps in its wake. It settles heavily in my stomach—a thick feeling of dread—and I just know: Someone bad is coming. The premonitions are vague, simple warnings of approaching evil or danger. They're feelings I've learned to listen to.

I glance around the city bus and see who I think is the problem. Aside from the few people on their way home from a long day at work, there's a group of guys being rowdy near the back. That's typical for public transit in Detroit, so I didn't think much of it when I got on the bus, but I've caught the attention of one of them. He's staring at me rather hard, and when he catches me looking his way, he gives me a nod. "Hey, baby, why don't you come back here, and we can get to know each other a little?"

To respond, or not to respond? Which would piss him off less? "I have a boyfriend, sorry." It's a lie; I don't date. But it's the easiest way to reject the man in front of all his buddies.

I quickly look away, praying he isn't one of those determined guys, or one who will feel the need to get his friends involved in harassing me.

"Aw, come on, baby, don't be like that. I don't see your boyfriend here."

Great. He's not going to leave it alone. Oh well, I'm almost home. If I can just get off the bus without trouble, I can hurry the one block to my apartment and lock myself in until whatever the danger is passes.

My phone dings as the closest person I have to a friend texts me.

SorcererX: P? You there? Where'd you go? You okay?

P is short for *PsychoPsychic*. It's my online handle on a few of the paranormal message boards X and I both frequent. We don't know each other in person, so we just call each other our screen names. I'm P, and he's X.

PsychoPsychic: Fine. Just getting harassed by some guy on the way home. No worries, though. He's being mellow, and mine's the next stop.

SorcererX: Be careful. If he follows you when you get off, call the police. And message me when you get home safe.

I smile at that.

PsychoPsychic: Will do.

As the bus nears my stop, the guy in the back quits trying to get my attention, but the feeling in my stomach intensifies. I'm still in danger. I take a deep breath and fight to keep my heart at a calm pace. Panicking won't do me any good. If he follows me off the bus, I'll need to have my wits in place.

"Hey, are you okay?"

I glance up from my phone at the new voice. The guy who's been sitting across the aisle from me since we both left the library at closing time is watching me with a concerned expression. I've noticed him before. He's cute, in a nerd-chic way. He's tall and lean, a year or two older than me—twenty-five at the most—with a head of wavy light-brown hair and beautiful amber-colored eyes. I've seen him three or four times a week, since I realized I needed to avoid my current living situation as much as possible, and started spending all my free time after work at the public library. Still, we've never spoken before.

"I'm fine," I say.

He smiles at my reply and brushes his bangs out of his eyes. "I'm Oliver."

I nod but don't give up any further conversation.

He tries again. "I've seen you around the library."

I narrow my eyes. Why has he chosen this moment—right as my premonition hit—to be so chatty, when he's spent the last few months only sneaking glances at me and trying to work up the nerve to say *hi?* Could he be the person my gift is warning me about? I don't want to believe it, but I can't rule it out.

I force a brittle smile and nod again. "Sure. Computer near the water fountain. I've been debating for weeks if it's online college classes or a *World of Warcraft* addiction."

My response shocks him. It doesn't match the stay-away-I-bite vibe I generally give off. I'm a loner who avoids people like the plague, yes, but I'm not inherently bitchy. It's just hard to hide my gift from people when I'm thrown into their heads every time I'm touched. I don't know why I have the gifts I have, or how I got them, but they've been saving me most of my life, so I don't complain. Lonely is better than dead.

My friendliness gives Oliver a boost of confidence. His smile widens just a bit, and his eyes light up. "Criminal justice courses." Smirking, he adds, "And *Dragon Quest X*. Not *World of Warcraft*."

I laugh once. I can't help myself. Despite my wariness of his sudden desire to strike up conversation at the same time my premonition hit, his answer makes me chuckle. "Nice. I'm Nora."

"It's nice to meet you, Nora."

The bus turns a corner onto my street, and the feeling in my stomach explodes with intensity. I pull in a long breath through my nose and let it out slowly.

"Are you sure you're okay?" Oliver asks. "You look like you're going to pass out. Do you want me to walk you home?"

The question raises my suspicions again. Oliver seems innocent enough, but I know exactly how deceiving appearances can be, and the premonition is only getting stronger.

My body is screaming at me to protect myself. My hands are trembling now, and a light sheen of sweat breaks out along my hairline. "This isn't your stop," I say with a shake of my head.

He shrugs. "Mine is the next one. It's not that far. I'd feel better knowing you made it home all right."

Now he's making me nervous. I need to get off this bus alone. "It's only half a block. I can make it. Thanks, though."

The hope in his eyes dims a little. "Okay. If you're sure."

He looks genuine, but without touching him, I can't be certain. "I'm sure. Thanks."

The bus rumbles to a slow stop, and the feeling of dread seizes my chest so hard that I can barely breathe.

The guy in the back is still watching me—frowning at me—and now Oliver is watching me closely, too. I can't tell which one of them means me harm. I need to get out of here. I'm so anxious that I stumble a little as I get to my feet. Oliver jumps up as well. "Please, let me help. You're really pale."

When he reaches for my hand, I catch a quick glimpse of his thoughts. He's imagining us walking down my street together. He wants to get me home safely. He's worried about me. He thinks a woman like me shouldn't be alone on the streets of Detroit ever, much less after dark.

The image of me in his mind is practically glowing. I'm tall and slender. I don't really have many womanly curves to brag about, but he thinks I'm beautiful anyway. He likes my sea green eyes even though they look haunted, and he thinks my long, shiny brunette hair is commercial worthy. He's never seen me smile, but he's sure it would be radiant if I did, and he wishes I would do it. He's kinder to me than I am. I don't think I'm as pretty as he sees me.

He's a nice guy. I feel terrible for thinking he could have been the monster my gift is warning me about. This is why I can't have friends. I would suck at being one. I pull away from him, needing to escape his mind. He takes my rejection the wrong way and sits back down, muttering, "Sorry."

Part of me wants to let him walk me home, but there's no point. No friendship I've ever had has lasted long. It's better to keep to myself. "I'll be fine," I assure him again. I lean closer and lower my voice. "But if any of those guys follow me off the bus, call 911 for me, okay?"

Oliver's frown deepens, but he nods reluctantly. "Be safe," he says.

I give him a small smile. "You too. It was nice meeting you."

Shouldering my backpack full of my grease-stained work clothes, I make my way off the bus. Each step takes so much effort it feels as if I'm wading through waist-deep snow. The second the bus pulls away from the curb, the reason for my premonition becomes clear. I let out a soft curse. I should have let Oliver walk me home. Should have stayed on the bus. I was an idiot for only thinking the trouble was with me instead of possibly lying in wait for me. I should have known better.

An unfamiliar car is parked on the other side of the street beneath a lamp. My creepy neighbor, Xavier, and one of his friends are hanging out in front of it. Xavier is leaning against the hood and peels away from it as if he's been waiting for me. My stomach churns.

I grew up in the foster system since I was six years old. Some of the families I was placed with were nice and genuinely wanted to help. The last family I was with when I turned eighteen wasn't. The wife worked all the time, leaving me with her drunk of a husband who couldn't keep his hands to himself. I got the hell out the day I turned eighteen, but unfortunately that led to me taking an apartment in a slumerific building in the worst part of Detroit. I've grown up here, so I'm used to it, but lately I've had a problem with my neighbor Xavier.

Technically, Xavier's dad is my neighbor. He happens to be my landlord, but I don't see him much. Xavier, on the other hand, is around all the time now. He just started his third year at Wayne State University. He lives in the dorms, but he was home all summer and doesn't seem to want to go back now that classes have started. He's got more interest in me than school.

Pretending not to see him, I turn toward the apartments and take off at a brisk walk. If I can just make it inside my place, I'll be safe.

"Hey, Nora!"

His voice, though innocent and cheerful, makes my skin crawl. Every time he touches me, I'm momentarily pulled into his head. I hear his thoughts, feel his intentions toward me. His disgusting mind terrifies me.

I pick up my pace and don't stop until his hand grabs my arm. "Where do you think you're going?"

Instantly, I'm flooded with his feelings and intentions. The images that flash in my mind make me shudder. He's not just perverted; he's twisted. The things he plans to do to me are degrading, painful, and sick. He prefers his women to feel like victims. He gets off on their fear.

A small squeak escapes me. "Xavier!" I gasp, clutching my chest as I feign surprise. "Hey. What are you doing here?"

My heart races as I glance down the street. I'm not close enough. Even if I could break away from him and make a run for it, I wouldn't make it to my apartment. He'd catch me.

Xavier's eyes narrow, and the side of his mouth twitches as if he's suppressing a smirk. He's surprised me. He knows I'm panicking on the inside, and he's enjoying it. "I was waiting for you. Pops said it's your birthday. I thought I'd take you out to celebrate."

I feel his pleasure as he says the words. I sense his arousal and excitement. He's waited for this since the first time he saw me. He thinks I'm a virgin because I don't date and don't even talk to guys, if I can help it. He's both wrong and right. Technically, I'm not a virgin. But at the same time, I have never experienced the act of making love. What my first foster father used to do to me doesn't count.

Anyway, Xavier knows there's a lot I haven't experienced, and he can't wait to be the first one to please me that way—not that he actually could. He especially likes the fact that it's my birthday. He feels as if he's giving me some kind of amazing gift.

He flashes me a smile that anyone else in the world would find charming. He's a handsome guy. He's tall and lean, with a gorgeous smile, golden-caramel eyes, and an athletic build from the vast amounts of sports he plays. Despite his good looks, I find him repulsive, and he knows it. It drives him crazy.

"Sorry, Xavier. I'm not feeling so well tonight. Maybe another time."

His jaw clenches so tight I'm amazed I don't hear his teeth grinding. He knows what I'm doing. I've been successfully dodging him for weeks. In fact, that's probably why he was waiting at the bus stop instead of closer to home. He wouldn't be able to force me out of my apartment once I was safely locked inside, and he knows I'd never go with him willingly.

People leave behind psychic imprints on the things they touch. Thanks to my gift, I'm able to pick up those imprints. The stronger a person's emotion at the time they touch an object, the longer the imprint stays, and the more vivid the vision I receive.

Xavier swiped my key from his father's collection and started breaking into my apartment a few weeks ago. He left behind enough imprints to give me nightmares for the rest of my life. I found the cameras he tried to hide in my ceiling fan, on my bookshelf, and in the vent above the bathroom shower. Last week I went to get a drink from the two-liter of soda in the fridge, and I caught a glimpse of the roofie he'd slipped in it.

I saw the suspicion in his eyes when I came out of my apartment later that evening with the empty bottle and wasn't the least bit drugged. He doesn't know how I've been avoiding his traps, but he knows I've been doing it intentionally, and it makes him angry. As angry as the fact that I haven't fallen for his charm. Tonight it seems he's reached his breaking point. "But it's your birthday," he insists.

I shrug. "I've never really celebrated my birthday."

His smile returns, wider than before. The victorious gleam in his eyes churns my stomach. "All the more reason to make sure this one is special. You're twenty-two, right? That's as good an age as any to celebrate."

"Sorry. I had a long day at work today, and I'm exhausted. I'm going to have to pass. Thanks, though."

I try to maneuver around him, but he grabs me by the waist and steers me toward his waiting friend. "I don't think so."

My heart starts racing. I dig my feet into the ground. When I try to escape him, his grip becomes painfully tight. "You're not ditching me again," he snaps. I startle at the venom in his voice, and he immediately calms himself. "There's no way out of this, Nora. You're all mine tonight."

I don't need my gift to recognize the double meaning in his words. When I glare at him, his cheeks flush with anger, and I suddenly feel a knife poking in my side. "Don't embarrass me. You'll regret it if you do."

Thanks to the knife, I have no choice but to go with him. I know he won't hesitate to use it. His thoughts prove that.

Xavier smiles at his friend. The guy nods back and slips into the front of the car while Xavier yanks me over by the arm and forces me into the backseat. "Hey, Parker, you don't mind playing chauffeur, right? My girl wants me to sit with her."

His knife hidden again, Xavier slides in after me. He looks at the guy in the driver's seat. "Parker, this is Nora." He points to Parker and says, "Nora, this is my new friend, Parker."

Parker is a little older than Xavier, maybe late twenties, and he looks like a GQ model. His clothes are obviously expensive. He's got dark, short stylish hair, and striking blue eyes. He's gorgeous. *Too bad he's hanging out with Xavier.*

Parker nods at me and then starts the car. "It's nice to meet you, Nora. You're even lovelier than Xavier said you were."

I'm more thrown off by the manners than the compliment, but I don't have time to dwell on it, because Xavier snakes his fingers up my thigh and says, "And tonight she's all mine."

I shove his hand away. "That's not happening."

Parker glances at me in the rearview mirror with shrewd

eyes while Xavier chuckles and slips his arm over my shoulder, dragging me into his side. "Nora loves to play hard to get," he says to Parker, "but I'm feeling lucky tonight."

He pulls me even closer and pushes his free hand beneath my shirt. I try to squirm away, but he's holding me too tightly. He brushes his lips along the length of my neck and says, "You know you want it, baby. I'll have you begging me for it before the night is over."

He laughs as if he's just said the world's funniest joke.

"Get *off* me."

I try to break free again, and this time, thankfully, he lets me go with a sigh. "All right, all right, relax." He rolls his eyes at Parker in the rearview mirror. "Apparently we need to get the virgin a little looser before she's ready for me. What do you think, should we hit up Club Noir?"

Parker frowns. "That's a bit rough for her. Let's go someplace better. Perhaps Vortex?"

"Too many rich douche bags," Xavier says. He smirks at Parker. "No offense."

Parker ignores the jab. Apparently he's rich, not that I couldn't have guessed by the car and the clothes. "What about Motown?" he asks.

Xavier thinks about it and nods. "Yeah, that could work."

My head starts spinning with ideas. If he plans to take me to a club before dragging me back to his dorm room or some cheap motel, I might have a chance to escape. Especially if I can get him drunk. But I have to get him to let his guard down first, which means playing along a little. Hopefully I can do that without getting sick. "Are we really going dancing?" I ask. "I've never been to a club before."

Xavier grins at me. "It's your night, birthday girl. You like dancing?"

"I *love* dancing."

Batting my eyelashes at him might be a bit much, but he falls for it enough that he slides a possessive arm around me again. He looks down at me through hooded eyes and speaks in a low, husky voice. "You never told me you like to dance."

The lustful thoughts I'm picking up from him are enough to drown me. Swallowing back my revulsion, I force another smile and shrug. "You've never asked. I'm not very good at it, though."

"I doubt that." Xavier shivers and graces me with a vision of the two of us grinding on a crowded dance floor. His hands are holding me in places that shouldn't be touched in public. "Motown, it is," he rasps, "and step on it."

"Actually..." An idea pops into my head that I can't ignore. I wait until I have his full attention before finishing my sentence. "If you're going to take me to my first club, I want to go to Underworld."

Xavier's jaw falls slack, and Parker glances sharply at me in the rearview mirror.

"Underworld?" Xavier hoots in amusement. "Girl, you've got a lot more spunk than I gave you credit for." He smiles at me again, but this time it's patronizing. "Baby, you are way too sweet for a place like Underworld. Hell, *I'm* way too sweet for that club."

"It's not so bad," I insist. "A guy who comes into the garage I work at goes there all the time. He says it's intense."

"Nora, Underworld is dangerous. Crazy shit happens there. Unexplainable shit. They say it's cursed."

"Rumors." I roll my eyes, faking a confidence I don't feel. I don't doubt the place is cursed, considering the creatures that run it and have their fun within its walls. Neither of the guys in this car knows what kind of true monsters frequent that nightmarish place. They believe humans are the only intelligent beings in this world. They believe we're the most dangerous things out there. They're wrong. I learned that for myself when I was only six. Since then, my awareness had grown thanks to the message boards and people like SorcererX.

X told me that Underworld is the central hub for the supernatural community in Detroit. Humans stupid enough to go there usually end up being some monster's prey. With my gift, I'll have a chance at getting out unscathed, but Xavier won't. At least, that's what I'm hoping for. Maybe it's a cruel fate, but it's no worse than the plans he has for me. "Are you *scared*, Xavier?" I taunt, hoping he won't be able to refuse.

Parker finally speaks up. "Aren't you?"

He pins me with an intense look that I can't decipher. I don't like the way he's staring. I've made him suspicious, and it's never good to have someone curious about me. There's too much I can't explain. Too much I can't hide. I try to look impassive as I lift a shoulder and let it drop. "Not really." Glancing at Xavier, I mutter under my breath, "Underworld is no more dangerous than my present company."

In the rearview mirror, Parker's eyes narrow and slide from me to Xavier for a brief moment, as if he heard exactly what I said and understands my meaning. He eventually returns his focus back to the road.

Xavier shakes his head. "All right, fine, but I'll have to call a friend to help us get in."

I frown at the thought that Xavier knows someone who could get us into Underworld. He even sounds like he's been there before. Humans can't get into Underworld on their own very easily—I was banking on my gifts to help us get in. I don't like that Xavier hangs out with monsters who could grant him access to Underworld, whether he knows what they are or not.

Xavier misinterprets my frown to be confusion. "They're really selective about who can enter," he explains. "Without a regular with us, we're not nearly pierced, tatted, or scarred enough to get in. Not to mention, you aren't dressed slutty enough."

"I can get us in." Parker's low voice is confident.

"For real?" Xavier asks. "I knew I liked you. Are you a regular there? Or a VIP?"

Parker ignores Xavier and meets my gaze. "If you're absolutely certain you want to go there. Xavier isn't wrong about Underworld's reputation. It *is* dangerous."

I'm curious how Parker knows this. He seems to have first-hand experience with the place—which in itself is frightening—but since it's what I want, I don't press the matter. The thought of going there scares the hell out of me; no one knows exactly how dangerous that place is better than I do. I don't want to have anything to do with underworlders, but the enemy of my enemy is my ally, so I steel my resolve and meet Parker's solemn eyes with determination. "Yes. I'm sure I want to go there."

He holds his stare a moment longer and then nods. "You're the birthday girl."

CHAPTER TWO

Underworld is exactly the type of club you'd expect it to be, judging by its name. Deep in the bowels of Detroit, it feels like a gateway from one world to another. It's dark, dangerous, and magical. Though most humans can't recognize it for what it is, they feel its power and instinctively shy away. The lucky ones, anyway. The outside of the club matches the abandoned warehouses that surround it. You'd never know it was here if not for the pounding bass and crowd of punk and goth partiers standing alongside of the building, waiting to get in.

Once we arrive, Xavier and I head for the back of the line, but Parker shakes his head and walks straight toward the bouncer. The way the people in line watch us as we bypass them makes me shiver. I can't tell what they are without touching them, but I can guess at a few. Some are curious, others are annoyed, and some smile pleasantly at us. Those are the ones who frighten me the most. It's the friendly ones that you really need to watch out for.

Guarding the front door is a man nearly seven and a half feet tall and at least half as wide. If I had to guess, I'd say he's a troll, but I don't care to get close enough to find out. His head is so bald the moonlight shines off of it. He has piercings in his ears, nose, and eyebrows, and he's playing with a stud in his tongue as we walk up. "Parker," he greets in a low, rumbling voice as he extends an arm the size of a tree trunk. "Back so soon? I thought you'd be busy with—"

"Oh, I am," Parker says, cutting the man off as he shakes his hand. His eyes flick briefly to Xavier and me before he smiles at the bouncer again. "You know me. Always busy with something."

The bouncer's gaze roams over Xavier and me, and he nods slowly. "I gotcha." He looks back at Parker. "Well, don't work all night. Make sure you blow off a little steam while you're here."

"I will."

I don't like this. Something's going on. Parker's obviously a regular here, and he's too interested in Xavier and me. That can only mean one thing. Parker isn't human, and whatever he is, it's something powerful enough to be a VIP at Underworld. Maybe I've been wrong all along. Maybe my premonition isn't a warning against Xavier. Maybe my real problem is Parker.

Parker and the bouncer fall into a whispered conversation. The words *humans*, *suspects*, and *her idea* startle me from my thoughts. I look up to see both Parker and the bouncer watching me with curiosity, suspicion even. I don't know what I'd be a suspect for, but this whole situation makes me sick to my stomach. What has Xavier dragged me into, and did I make it worse by coming here? It would be just my luck.

I know better than to admit I'm aware of their world or show any fear. Pulling my shoulders back, I meet Parker's gaze with not just confidence, but attitude. Underworlders respect arrogance. "Is there a problem, Parker? I thought you said you could get us in."

The bouncer's pierced brows climb up his huge, shiny forehead, and his mouth quirks up on one side into a crooked smile. "I don't like trouble in my club, little lady. You're not looking to start any, are you?"

I match his smirk. "Define *trouble*."

The bouncer's smile grows into a wide grin, and he folds his watermelon biceps in front of his chest. "Feisty little brunettes with not enough sense of self-preservation."

I grin. I can't help myself. "We're good, then," I assure him, "because I'm all about self-preservation."

The bouncer shakes his head, chuckling, and nods to Xavier. "And him?"

I shrug. "A harmless frat boy looking for a good time who doesn't have enough brains to know he needs any self-preservation."

At that, the bouncer throws his head back and laughs. The sound is so bellowing it shakes the walls of the club. Definitely a troll. "You've found yourself a winner, Parker. Just make sure you keep an eye on her. She's trouble, all right."

When he pulls the rope back to let me pass, I wink at him and stride through. Xavier enters behind me. I turn around just in time to catch Xavier glare at the bouncer. "She's not with Parker, she's *mine*."

The troll could snap Xavier in half with his pinky finger, but he can also see that Xavier isn't worth the time and effort. He raises a questioning brow at me. When I roll my eyes, he laughs again.

Parker is last to pass the bouncer. As he does, the troll clasps his big, meaty hand on Parker's shoulder. I have to strain to hear their conversation, but I'm fairly certain the troll says, "You sure about that one? I like her."

Parker's response is too low to make out, but he smiles and pats the bouncer's arm reassuringly. I'm not sure if I feel safer or more worried to have Parker's attention. I need to find out what he is so I can figure out how to ditch him, but when I hang back to wait for him, Xavier slips his arm around my waist and pulls me into the club.

When we walk through the door, I feel the slight tingle of magic, as if we've passed through a glamour or a protection ward. Xavier doesn't notice a thing. Most humans wouldn't. I think I feel the magic because of my gift, but it could just be that I know it exists, so I'm more tuned in.

I don't know a lot about magic other than what it feels like. There's a lot of info online, but I never know what information I can really trust, and aside from SorcererX, I don't make a habit of befriending people who could give me facts. I think X might be an actual sorcerer, but he's always been very vague on the details when I ask him about magic. Sorcerers don't like giving up their secrets.

Inside, the club is very posh. There are several different rooms, with different types of music playing. My guess is they cater to different species of underworlders and their unique tastes for pleasure. I'm curious, but not enough to want to stick around here any longer than necessary, so when Xavier drags me straight into the largest dance hall, I don't argue.

The walls are black, and the furniture scattered around the edges of the dance floor is plush and bloodred. There's a stage set up in the front for the DJ, and there are dancing cages on either side. At least, I hope they're used for dancing. The bar lines the entire back wall, and since it's early yet, that's where the majority of the crowd is gathered. The dance floor is still pretty open.

Scanning the dim room, I quickly find what I'm looking for. A woman sits at the bar, staring out at the crowd on the dance floor as a lion would watch a herd of gazelles. Her slinky dress shows off more curves than a Victoria's Secret model. She has flawless skin, long, sleek hair that's dark as night, and eyes just as black. She's beautiful—too beautiful to be human—and she's on the prowl.

Xavier's eyes find the same woman, and he gulps. This is going to be too easy. I don't feel bad for what I'm about to do. Even if that creature does take interest in him, he'll probably still survive. The monsters here aren't stupid. There are rumors, but if there were too many actual human disappearances, the club would garner too much attention. Rule number one in the underworld is: Don't let the humans know you exist. Underworlders are nothing if not cautious and discreet.

Xavier blinks himself back from his stupor and smiles at me. His fingers dig into my hip. "I didn't expect this from you, Nora. You're full of surprises."

His fantasies have changed since my conversation with the bouncer. They've gone in a much more dominatrix direction. He no longer thinks of me as a victim, but is excited at the possibility that I might play rough with him. He's revolting, but now that I'm in the presence of real danger, my fear of him seems almost silly. I twist out of his grip and give him a coy smile. "Of course I'm surprising. You don't know anything about me."

His eyes flash eagerly—he's excited that I'm playing along. "Dance with me."

Dancing with him is the last thing I plan to do tonight. Shaking my head, I point to the open space at the bar next to the seductive underworlder. "Drinks first."

Xavier grins, but when he grabs my hand and starts to lead us to the bar, Parker steps in the way, a slight frown on his face. "You don't strike me as much of a drinker."

He's right. I don't drink. Ever. Especially not in a place where I could be served faerie drinks. Again, I don't know facts, but there's a lot of speculation about the effects of faerie drinks on humans, and none of it's good. That's enough to sell me off the stuff forever.

I keep my face impassive, though I'm impressed Parker can read me so easily. I'm curious as to why he's trying to stop me from having a drink. If he's the danger I'm supposed to be looking out for, I would think he'd want me impaired. Still, I need to get to the bar. "I told you, I'm self-conscious about my dancing. I need alcohol."

He starts to argue, but the suspicious look I give him keeps him quiet. He may know I'm up to something, but he is, too, and he doesn't want me to figure out whatever secret he's hiding. He steps aside, sweeping a hand out from me to the bar as if to say *Go ahead.* The look on his face is much closer to *It's your funeral.*

I lead the way, heading straight for the woman I noticed before. She's still there. Her attention is focused on a couple out on the dance floor that could use a lesson in PDA etiquette.

As I reach the bar, I roll my ankle and stumble slightly into the woman. I grab her arm to brace myself. She turns to me with a glare, but I've already accomplished my goal. Her thoughts fill me. She's angry. She was skimming energy from the lusty couple, and I've interrupted her feeding. "I'm *so* sorry," I say, letting my hand rest on her arm so I can continue to gauge her thoughts.

I know what she is, and she's more perfect than I expected. I figured her to be one of the fae, but she's a succubus, a demonic creature that feeds off of lust. She lures her prey to bed and sucks their life force from them while they're in the throes of passion.

"That was so clumsy of me," I gush. "I guess I'm a bit nervous to be here—obviously, this isn't my normal scene—but I couldn't let my friend down. He *insisted* we party tonight." I drop my voice into a whisper and giggle as I add, "He can get pretty wild."

She thinks I'm a vapid human, but I've piqued her interest

with the mention of my friend. A human male unspoken for by another underworlder. That's rare for this club. She hadn't come here tonight to hunt, but this is too good an opportunity to pass up. Plus, she thinks it would serve me right for being so annoying.

The woman looks Xavier over, and a brief smile flicks across her face. "Is that so?" Her hand falls gently to Xavier's forearm, and her voice becomes a purr. "I can get pretty wild myself." Slipping her finger from Xavier's arm over to his chest, she drags it up and down his abdomen. Xavier shivers beneath her touch. The woman's pupils swell in response. "I have a private room here in the club. Would you like to join me there?"

"I..." Xavier blinks and shakes his head. He meets my eyes, frowning in confusion. "I came here for Nora. I...we..."

The woman pulls his gaze back with a finger under his chin. She leans in close to him and takes a deep breath. "Nora can come with us," she purrs. "I don't mind parties of three."

Xavier is gone now, lost to her seductive allure. He nods his head, unable to take his eyes from her. She grins victoriously. As she stands up from her stool and takes Xavier's hand, she smiles at me. "Shall we, lovely Nora?"

I flash her a big, fake smile and step back so that I'm out of her reach. "Oh, you guys go ahead. I'm more of a one-on-one kind of girl. I'd spoil your fun."

The succubus cocks her head to the side. The way she's watching me, I'm afraid she's figured out what I'm doing. After a moment, she lets the suspicion pass. "Suit yourself." Her eyes slide to Parker. "And you, Parker? Care to join us? You know you're always welcome."

I'm not surprised that the succubus knows Parker, and I don't wait around to hear his answer. As soon as his attention turns from me to the woman, I slip away as quickly and quietly as I can. I hurry past the bar and out the club entrance. My new friend, the troll bouncer, sees me before I can completely escape. "Leaving so soon, Trouble?"

I smirk and lift a shoulder into a shrug. "No offense, but it's a little too tame in there for me."

He matches my grin, and my smile becomes sincere. If he weren't an ancient magical creature that likes to eat the occasional human, I could almost like him.

"Aren't you missing a few companions?" he asks.

I feign a look of surprise and glance to either side of me. "Well, I suppose I am. How 'bout that?" When he frowns, I wink at him. "It's like I told you. I'm all about self-preservation."

His confusion turns to comprehension, and a look of pride washes over his face. "You hurry yourself home, then, Trouble. And be careful. These streets get rough at night."

I give him one last smile and a salute, then spin on my heel and hurry away from the club. My gift has settled, but I'm not out of the woods yet. I'm still a woman alone on the streets of Detroit after dark. If I can just get to the nearest bus stop without running into a gang or any stray underworlders, I should be okay.

A soft, low voice suddenly speaks from right behind me. "Going somewhere, Nora?"

I jump at the noise. My feet freeze, and I cringe. I knew Parker wouldn't fall victim to the succubus, but I was hoping he wouldn't find me before I disappeared. He's on to me. He knows I did what I did intentionally. But exactly how much of the truth has he put together? What does he suspect about me?

Steeling my gaze, I glance over my shoulder. "I'm going home. The club scene isn't really my thing."

His eyes narrow. "You want to tell me what all that was about, then?"

"Not especially. Have a good night, Parker. It was nice

meeting you, but you'd better get back in there before Xavier gets in trouble or something."

I start walking again. Parker won't let me go, but maybe he'll let me get as far as the bus stop. If I can stall him until a bus comes, I'll be safe. There's not much he can do to me with an audience.

"Nora." He grabs my hand, whirling me around to face him.

I could pull out of his grip—he's not holding me tightly—but I stand still and let his thoughts and intentions hit me. I need to know what I'm up against.

He stares at me for a long time, unsure what to say. He's confused. His thoughts are on a beautiful Middle-Eastern woman. She's missing, and for some reason he's wondering if I'm involved.

"Nora, what you did to your friend back there—"

"Xavier is *not* my friend," I snap, anger and fatigue bubbling up inside me. My premonition has finally left me, and my system is crashing like I'm coming down from an adrenaline rush. "I don't know if you noticed, but he basically abducted me back there. All I did was bring him to a place where I knew he'd find someone shinier and more in the mood to play his sick games. Now, if you'll excuse me, I've had a long day, and I just want to go home and crawl into bed. Alone."

Parker's still gripping my hand, not ready to let me leave. He's frustrated. He doesn't understand how I know about his world—if I even do. He thinks I do, but he's not positive. He intends to get answers, but he's not sure how to go about it.

It's hard not to get lost in his eyes. They're beautiful—piercingly blue and hooded by mile-long thick, dark lashes. The rest of him is just as gorgeous.

His pupils dilate, and his grip tightens the tiniest bit. He senses my attraction to him, and it's driving him mad. Watching me stand up to Terrance—who I assume is the troll—

and ditch my psycho neighbor is the most amazing thing he's ever seen a human do. If I weren't a suspect in his case, he would take me somewhere right now and have his way with me until the sun comes up.

But there's another desire growing in him as well. Thirst. I smell mouthwatering. He's trying to convince himself that I'm not involved with Nadine's disappearance and to let me go. I'm too tempting. With his current state of excitement, he's afraid he might lose control. He doesn't want to hurt me.

When I realize what he is, I tear myself out of his grip, unable to stop the horrified gasp that escapes me. He's the worst of all monsters. I loathe his kind above any other. They're ruthless, bloodsucking, twisted killers. Parker is one of the same soulless abominations that killed my mother.

Vampires can smell fear—this I *do* know for a fact—but I can't help the terror that surges through me. It's suffocating. Paralyzing. My entire body trembles as I back away from him. I need more distance between us—not that it would matter, if he decides to attack. He can move inhumanly fast. I'll never escape him.

A deep crease forms in Parker's brow. "Nora? What's wrong?"

I'm unable to make more than a whisper of a sound. "Stay away from me."

He jerks with a start as realization sweeps over him. My heart skips a beat or two. He knows I know. I'm so dead. "You know what I am," he says.

I shake my head frantically. "I don't know what you're talking about."

I take another step back, and he grabs me again, gracing me with his thoughts once more. He's beyond frustrated now. He knows he should hand me over to Henry, but he wants me for himself, and he's afraid Henry would claim me. Or destroy me.

That's enough of that. I yank myself out of his grip.

Parker's eyes flash red, and in a blink he's holding me painfully tight against his chest. "Don't *lie* to me. You know the secrets of the underworld, don't you? *How?*"

I keep up with my lie. "I don't know what you're talking about."

His fangs haven't descended, but I know they're there. The hideous creature makes my skin crawl. I don't want him touching me. I don't want to be inside his head. I'm so afraid I can't breathe, and my eyes prick with unwelcome tears.

Parker sees the revulsion in my eyes, hears my unsteady heart, smells my fear. He's confused by it, and angry, but he's also hurt. He doesn't like my instant rejection of him or his kind. "I'm not going to hurt you."

I don't believe him. He's going to kill me.

He keeps me pinned to him. I try to fight him off, even though it's futile. He's too strong. I can't escape. "Let go of me!"

"Nora, calm down. I won't hurt you."

"Liar!" I try again in vain to break free. "If you don't want to hurt me, why won't you let me go? I didn't do anything to you. I don't even know you."

"But you know other things. You're involved in things you shouldn't be, aren't you? You took Xavier to that club knowing what waited for him there. What were you doing, tying up loose ends?"

"Are you delusional? I was *escaping* him, not trying to get rid of him."

"Harsh way to ditch someone. Do you have any idea what that woman was? What she will do to him?"

My fear vanishes. It's pushed out of my body by my hatred. I glare into Parker's eyes—eyes that I hate for being so mesmerizing. "Do you have any idea what *he* intended to do to *me?* What he's been trying to do to me for months? I hope that she-demon sucks every last ounce of life from him until there's nothing left. I hope she tortures him the way he wanted to hurt me—the way I *know* he's tormented others. I hope she kills him. Then he won't be able to hurt me, or anyone else, ever again."

I feel Parker's sympathy for me in his thoughts, and his repulsion for Xavier, but I've admitted outright my knowledge of the underworld now, and that Xavier has been hurting women. Parker thinks I must know more about Nadine than I'm telling him, even if I don't know who Nadine is specifically. He thinks I can give him answers that I honestly don't have.

I wouldn't be surprised if Xavier is involved in the disappearance of Parker's friend—the prick dragged me off tonight at knifepoint—but I don't know anything about it. "I can't help you. I don't know what Xavier's up to. I'm just his neighbor. He forced me to come with you guys tonight. I was probably just the next girl on his list. I don't know anything about your missing friend."

Parker's frustration turns to shock. "How did you—what *are* you?"

Oops. Shit. I didn't mean to let that slip. I'm being careless because I'm scared, and now he knows I'm reading his thoughts.

I tug my arm, but Parker won't let go. "I'm just a human who accidentally found out about your world. I'll never tell. I'm not that stupid. I swear I don't know what Xavier was up to. You're better off going back to get him."

"I will, but I can't just let you go. I need answers."

"I'm just a victim. I swear."

A hint of sadness bleeds into me from him, and I hate that his face softens. I don't want to see or feel his compassion. "I want to believe you, but I have to make sure. I'm sorry."

When I realize he intends to take me to his master, I finally succumb to panic. "No! Not to the vampires. I can't go there. You can't take me there."

I frantically shake my head. I want to be brave, but I can't. My fear is too strong. My nightmare is still too vivid. I lose myself to my panic as I'm thrown into the memory of the night I discovered the underworld.

I was six years old. I was sleeping when the premonition hit, jolting me awake. The power of it was so strong I couldn't move. I screamed for my mother, and when she came to me, I begged her to run. I told her danger was coming and that we needed to hide, but she said I'd had a nightmare and told me to go back to sleep. I didn't know back then to listen to the warnings. I didn't know, then, that they were never wrong. I didn't convince my mother. I let her hold me and sing to me while I tried to ignore the dread in my chest.

They came into my room like shadows in the night and ripped me from my mother's arms. There were three of them. One of them fed from me while the other two went after my mother. My vampire quickly lost interest in me, though, when the others decided not to simply drain my mom. I was thrown to the ground like a broken toy and had to watch, half conscious, as those vampires did unspeakable things to my mother.

My young eyes couldn't comprehend the true awfulness of their crimes at the time, but the nightmares stayed with me, and I eventually grew to understand the depth of all they'd done. They left her body on my bedroom floor and didn't spare me another thought before moving on to find their next victim. I still remember their laughter as they shut the door on their way out.

I don't know when my knees buckled, but Parker is now holding my limp body upright. He's cooing at me in a gentle voice as he lightly strokes my hair. "Calm down, Nora. Shh. It'll be okay. Relax. I'm not going to hurt you."

"Please," I whimper. "If I have to die, be merciful, and do it now. Fast. Don't take me to your master. I can't go to the vampires. I know what your kind do to humans. *Please*, Parker. Not vampires. Anything but vampires."

I've never begged in my life, and I hate that I'm doing it now. I hate Parker for making me do it. But I can't go through the torture my mother endured. I *can't*.

"Nora, look at me."

I don't want to. I don't want to see the monster again. But his voice is so soft, so soothing. Parker's fingers press my chin up toward his face, and then I feel the back of his hand brush my cheek. "Nora," he whispers softly. "Open your eyes."

I know I shouldn't. I can't remember why, but I know I'm not supposed to look into his eyes.

"Nora."

I crack. When I look, his beautiful azure eyes are right there, waiting to greet mine. My head swims, and I remember why I wasn't supposed to meet his gaze. "You're compelling me. You son of a..."

I fall unconscious before I can finish my sentence.

CHAPTER
THREE

W**aking up is difficult**. It feels like I'm coming out of a drug-induced sleep. My memory is foggy. I don't know what happened or how I got here—wherever *here* is. A quick inventory of my body tells me that I'm fine, aside from the slight ache in my head. I can't be hung over. I don't drink. Not ever. Nor do I do drugs. Nothing good can come from impaired judgment. The only answer I can think of is that I've been roofied. Or...

The fog lifts, and memories of last night crash to the front of my brain. I see it all with crystal clarity up until Parker compelled me. Everything after that is blank. "That bastard."

He brought me to the vampires.

I bolt upright to find that I've been sleeping in a large canopied four-poster bed in a grand suite five times the size of my apartment. The furniture is extravagant, made of dark cherry wood, and very masculine. The carpets, linens, and wall hangings are a mixture of beige and brown tones with deep burgundy accents. To the right of the bedroom area is a retreat with a full living room setup centered around a large stone fire-place. To the left is the entrance to the most beautiful, luxurious bathroom I've ever seen. It's a room fit for royalty. Or a master vampire.

I've got to get out of here. I throw back the covers, relieved to see that I'm still wearing my own clothes. My shoes have been taken off, but everything else seems to be in place.

Shooting to my feet, I realize too late that I'm still very affected by Parker's compulsion. My motor skills haven't completely returned. I grab one of the bedposts to keep from falling. The moment I grasp the post, I connect with a psychic imprint and am thrust into a vision.

A man leans against this bedpost. For a moment, all I can do is stare as he slowly removes his tie and dress shirt. He appears to be in his late twenties to early thirties and is painstakingly attractive. His dark blond hair is pulled back into a short ponytail, and his dark eyes pop in contrast to his flawless pale skin. I swallow at the sight of his muscled chest and stomach, clearly defined beneath a tight white tank top.

The look of heat in his eyes leaves me breathless. The vision is so intense that it feels as if that needful gaze is directed at me. But it's not. He's staring at a woman standing in front of him. "I'm glad you've come to join us, Desi." His voice is low, soft, and alluring. "Are you settling in all right? Have you been welcomed?"

"Of course, Sire." Her voice trembles slightly, but I don't think she fears him. She looks nervous, but hopeful. There is longing in her gaze. "Everyone has been wonderful and..." A blush rises in the woman's cheeks, and she looks at her feet.

The man lifts her chin, forcing her to meet his eyes. "And?"

"I'm glad that my presence here pleases you," she whispers. "It's an honor to be claimed by you."

Heat sears from the man's eyes, making both the woman and me shiver. The man strokes the woman's arm, and she sucks in a breath, finding a moment of confidence. "Sire..." She opens the top button of her blouse and pulls back her collar, exposing her neck and shoulder. "If you are in need, I am yours."

The man stiffens, causing my focus to fall to his stomach once again, and to all of the perfectly sculpted muscles there. He brushes his hand along her smooth skin and then buries his fingers in her hair. As he pulls her to him and places a soft kiss to the crook of her neck, he says, "It's not blood I am in need of right now."

His mouth falls to her collarbone and dips lower, exploring the skin exposed by her open blouse. She shudders. "I'm yours however you want me, Sire."

He lifts his gaze, meets hers for a moment, contemplating, and then in a move so fast that he blurs, he rips off her blouse, spins her around, and slams her against the bedpost.

I try to escape the following show, but the stronger the vision, the more impossible it is to pull myself out. I'm forced to stand witness, and I can't help the physical feelings that stir in me. It's impossible to deny the appeal of this man—the grace and stamina he displays. There's no question he will leave his partner in want of nothing.

As the woman reaches her climax, her lover finally allows himself to follow her, and in the exact moment of his release, he leans forward and sinks his teeth into the woman's neck. Two screams shatter the air—the woman's cry of ecstasy and my shriek of utter horror.

The scream rips from my lungs and finally pulls me from the vision. Alone in the lavish room once more, I release the bedpost and stumble back. I barely have time to let my eyes adjust before the bedroom door is thrown open and the man from my vision bursts through it, Parker following closely. "Nora?" Parker asks. "Are you all right? What happened?"

His panic lessens as his eyes sweep the room and find no danger present. *My* panic, however, increases a hundred times. I'm stuck in a room with two vampires, and I'm certain that one of them is the clan leader.

Parker steps toward me, but the man from my vision thrusts

his arm out, blocking Parker's path. "She seems fine, Parker." The warmth that was in his voice in the vision is gone. He doesn't look or sound angry, but his words to Parker feel like a warning. "Close the door."

I flinch at the soft click the door makes when Parker shuts it, closing me in with them.

The man from my vision smiles at me. "Hello, Nora." He says my name as if testing out the feel of it on his lips. "That's a very beautiful name, love, for a very beautiful woman. I am Henry, and I'm very pleased to meet you."

I give no reply. My heart is pounding so hard in my chest it's painful. My eyes bounce back and forth between Henry and Parker. Parker is now standing by the door, acting as sentry and keeping me from running—as if I could run from these guys.

When Henry crosses the room to me, I dash away from him, placing myself behind one of the couches in the retreat area. It's hardly a protective barrier, but I have no other options at the moment. My voice shakes as I say, "Stay away from me."

Annoyance streaks across Henry's face, but he stops coming toward me. "Have I hurt you? Touched you? Disrespected you in any way?"

He hadn't. Not yet. But he would. It's what his kind does. "How long was I out?"

"A good nineteen to twenty hours," Parker mumbles.

"A *day?*" Parker winces at my screech. "I've been gone a whole day?" Damn it. I'll be lucky if I still have a job when I get home. "Where are my shoes? I have to go."

Henry's voice stops me from looking around the room. "I'm afraid we can't let you go yet, Nora."

I freeze. In my panic about work, I'd momentarily forgotten who and what Henry is, and how I got here. "Why are you holding me hostage?"

Henry walks toward me again, and my stomach leaps into

my chest. I glance at the window behind me. There's a thick dark curtain blocking out all the light, so I have no idea if I could use it to escape. Even if I tried, Henry would catch me. Still, my brain can't stop trying to come up with a solution.

"We have a bit of a situation," Henry says.

I nod quickly, remembering last night's conversation with Parker outside the club. "Yeah, your missing vampire. I'm sorry for you, but I really don't know anything about it."

"I do hope for your sake that's true."

He smiles as if we're having a cordial conversation, while shivers race down my spine at the threat. He's being pleasant, and using the manners and grace of a gentleman, but he can't mask his underlying aura of danger. This man can and will kill me if he wants to.

My face pales, and my voice escapes me. I can only whisper as I shake my head. "I *swear.* I don't have the answers you want." My eyes flick quickly to Parker. "How many times can I say that?"

Henry comes to a stop at the end of the couch. He's maybe four feet from me now. My pulse spikes even higher, and Henry pauses, cocking his head to the side as if he can feel it. Or hear it. "I believe you may be genuine," he says, as if he's surprised by his own faith in me. "However, I need to know for certain, and there are other things that don't add up." His eyes narrow. "Parker seems sure that you are hiding something, even if it's not information about Nadine."

I glare at Parker. He stares right back. "How do you know about the underworld?" he asks. "I swear you read my mind last night."

The spike in my pulse confirms his suspicion. Henry nods as he files away that truth and takes a step closer to me. He rests his hand on the back of the couch and smiles again. The grin is slightly more predatory now. "How do you have such an extraordinary gift? And how is such a frail little thing like you involved in the underworld?"

He uses that same calm voice from his vision, as if he's attempting to seduce me. His eyes are penetrating as well. I'm afraid he's going to try to compel me. I drop my gaze to my feet and shake my head. "Believe me, I wish I wasn't."

In the blink of an eye, he comes around the couch and gently lifts his hand to my face. I flinch away from his touch, but his skin comes into contact with mine anyway. "I am not a monster," he whispers, stroking my cheek with the back of his hand. "But I do need to know what you know of our world. I need to know how you're involved with my missing vampire. I need to know what you're hiding from me. If you will cooperate and try not to fear me, then I shall try to control my needs and desires." His eyes rake over my body, and he swallows. "Though you tempt me so greatly."

I don't trust him, but hope explodes within me anyway. "Cooperate with you how? I already told you I don't know about your vampire. What else do you want from me?"

He crowds my personal space again. I begin to tremble as fear twists my stomach into tight knots. I yelp when he suddenly grips my head in his hands. "I just need the truth, but I'm afraid I can't trust your words. I will have to use my gift."

Fear keeps my voice a whisper. "Your gift?"

"Don't be afraid, Nora. If you don't fight me, I won't hurt you. I'm simply going to take a look at your memories. Memories cannot lie."

He intends to sift through my memory? I've heard rumors of stronger vampires who could do amazing things with their compulsion powers. Clan leaders—masters—usually have extraordinary gifts that set them apart from other vampires. Make them stronger. I'd always hoped those stories weren't true. But they *are* true. I can feel it in his thoughts and intentions.

Henry is going to get in my head and look at my memories. He's very excited to do it. He's curious about me—a human with the power to read minds who walks among his world.

I know the moment he accesses my mind. I feel his presence slip inside my head. The invasion of privacy is unbearable, and I automatically try to kick him out. Pinching my eyes shut, I mentally push against the unwelcomed presence. He fights back, pushing hard against me. "Do not resist me."

"Get out of my head!"

Pain pounds behind my eyes, crushing against my brain and my skull. It hurts so badly I have to fight the urge to vomit. My nose begins to bleed. A tortured scream rips from my lungs. Still, every instinct I have propels me to eject him from my mind.

I fight as hard as I can. I'm strong, but Henry's stronger. He breaks through my mental barrier, shattering my will. I collapse in his arms.

Parker dashes toward me. "Nora!"

"She's all right," Henry reassures Parker as he lays me on the nearby sofa. "She will not resist me anymore." He smiles at me, swiping my hair off my forehead. "Will you, love?"

I want to shout and curse and scream at him, but I don't have the energy. My brain is mush, and I'm barely hanging on to consciousness.

Henry wipes the tears from my cheeks and places his hands on my head again. "No," I croak.

"Forgive me. I must."

He enters my head again. I try to fight it, but I can't. My memories surface against my will. While Henry absorbs them, he's still touching me, and so, gives me a running commentary of his own thoughts at the same time. He starts with my most recent memory, because he's curious as to why I'd screamed. He sees me wake up, sees me touch his bedpost, and gasps when he watches me fall into my vision.

I'm stuck in the memory, but I can hear Parker close by our side. "Sire, what is it?"

Henry can see my vision. He watches the scene of him and his lover play out, standing, as I did, like an outsider. "My, my," he rasps. As shocked as he is by my ability, he's aroused by the vision. He likes watching himself. "So it's not just mind reading that you are capable of. You are an extremely powerful human, aren't you? How does it work, exactly? Have you always had this gift?"

"T-that's n-none of y-your b-business."

Henry chuckles. "Actually, *this* vision is very much my business, don't you think?"

I refuse to answer that and pray he's watching the vision and can't see my blush.

"Sire, what's happening? What do you see?"

Henry chuckles. "Would you like to describe it to him, Nora?"

The tone of his voice makes me wish I could punch him in his smug face. There's nothing I can say right now that wouldn't sound pathetic, encouraging, dirty, or like a denial of attraction, so I keep quiet.

Henry sighs, sad that I've not taken his bait. "Nora has been gifted with a form of psychometry," he explains to Parker. "She can see visions of the past when she touches objects—such as my bed. Isn't that right, Nora?"

Parker gasps. "With a gift like that, she could help us find Nadine. We could take her to—"

"All in good time, Parker. Allow me to concentrate, if you will."

"Forgive me, Sire."

Parker goes quiet, and Henry's attention shifts back to the vision we're both stuck in. His arousal increases. He sees me watching the scene and likes the thought that I saw him—as if I'd had a choice in the matter. But, whether I'd wanted to or not, I had been turned on by it when I saw it, and he can tell. He feels my attraction and groans. "Nora." He sounds agonized. "Sweet Nora, you torture me. I can feel your desire."

As the words escape his lips, he reaches the part of the vision where he'd bitten the woman and feasted on her blood. He watches me scream. Just as he'd felt my desire before, he feels my revulsion now. He feels my memories just as I'd felt them when I experienced them. My stark terror over what is the most intimate treasured act among his kind hurts him. It's the closest that two vampires can get to one another, and he's desperate to share that bond with me.

Henry lets go of me and pulls out of my head. The look in his fevered eyes screams of his hunger. His desire. "I could give you pleasure like you've never known," he says.

I'm not sure if he means the sex or the biting, but either option terrifies and repulses me to a state of panic. I shake my head. "No thanks."

He smiles, as if my declaration amuses him. "Don't be so hasty, love. I felt your arousal as you watched us. You're attracted to me."

"My body responded instinctively. That's all it was. You're hot, but knowing what you are, you lost any attraction I might have felt."

He gives me a knowing smile, as if he doesn't believe me for a second, and places his hands back on my head.

"Not again." I groan.

"I must. I don't have the answers I need yet."

I know there's no point in arguing this time. Fighting him before did nothing but give me a horrid migraine and make me physically collapse. I really don't want to lose consciousness, with Henry so close.

He dives once again into my memories. My attempts to fight him do nothing. I'm too weak, and he isn't being gentle anymore. He works faster now, watching the night that Parker found me with shock and wonder. He's amazed by how a human could know about the underworld, fear it as much as I do, and still face it head on.

He's curious about Xavier and what kind of man he is that I would be desperate enough to face my greatest fear just to be rid of him. He skims over my memories of the months I lived next door to Xavier. As he swims through my past, I feel his anger. He works himself into a rage watching all of Xavier's attempts to spy on me and drug me. He can barely control himself as he witnesses the visions I'd witnessed. Feels the things I'd felt. Hears the thoughts I'd heard. He wants to kill Xavier.

"You see?" I say, trying to change the direction of his thoughts. "I don't know anything about your missing vampire."

"No," he agrees. "You are as innocent as you claim, though you are so much more than you pretend to be. Your gifts are remarkable."

"Look, you got what you wanted. Stop invading my privacy now."

"I'm afraid I can't do that."

I try to yank myself away from him, but I don't have the strength left. My head is pounding. "Why the hell not?"

He doesn't answer my question, but he can't hide his thoughts from me. He could stop now, but he doesn't want to. He wants to know everything about me. He thinks he's been given a miraculous gift and that he would be a fool to not learn everything he can about me.

I try to push him from my head again, but the effort is

almost nonexistent now, and my stomach rolls. I'm helpless to do anything but lie there while he delves, unwelcome, into my past.

At first, he analyzes everything. He tries to think of how he might be able to gain my trust, but soon his thoughts trail off, and he simply watches. He sees my lonely life and is starting to recognize a reoccurring theme—men.

All my life, I've been sought after. There's something unnatural about me that puts men under a spell. I mean that literally, as in, magic is involved. I call it a curse. I'm cursed to attract men to unhealthy levels. I can't explain why, but I know I'm not imagining it.

Henry watches me bounce from foster home to foster home, always having problems with my foster fathers or brothers. He sees school after school and all the boys that never leave me alone. His anger rises each time I am harassed or assaulted. He roars, furious with what he's seeing. That he's angry on my behalf doesn't make me feel any better. "Please, stop!" I scream. "Once was bad enough. Stop making me remember! Please stop this!"

"I am so sorry, Nora," he coos in my ear. His hand strokes my head over and over. "You're safe now. You have my word. I will protect you."

His promises bring me no comfort. Who will protect me from him?

My curse hits Henry hard. Seeing everything I've been through, he doesn't just become drawn to me; he instantly becomes protective of me. And possessive. I'm his now, and he plans to take care of me. He vows to himself that I will never be put through that again. No one else will ever come near me. He'll make sure of it. He thinks he understands why I hadn't wanted him to touch me. He wants me to see him differently from all of the past men in my life. He wants me to long for his touch, not abhor it. Fat chance of that.

When I realize just how far back in my memory he's going, and I recognize what else I'm about to have to relive, I panic. "No!" I scream. "Get out of my head!"

"Nora, what is it?"

"Stop. *Please.*"

"Stop fighting me, love. You're too weak right now. You will hurt yourself."

"Then STOP!"

"Shh," he whispers, wiping the tears from my face. "What are you hiding from me?"

He pushes harder, and I try to match him. I'm fueled by desperation. I can't watch them kill my mom again. Seeing the memories like this makes them feel too real. They're too vivid. I can't go through that again. I just can't.

The premonition hits, and my child self jerks up in bed, crying for my mom. She enters the room, and my heart aches at the sight of her. For a moment, I'm powerless to do anything except take in the memory. I can feel her arms around me. Hear her voice. It's so real. I begin to sob as she holds my younger self. And then they come. I can't watch this, and yet I can't help it.

"Stop!" I cry. I can feel her pain and her fear. Worse, I can now feel the monsters' excitement as they attack my mother. "Please," I beg. "Why are you making me relive this? I hate you, you sick bastard!"

Unable to take the torture anymore, I tune Henry out and break down into gut-wrenching sobs.

It's the crying, I think, that finally makes Henry extract himself from my head. With everything he'd put me through, I hadn't shed a tear, but now I'm sobbing like a baby. My grief and fear are so fresh it's as if it all happened yesterday.

My nightmare stops, and the pressure in my head goes away, but the aftereffects are a bitch. I blink my way back to reality, feeling as if my brain has been shredded by a set of sharp claws. But that's nothing to the feeling in my chest. My heart has been ripped to pieces far worse than my brain.

I sit up, ignoring the throbbing in my head, and take a deep breath. My sobs quiet, but I can't stop silently spilling tears. I close my eyes and sniff as more shudders wrack my body.

"Sire, what's the matter with her?" Parker whispers, kneeling beside Henry now, and biting his bottom lip as if it pains him to see me crying.

Henry shakes his head, and his eyes fasten on mine. "They were rogues," he murmurs. "Those who attacked you and your mother. The worst of our kind." Parker gasps. Henry looks like he feels sick. I hope he does. "They were monsters, yes, but they were the exception, Nora, not the norm. I promise you. We do not condone such actions. I am so sorry that happened to you."

His apology doesn't make me feel any better. I've been trying to forget what happened all my life. And now, thanks to him, the memories are so much worse. I'll never forget the feelings those monsters felt. I'll never forget their faces, or the looks of pleasure on them. I'll never forget my mother's pain.

Unable to look at the monster in front of me any longer, I turn my face into the sofa and let more tears fall. Behind me, Henry sighs. "Bring the car around, Parker." A hand falls on my shoulder. "Come, Nora. Some fresh air will do you good."

CHAPTER FOUR

Henry **ushers me into** the back of a sleek black Mercedes sedan and then slips in beside me. When Parker climbs behind the wheel, I can't help but think of the similarities between this moment and the night before when Xavier forced me to go out with him. The only difference is that the premonitions of someone close by meaning to do me harm are missing. Oddly enough, I haven't felt the warning feelings since ditching Xavier. The vampires truly don't mean me any harm. Right now. That doesn't mean that I'm safe by any stretch. Vamps are moody, and I'm sure their definition of bringing me harm would be different than mine.

"Where to, Sire?"

"Underworld. That was the last place Nadine was seen, was it not?"

As Parker nods and puts the car into gear, I lean forward, trying my best to keep my temper in check. "Uh, you're going to take me home first, right?"

Henry gives me a long look that says so much. The bastard has no intention of ever letting me go home.

"Oh, this is bullshit. Take me home, *now*. You got your answers. I didn't take your missing vampire, and I'm not a threat to you. I've never told anyone about the underworld. Plus, you know about my gift. You keep my secret, I keep yours. Those are the rules of the underworld. You have to let me go."

"You want to go back?" Henry asks. "To that hole of an apartment next door to that loathsome human?" He sounds like he's insulted that I'd pick my home over his.

I shrug. "It's my home. I have responsibilities, a job—maybe. I probably got fired for not showing up to work today, thank you very much. But still, it's my *life*. You can't just take it from me."

Henry gives me a rueful look. "It wasn't much of a life, Nora. You lived alone with no family, no friends, no lovers..."

My chest clenches like Henry is punching me with each word he says. As an orphan who grew up in foster care, I've never wanted anything more than a real family. Being a scrawny little outcast was bad enough—I never fit in and was always picked on—but add having to hide my gifts, and I never had a chance at having any kind of real relationships. I've grown resigned to my lonely life, but I've never wanted to be alone. Henry's hitting below the belt, and he knows it. He waits for a response from me, but I can't give one without sounding emotional, so I turn my head and stare stoically out the window.

"You'll have all of those things from now on," Henry says. "I'll keep you safe. Provide for you. You will be well taken care of, I assure you."

"You can't do this." My protest is weak. He *can* do this, and we both know it. Who would stop him? "The laws of the underworld—"

"Apply to *underworlders*, Nora. You are human. You know

the truth. You know my identity. It is too dangerous to allow you to leave."

"But I won't tell anyone!" I blurt as panic takes over my aching, exhausted body. "You've seen my life. You know I've never said a word about your world to anyone. I won't tell people about you. You *know* I won't."

"You won't," Henry agrees, "because you won't be leaving me."

Henry reaches across the seat and pulls one of my hands into his. His voice turns to silk again. "I know you're scared, Nora. You have reason to fear and despise my kind, but you will get over it."

"Oh yeah, because kidnapping me is definitely the way to win me over. You are the worst kind of villain, because you actually think you're doing the right thing here. You're delusional."

Henry pulls his hand away from mine and glares at me. *"Delusional?"*

I shrug. My piece spoken, I go back to glaring out the window. After a few minutes, Henry says, "Regardless of your opinion of me, your life is here now, with me and mine. You had better get used to it. Cooperate, and you will be treated well."

I can't help taking the bait. "Cooperate how? Am I just supposed to jump into your bed? Would that get you off, Henry? Knowing you were forcing me to be with you?"

Henry whirls on me in his seat, and his eyes begin to glow a scary red. "I would *never* disrespect you in that manner! When you come to my bed, it will be because you want it. I guarantee you will be desperate for me before I ever touch you."

I scoff.

"I want you, Nora," Henry says, still seething. "But until you are ready to become my lover, your role in my clan will be a different one."

"What role?"

Henry takes a deep breath and sits back against his seat. Once he's calm again, he says, "Your gifts. I need them. You will be of great service to my clan."

Of course it's about my gifts. I should have known. Vampires are all about power and politics. Henry, no doubt, wants to remain the big man on campus, and to do that he needs all the most powerful tools in his arsenal. I'm a shiny new toy that no one else has. Sadly, this news is better than the idea that he just wants me for my body or my blood. But not much, because I know he still wants both of those things as well.

Henry continues when I don't respond, his voice becoming practical, businesslike. "You will help me in exchange for room and board and anything else you might need. I promise you will be better cared for by me than you ever have been before. You will be protected and afforded the finest luxuries I have to offer."

Yeah. As if expensive dresses and jewelry could make up for my freedom. I meet his gaze again. "And if I don't want it?"

Annoyance sweeps across his face, but he stamps it down and continues to speak calmly. "Then you will help me in exchange for your life."

He says it so simply. So matter-of-factly. As if my life means nothing to him, and killing me would be inconsequential.

"Humans are not supposed to know about our world," he continues. "I could kill you to keep my secret safe, and no one would care."

"*I* would care."

He smiles. "Then I suggest you accept your new life, my dear."

His smugness is too much. Huffing, I turn back to the window, determined not to speak again for the rest of the ride.

Henry must understand that I've reached my limit, because he leaves me be until we reach the club.

When we arrive at Underworld, it takes me a moment to realize what's different. There's no line out front and no cars parked in the parking lot except for a few near the back that must belong to employees. It seems odd for the place to be closed, considering it's almost midnight.

Inside, the club is empty save a handful of employees running around. The house lights are on, and the music isn't playing. The place is also completely wrecked. There's broken glass and spilled liquor the entire length of the bar, the furniture is either ripped apart or upturned or both—a few chairs even stick out of the walls where they were clearly thrown in a fit of temper and went through the drywall. There are holes punched in the walls and doors are ripped off hinges—it's a complete disaster area.

We walk into the main room, debris crunching under our feet, and a man working to clean the mess behind the bar shouts, "We're closed!"

Parker ignores the warning. "Good evening, Wulf. I'm sorry to intrude, but I was wondering if we could take a look around again?"

When Parker leads our group toward the bar, the bartender jumps the counter in one lithe movement and stomps over to us. He's a tall, ruggedly handsome man with golden tanned skin, brown hair, striking green eyes, and a dark five o'clock shadow. His eyes drift over our little threesome and get hung up on me. He frowns before shaking his head at Parker. "You guys need to leave."

"Please. It's very important. We need to speak with Terrance."

Wulf shakes his head again and waves his hands in a refusing gesture. "Parker, now *really* isn't a good time."

Looking around the place again, I mutter, "No kidding."

I barely speak louder than a thought, but the bartender hears me anyway. His eyes snap to me with enough fire in them to make me cringe back. "Sorry," I grumble, and try to deflect his attention from me with a question. "What happened in here?"

"A couple of trolls got pissed off," he says, voice completely flat. He turns his gaze back to Parker. "And they're still not over it, so I need you guys to leave."

Henry steps in front of Wulf, looking all arrogant and pissed. "You *will* let us stay."

In the blink of an eye, the bartender's hand is around Henry's neck. He looks super mega scary pissed. His body trembles, and his eyes glow a dim yellow. He lets out a deep growl that sends a chill of terror through me. There's no mistaking that noise. The bartender has got to be a werewolf. Wulf the werewolf bartender. I'm not touching that one. At least not while he looks about to rip out of his clothes.

"If you even *think* about using vamp compulsion on me, I will rip your head from your body before you can get the command out."

Henry doesn't appreciate the threat. He quickly transforms into a man similar to those who killed my mother. His eyes glow a bright red, his fangs descend, and his fingernails elongate into vicious claws as he hisses and snarls. Wulf growls right back. Without a doubt, these two are seconds away from ripping into each other. I'm both terrified and fascinated at the moment, and I have to admit, as violent as it is, I'm sort of hoping for Wulf to follow through on the decapitation threat.

Parker jumps between the two before the vampire and the werewolf go ape shit on one another. "Henry! Wulf! Wait! Please!"

"WHAT THE HELL IS GOING ON OUT HERE?"

Everyone freezes at the roar that shakes the whole building. I know that thunderous boom. My heart lightens until I see the murder on Terrance's face. It seems my favorite troll isn't feeling nearly as friendly tonight. His frown is as big as his biceps, and his body is shaking with rage. Considering he's a troll, that's a bad thing. If he loses his temper too badly, he'll rip everyone here to shreds in a matter of seconds. Just ask the club he trashed earlier.

Parker decides to be the brave one and slowly steps forward, holding his hands up in surrender. "Hello, friend." He lowers his voice to something so calm it practically bleeds the tension out of the air. "I'm sorry we've caused a stir. I promise we don't mean any trouble. We've just come hoping to take another look around. We might have a new lead on Nadine."

Lead? Ha! They don't have a new lead on Nadine. They have a new tool to try and find a lead—me. It's actually a smart move on Henry's part. If I could help him at all, this would be how. He must have gotten a really good grasp on my gifts while watching my life history. Though, the chances that I'll pick anything up here when it's been so long since she disappeared and countless other people have probably left imprints behind are slim to none.

Something flashes in Terrance's eyes. Worry? Hope? Desperation? "What do you know?" he demands.

Parker's brows pull low over his eyes. "What's going on, Terrance? The club is trashed, you're on the verge of a rage, and your man is a breath away from killing my sire. I assure you, Henry meant no harm. He's simply on edge because he's worried about Nadine."

Terrance swallows hard. His hands are still in fists at his sides, but he takes a deep breath and cracks his neck as he tries to relax a little. “We’re all on edge,” he grumbles. “There have been other disappearances. No one put the pieces together until tonight, because the damn races won’t talk to each other or ask each other for help. I had a girl go missing tonight, too. A member of my home clan was stolen right out from under my damn nose. No one saw anything. She just disappeared. It was just like Nadine.”

“A troll?” Parker mutters, his jaw falling slack. “Who could possibly steal a troll? Who would be that reckless?”

Terrance shakes his head. “My sister, Nell, and her friend were in town. When we realized Shandra was gone, we nearly tore apart the whole club. Nobody was killed, thankfully. The crowd cleared out fast, but Nell couldn’t keep her temper under control. I had to lock her in my safe room, and I have the Elders coming down to get her right now. Then, Wulf mentioned he heard about the Huron River Pack missing one of their females, too, and I remembered you said Nadine vanished, so I called in the FUA. They just left. They found nothing. What’s this new lead you’re talking about?”

“I can explain everything, if you’ll have your man stand down.” Parker nods toward Wulf and Henry. Wulf’s hand is still circling Henry’s throat.

Terrance huffs out a breath and nods once to his bartender. Wulf grudgingly releases Henry. Henry snarls the second he’s free, and Parker has to drag him back several feet to keep him from attacking Wulf. They argue in hushed voices. I hope it doesn’t take Parker long to calm Henry down, because both Wulf and Terrance turn their suspicious gazes my way. I throw my hands up. “Don’t look at me. I think you should have torn the asshole’s head off.”

There’s only time for both men to startle in surprise before

Henry growls at me. "Nora, you will watch your mouth! You do not speak of your master like that."

I almost growl back. "Maybe if I had a master, I wouldn't."

"You will start showing me respect, or I—"

"Trouble?" Terrance blurts, interrupting us before Henry can finish his latest threat. His eyes are bulging, and his mouth is open wide. "Is that you, honey?"

"Unfortunately." Nodding slowly, I slip close to Terrance. It says a lot that I'd rather stand next to an angry troll than Henry. "I didn't escape fast enough last night. Stupid Parker caught me and took me to his *master*. Now Henry thinks I belong to him and won't let me go home. Please tell me you can kick his ass, and call the cops for me."

"They kidnapped you?" Wulf asks. He's glaring at me, but I don't think it's me he's mad at.

When I nod, Terrance's nostrils flare, and he drops a heavy arm over my shoulders, pulling me tightly to his side. Since it's a protective gesture and not a possessive one, I don't try to squirm free. Terrance can be my shield any day. "You did *what?*" he asks Parker. His low voice gives me a fearful shiver. It screams *I'm a badass about to go to town on someone.*

"She's human," Parker pleads. "Not only did she know about the underworld, she was involved with my main suspect in Nadine's disappearance. I had no choice. I needed answers."

Before the two of them can get into an argument, Henry's voice cuts in, sounding every bit as lethal as Terrance's just did. "I will ask you once, troll, to take your hands off my mate before I rip you to shreds and burn this pathetic dump to the ground."

Terrance freezes. "Your *mate?*"

"Your *what?*" I screech. I knew he planned to keep me, but he didn't say anything about *mates.* My curse has him much further gone than I realized.

Henry pulls his shoulders back and tugs at the cuffs of his

sleeves as if straightening himself out. "She is mine," he says simply. "I have claimed her, and my clan will defend my claim."

I expect Terrance to respond aggressively to Henry's threat —the man's a freaking troll, for crying out loud, surely he can beat one lousy vampire—but instead, he blanches and lets me go. When I realize he's stepping away from me—giving in to Henry—I grab his arm in a panic. "Terrance, *please*. The guy is crazy as hell. He's holding me hostage. He really plans to force me to be his slave for the rest of my life."

"Mate," Henry snaps. "Not *slave*."

"As if there's a difference in this case?"

Henry's face turns red. He's going to blow his top soon, but I don't care. I look at Terrance with pleading eyes. "Terrance?"

Terrance shakes his head, pain heavy in his expression. "Sorry, Trouble. I can't. Vamps are the powerhouse in this city, and Henry's clan is the strongest. If I kill these two right now, his clan will come after me for revenge. I'm alone in this city. They'd kill me and burn this place to the ground with everyone who works for me inside it. It'd cause riots in Detroit and start a war between vampires and trolls. We're a strong race, but small. We'd be greatly outnumbered. My family would most likely die."

Henry puffs his chest up, proud of Terrance's claims. Sick bastard.

I slump in defeat. If Terrance can't help me against Henry, I doubt there is anyone in this city that could. I'm completely on my own. And completely screwed.

"I'm so sorry, Trouble."

I shake my head. "Don't be. I would never ask you to put your life, or anyone else's, on the line for me. I'll find a different way out of this."

Maybe I can bargain. If I can find something here, I can use the information to earn my freedom. I mean if Henry can kidnap me, then I can hold his clues for ransom. It's only fair.

Henry clamps a hand around my arm and glares at me. "There is no way out of this. Stop fighting your fate or—"

"Whatever." I cut him off, tired of his threats. "We can fight over the semantics later. Let's just get this over with." I yank my arm so hard Henry lets me go.

Wulf frowns. "Why do you have a human here, kidnapped or otherwise?"

He directs the question at both Henry and Parker, but I give him the answer. "Because I can help." When all eyes turn to me, I sigh. I meet Terrance's curious gaze and shrug my shoulders. "I'm not your average human."

"What do you mean, you're not an average human?" Wulf asks.

I could drown an elephant in his skepticism. Terrance, however, is leaning in, eyes wide, and holding his breath, waiting for me to hand him a miracle. "Can you really find Shandra?"

I feel bad for the guy. He's bleeding with so much hope, but I don't know that I can deliver. I hold my hands up to ward him off. "Whoa, slow down. There's a chance I can find some clues. A *chance*. Not a guarantee. It's not an exact science."

Terrance clasps my hands in his. "Whatever you want. I'll give you anything I can, if you'll help me."

I'm graced with his thoughts as he grips my hands. He's been out of his mind, sick with worry and guilt, since the moment he realized Shandra was gone. She'd been in his club. She was supposed to be safe here. And worse, she was *clan*. She was visiting the city for the first time with Terrance's sister, and now she's been abducted. He feels like a failure to his clan and hates that he let his little sister down in such a horrible way. But at the same time, he's relieved his sister is not also missing.

Still, as relieved as he is for Nell, he's genuinely afraid for the missing troll woman.

His fear and worry for this woman that he barely knew changes everything I've ever thought about underworlders. No one with such a big heart could truly be a monster. I want to bring Shandra home safe for Terrance. If Henry weren't standing here, I'd do it no questions asked, but it can't go down like that right now. I feel skeezy for what I'm about to do, but I don't have any other options.

"I want my freedom, obviously."

I pull my hands out of Terrance's and back away, feeling like the biggest jerk that ever lived. I quickly meet Terrance's eyes, and then Henry's. "I'll be happy to do everything I can to find the missing girls if you promise I can go home—to *my* home—when I'm done." I stand up straight, pull my shoulders back, and lift my chin. "My help for my freedom, or else I'm not doing it."

Henry's jaw clamps, and he pulls his shoulders back, puffing out his broad chest. I'm pissing off a master vampire again, but I don't care. I'm not backing down from this. I feel awful about the missing women, but this is my only bargaining chip. It's my only shot at freedom. Refuse to help a bunch of missing girls, or become one myself. I'm not that altruistic.

Terrance waits, holding his breath and silently pleading to Henry with his eyes. Wulf stands there, glowering at Henry so hard the guy has to have a migraine. Neither speaks up. It's Parker that surprises me. I expect him to stand behind his sire, all stoic and silent with a conflicted expression, allowing his boss to do something he disagrees with. Instead, he places a hand on Henry's shoulder and says, "It's a fair deal. You should release her."

My jaw drops. So does Henry's. "Let her go?" he asks. "Are you out of your mind?"

Parker doesn't flinch away from Henry's anger. "If she doesn't want to stay in our home, why force her?"

"She doesn't know what she wants!" Henry hisses, his pale cheeks ruddy and his eyes wild. He waves his hand my direction. "She's just scared of the underworld. Of vampires, especially. She doesn't understand, yet, that we are not the monsters who killed her mother."

Parker frowns, somehow staying calm despite how enraged Henry is. "Are we not monsters if we kidnap her? Are we not just like those who stole Nadine from us?"

Henry sputters, and his hands clench into fists at his sides. He's going to come to blows with Parker any moment if Parker doesn't back down—not that I want Parker to stop. I can't believe he's sticking up for me. And, I have to admit, I hate Parker a lot less right now.

Terrance and Wulf watch the drama unfold between them like it's a good soap opera. They look just as shocked by Parker's interference as me. It must be really unusual for a vampire to argue with his sire. I can't help the feelings of hope welling up inside me. Parker is Henry's right-hand man. If anyone could convince Henry to release me, it would be Parker.

"We're not kidnapping her," Henry says. I could choke on his haughtiness, there's so much of it in the air around him. "We're taking care of her. She's alone in the world. I've seen her life. She has no one to protect her. She *needs* me. I'm giving her a home and a family, safety and security. Those are things she wants anyway!"

"Sire, if she wants those things, offer them to her. Don't force them on her. You'll never win her over with force. And think of Nadine. You know Nora is powerful. Think of how much help she could be if she was cooperating willingly."

Boy, was that ever the wrong thing to say. Henry's temper finally explodes. "I am a master vampire!" he shouts. "You do not question me, and she will not defy me! I can make her do anything I want!"

He's standing in front of me with his hands on either side of my head before he finishes his last word. He moves so fast it takes my breath away. There's no time to escape him, or even understand what he's doing, before he grips my face and captures my gaze in his glowing red one. "You will do as I say, Nora. There will be no bargaining." I feel the weight of his words and curse. He's compelling me. "You *will* assist me. From now on, you will do everything in your power to find Nadine. Do you understand?"

The command settles in my mind like a cake in the oven that's just fallen flat. It's heavy, and hard, and irrevocable. I nod, because I can't speak past my anger. It's my first command. I'm officially his little psychic tool.

CHAPTER
FIVE

I**'ve been compelled**. Henry *compelled* me. I now have to help him find his missing vampire. I have no choice. The thought makes me ill.

Henry releases his grip on my face but keeps his gaze on me. "I would hate to have to compel you to do anything else since I know you're not keen on the action. But make no mistake, love, you are *mine*. You will do as I say, and accept your new life, or I will compel you to accept it."

I hate him so much that I can't even feel the fear his threat should ignite in me. Someday I am going to kill this bastard. As he waits for acknowledgment from me, I stare him down, letting him see exactly how much I loathe him. I wonder if he can see the promise of murder in my eyes.

Henry grins, as if he finds my hatred a juicy challenge. "I can make you want me, you know."

The blood in my veins turns to ice. "It wouldn't be real. You don't want to compel me to like you, because it wouldn't really be me. You wouldn't really be winning."

"I would prefer not to, no, but I will if you make it necessary, Nora. Do not doubt me on that."

Henry stares me down for a long minute, and I stare right back while trying to get my fear under control. I would have doubted he'd really do it before he compelled me. But if he's willing to force me to help him find his missing vampire, maybe he really is willing to force me into a relationship with him. I don't want to find out, so I try to get the attention off me. With a hard swallow, I drag my eyes away from him and turn to Terrance. It's hard to look him in the eye. I feel like I have no dignity left and hate that I now have to help him against my will. "Do you know where your friend was tonight?" I ask. "Specifically, the last place anyone saw her?"

Terrance hesitates. Pity streaks across his grumpy face, but he quickly squashes it and turns all business. "She was at the bar."

"Where?" I glance down the long length of the bar. "Do you remember which seat exactly?"

"She was—"

"Forget the troll, Nora," Henry interrupts. "You are here to help me find my vampire."

I'm almost stunned by his heartlessness. Almost. Terrance growls, and I place a hand on his arm, willing him to calm down. I can take care of this. "Unbelievable." I shake my head in disgust. "You are such a dick, Henry." He hisses at me, but I ignore it. "Helping Terrance find his missing friend *is* helping find your stupid vampire. Do you think their disappearances, both from this club, are coincidence? No. And his is more recent. How long has Nadine been missing?"

Henry is too angry to answer me, so Parker speaks up. "Over a week," he whispers.

"Over a *week?*" I shake my head, a scornful smirk on my face. "You dragged me here looking for clues over a *week* old?"

I've never caught an imprint that was older than two or three days. Henry knows that since he'd rummaged around in my head, taking any and all information he wanted about my gifts. "It's still worth a try," he grumbles defensively.

"Right. Sure." He and I both know I won't find anything from his missing vampette. "Don't murder me when I try to help with something I might actually have a chance at seeing."

Henry's jaw clenches, but he concedes me this victory with a curt nod. I don't celebrate. That would be acknowledging the fact that he has control over me. Glancing to Terrance again, I give him a grim smile. "Please show me *exactly* where your friend was sitting tonight, if you can."

Terrance scratches his head and looks to Wulf. The werewolf's eyebrows pull low over his eyes as he thinks about it, and then he walks over toward the bar. "I think it was one of these two seats," he says. "I remember the girls sitting near the soda dispenser."

Now we're getting somewhere.

Sliding onto one of the stools in question, I close my eyes and run my hands over the bar. It's a long shot, but it's the only place I have to start.

"What are you doing?" Wulf murmurs. He's close enough that the sound of his voice startles me. The big guy is really quiet on his feet.

"Trying to concentrate," I hint.

He smirks and gives me a friendly salute before backing up a step. I wink at him and close my eyes again. At first, I pick up nothing, but if I focus, sometimes I can catch weaker imprints. After a moment, I'm sucked into a memory.

Deafening bass pulses through the club. It's crowded—every stool at the bar is taken, and a row of customers stands behind them, calling out to Wulf for drinks.

I enter the vision standing next to the seat I'm sitting on back in the real world. A young woman sits there now. She's not very attractive—tall and bulky, not fat, big in a masculine way—but she's made effort with her dress and makeup. The girl beside her has similar features, though her face is slightly more appealing.

The girl next to me has one hand wrapped around a mug of dark brown liquid and has the other hand resting flat on the bar—the place I picked up the imprint. She stiffens suddenly as Terrance appears behind the bar, offering to give Wulf a hand. The girl beside her sees her nerves and flashes her a giddy smile. "He's going to love you, Shandra. I'm sure of it."

"Nell, you're his sister and my best friend. Of course you think that. But I'm just a kid compared to him."

"So am I, and he loves me just fine."

I smile at Nell's enthusiasm, but Shandra isn't as amused. "He hasn't even come over to say hi yet. Do you think he's upset that I was sent here? He's lived on his own for so long. Maybe he doesn't like the idea of having a mate."

Nell glances across the bar to where Terrance is pouring a shot for a decent-looking guy with blond hair and huge muscles. "I don't think so," she decides, frowning. "It's just really busy tonight. Terrance is a loner, but no troll wants to go without a family forever. Maybe the clan is trying to push him into motion with this, but I think once he considers it, he'll like the idea."

Before Shandra can stop her, Nell waves her hand in the air and calls out to Terrance. His entire face lights up at the sight of her. "Nell! Is that you, baby sis? What are you doing here?"

Giggling, she throws her arm over Shandra's shoulder and holds up her drink. "I've brought your future mate to meet you—clan's orders—so get your scrawny butt over here!"

Shandra glares at Nell, but Nell doesn't notice. She's too busy giggling at the look of shock on Terrance's face. He's gaping at Shandra with his jaw on the floor. "I guess the clan elders forgot to mention this whole mating idea to him," Nell whispers.

Terrance finishes pouring the drink for the hot guy customer who is also staring at the two trolls with a hint of surprise, and slowly makes his way over to his waiting guests. Terrance warily lets his sister introduce him to Shandra, but I don't pay attention to them. My eyes stay locked on Mr. Muscles across the bar. He hasn't stopped looking at the girls since the moment they got Terrance's attention. There's something about the way he's watching them that doesn't sit quite right with me. His gaze is calculating and hungry. He's clearly not a troll. He's much too small for that, despite the body builder appearance. So why is he so fascinated by a couple of unattractive troll girls?

I pull myself from the vision, taking a moment to orient myself. I don't answer all the questions being thrown at me as I head toward the stool Mr. Muscles was sitting on. I don't want to lose my concentration. Quickly, with Mr. Muscles' face at the front of my mind, I slide onto his stool and run my hands over the counter he'd been leaning against. The vision comes much quicker this time. It's a stronger imprint. Whoever the stranger was, he was pretty excited last night.

His hand clenches into a fist on the bar as he watches Terrance talk to Shandra and Nell. It's clearly an awkward conversation. Poor Terrance looks so frazzled. I feel badly for Shandra, too. Whatever this mate business the girls were talking about was, it had obviously been something she was looking forward to, and Terrance didn't seem to share her excitement.

Shandra says something to them both and abruptly jumps up. Her eyes are glossy with unshed tears as she heads toward the restrooms. Terrance and Nell automatically begin arguing with one another. I find it fascinating and am dying to know how marriage and family works among troll clans, but I force myself to pay attention to Mr. Muscles. He knocks back the rest of his drink in one gulp and follows after Shandra.

When the vision ends, my head starts to throb—an unfortunate side effect of getting sucked into visions. I'm going to have a killer headache after this, because I've got to try and dive into a few more before I can call it a night.

I lean over the bar with a groan, resting my head on the cool counter until the throbbing subsides. Parker and Henry reach my sides first, both calling my name in concern.

"Just give me a second."

"What's going on?" Terrance asks as I concentrate on not vomiting.

"Nora, love, what's wrong?" Henry places his hand softly on my back. "Are you ill?"

His chilly fingers on my back give me the creeps. Squirming out from beneath his touch, I scramble off my stool and glare at the man. "Getting sucked into memories isn't exactly a picnic, but I'm *fine*. Stop touching me."

Ignoring his annoyed frown, I turn to Terrance. "When your sister and Shandra showed up, you were serving a drink to a guy—early twenties, decent looking, blond hair, brown eyes, big arms, thick neck. That's your guy. That's who took her. He followed her to the restroom when she left you and Nell to argue. Do you remember him? Did you know him?"

Terrance gasps and his face pales. "How do you know that?"

"Sometimes I can see things. Imprints of the past. Whoever the man you served last night was, he was awfully interested in your sister and her friend."

"What kind of underworlder was he? What race?" Parker asks while Henry has his own set of questions. "Who was he? What did he want? Why did he take her?"

Ugh. I knew this was going to happen. "How the hell am I supposed to know?"

"You had a *vision*," Henry snaps, displeased with my bad attitude.

"Yeah, a *vision*," I snark back. "A *picture*. Imprints are like movies. I can see what's going on, but I don't hear what's going on in their heads."

"But what was he?" Parker asks again. "Knowing his race will give us a place to start looking."

"I don't *know*."

Parker doesn't set off my bitch meter as much as Henry, but I'm still losing my patience. I'm not in the mood to go into all the details of my gift's limitations, so I ignore the lot of them and head toward the back of the club. They follow silently and, wisely, don't bother me as I begin running my hands slowly along the walls of the dim hallway where the restrooms are.

I really don't have much of a chance of picking up anything useful, but I have to try. Shandra seemed so young and nice, and Terrance is so worried about her. The first imprint that sucks me in is a flash of a woman holding herself steady against the wall while she throws up. I guess even underworlders can't always hold their liquor.

Next, I'm pulled into a couple who I first assume are making out against the wall, but on closer inspection I realize the woman has her fangs sunk deeply into the man's neck. The imprint is so strong I can't pull out of it, and I'm forced to wait out the feeding. Like my vision of Henry this morning, this couple seems to really be enjoying themselves. The fact that the experience seems orgasmic for both of them doesn't lessen my repulsion. All I see is a monster drinking blood.

When I'm finally free of that imprint, I'm quickly sucked into another one. This time, a man with all black eyes stands in the darkest corner of the hall, and a scantily clad woman kneels in front of him. I roll my eyes and vow never to wander into the dark recesses of a nightclub. I'm just about give up the search when I find what I'm looking for.

Mr. Muscles leans against the wall outside the women's room. One hand is tucked into his jeans pockets, and the other holds a lit cigarette. Though, it's a hand-rolled cigarette, so it might not be a cigarette at all. He's got a bored look on his face, as if he's waiting for his girlfriend to come out of the restroom.

When Shandra finally exits the bathroom, Mr. Muscles takes a long drag from his cigarette and pulls away from the wall. He steps into her path, accidentally colliding with her.

Shandra shoots him a nasty look and growls at him in a way only an angry troll could manage. "Watch it!"

"Sorry," he grumbles, blowing the smoke from his lungs into her face.

"Gross!" Shandra waves the smoke away from her face with a cough. "Thanks, asshole."

She pushes him out of the way, slamming him against the wall hard enough that the guy's eyes widen in shock. He presses his hand to his chest where she'd shoved him. She probably left a bruise.

Shandra takes two steps before she sways on her feet. Mr. Muscles quickly grabs her from behind to help steady her. As he walks a confused, drowsy, and dizzy Shandra toward an emergency exit at the end of the hall, he looks to anyone watching like nothing but a concerned boyfriend helping his drunken date outside.

Pain flairs behind my eyes and in my temples when the vision fades. I've never had so many visions in a row, and my body is protesting. But I can't stop now. This is working. I wait a moment for a bout of nausea and dizziness to pass, but as soon as I can walk without falling over, I head to the emergency exit.

"Oh, my head is going to hate me forever," I groan when I push the door open and am sucked into the most intense vision yet.

As soon as Mr. Muscles pushes the stumbling Shandra through the door, she collapses. Mr. Muscles is strong, but he can't hold her dead weight and struggles to get her unconscious body to the ground without dropping her.

"Damn," a new voice says. "How much does that bitch weigh?"

Another guy, who looks like he comes from the same gym as Mr. Muscles, jumps out of a car that is backed into the dark alley behind the club just feet from the exit. It's a ghetto mustard-yellow, low-riding Chevy Nova with ridiculous spinning rims and a chrome exhaust pipe. There's a decal on the back window that seems out of place on the tricked-out classic car. It looks like a fraternity logo of some sort, but I don't recognize the symbols. I snort. Yeah, these guys are definitely fraternity types. Stereotypical to the point of painful.

"Too damn much, bro," Mr. Muscles says with a grunt and a laugh. "Help me get her fat ass in the car. Did you get the security camera?"

"Taken care of," Muscles Two says as he grabs Shandra's feet.

Together, the two meatheads are able to tuck Shandra into the backseat of the car. "Damn," Muscles Two says as he finally gets a good look at Shandra beneath the car's dome light. "She's ugly, too."

"Trolls aren't exactly known for their looks, dumbass."

"A troll?" Muscles Two whisper-hisses as he shuts the door. He glances all around the alley, as if suddenly afraid a boogie man is going to jump out at him. "You swiped a troll?"

Mr. Muscles hurries around to the passenger side of the car. "Yeah, and I bet we only have a few minutes before her two troll friends come looking for her, so get your ass in the car, and let's get the hell out of here."

Muscles Two's face drains of color. "Two more? Shit! Are you insane? Those things go berserk. Just one troll could level an entire city in a rampage."

"Yeah, but, dude, imagine having that kind of power. She's the best thing anyone could get their hands on. There's three guys competing, and only two spots to fill. Elijah said species matters. This'll get me voted in for sure."

"If we live through this," Muscles Two grumbles as he climbs behind the wheel.

The car peels out of the alley, and the scene goes black.

CHAPTER SIX

I **come back to reality** with a gasp, feeling like I'm about to puke. I've never pushed my body to the limit like this before. Parker reaches for me when I stumble, and I fall against his chest. His arms come around me instinctively. "Nora?"

The numbers of the car's license plate are on the tip of my tongue, but all thought flies from my head when I look into his deep blue eyes. He's holding me in his arms, and our faces are just inches apart. I shudder, shocked by the closeness, and the sudden desire that sweeps through me. His pupils dilate, and he sucks in a sharp breath, as if he can feel my desire. He probably can. Dammit. This can't happen. I refuse to be attracted to a vampire, even if he is looking at me with smoldering eyes that are warming parts of me that have no business being warm right now.

"Nora..." His voice, thick and husky, sounds agonized. "Are you okay?"

"Fine," I rasp. Shit. I even *sound* like I want him. What the hell is wrong with me?

Henry's growl as he rips me from Parker's arms could match

Wulf's. The violent jostling of being pulled from one man's arms into another's makes my vision blur and my stomach roll. My head pounds so hard that I can't even fight Henry as he slams me against his chest. "She is *mine.* You're pushing my limits tonight, Parker."

"Forgive me, Sire. I was only worried about her. She looks as if she's about to pass out."

Henry's eyes snap to my face, and his brow furrows. "You do look unwell. Come, let's find you a place to rest for a bit."

Henry carries me out of the hallway into the main dance hall. Parker rights an overturned couch. After he brushes it off, Henry lays me down as if I'm Sleeping Beauty and pushes my hair off my forehead. I glare at him, but I can't hold it because my head hurts too bad. I close my eyes with a groan and throw an arm over my face.

"It's going to be all right, love," Henry says. "Terrance, could you please get Nora a glass of water? We need to have her feeling better if she's to continue."

Gee. How thoughtful of him.

"No need to continue," I say, swatting his hand away from me. "I got the license plate. Michigan. 4BX 36K."

When silence follows my statement, I move my arm from my face to find everyone gaping at me. "The *kidnapper's* license plate?" Wulf asks. He and Terrance are wide-eyed and slack-jawed. Parker and Henry are only slightly less surprised. I feel like I should be insulted. Did none of them have any faith in me?

"Yeah. 4BX 36K. Someone write it down. Once I soak up an imprint, it's gone for good."

Terrance finds a pen and paper behind the bar, and after he writes down the number, he pulls out his phone. "I'll call it in to Gorgeous."

Whatever the hell that means, Henry doesn't seem thrilled

about it. He dashes over to the bar to stop Terrance from making his call. "No. I will have Parker look into it."

"But Gorgeous is already working the case."

"No!" Henry snaps. "I don't want the FUA to know about Nora. They're power hungry. They will ask too many questions."

Terrance's face flushes red, and he takes a menacing stance. "The FUA is our best chance at finding Shandra and the others. I won't ignore that just because you want to break a few rules."

Henry sputters at the accusation. "Nora is human. I have broken no underworld laws."

"Then you won't mind if I call Gorgeous and let him run the plates."

Henry and Terrance fall into a heated argument that has Parker and Wulf trying to voice their own opinions and play peacekeepers.

I'm not quite sure what they're talking about. I've never heard of the FUA. It almost sounds like they mean the cops. But there's no way underworlders would work with the human police.

Whatever they're arguing about, they're getting really riled up over it and aren't paying the least bit of attention to me. Now could be the chance for escape I've been waiting for. It's a long way from my couch to the exit, but it's my only chance. I have to try.

There's nothing for me to do but stand up and walk away, so I take a deep breath and get up. When no one notices anything, I casually head for the door, trying to be as quiet as possible. It's slow going because it's difficult to step quietly with all of the debris on the floor. As I weave my way around what used to be some stools and a bar table, I notice one of the chair legs has been splintered off and has a rather pointy end. I can't help thinking it looks like a great wooden stake. It's in my hands before I can even debate whether the wooden stake myth is true or not.

"Fine, ask him to run the plates!" Henry shouts. "But leave Nora out of it!"

Shit. I'm out of time, so I make a mad dash for the door. Henry's on me before I get two steps, grabbing me from behind. His hands clamp around my arms, and he hisses in my ear, "Are you trying to leave me?"

The anger in his voice sends a chill up my spine. I clutch the broken table leg close to my chest as Henry pulls my back against him. "Can you blame me?" I ask.

Henry's hands tighten around my arms enough to make me cry out in pain. "I am tired of this game, Nora," he growls. "You. Are. Mine."

"The hell I am. I'd rather die." My words may be brave, but my entire body is shaking.

"So be it."

The tingling of my intuition kicks in. The hairs on my arms and neck stick up, and pure dread washes over me. For the first time since I met him, Henry means to do me harm.

Henry releases one of my arms to sweep my hair away from my skin and runs his nose along the side of my neck. "In death you will adore me," he murmurs. "With a proper sire bond, you will want me as desperately as I want you."

I shiver, and not from the breath blanketing my neck. He's going to turn me—make me one of his vampires. "Don't you dare!"

I thrash in his grip. I don't have a chance in hell to escape him, but I can't help my body's natural fight or flight instincts. I can't become a vampire. I just can't turn into one of the monsters that killed my mom. I couldn't live with myself if I did.

My only option is the piece of wood I'm holding. It's not

much, but I'm not going to just stand here and let him make me a vampire without a fight. "Turn me around," I say, gripping the makeshift weapon. "Look me in the eye when you take my life."

Henry can't resist the challenge. He whirls me around, never realizing I have something in my hands. I don't think. I just shove the wood into him with every ounce of strength I have. I half expect him to be impervious to it, but the stake pierces his skin and sinks a good six inches deep into his chest.

Henry lets out an anguished scream and backhands me across the face so hard I fly back a few feet. I crash to the floor with a cry of pain. Terrance releases a mighty roar as I go down. The sound is guttural, and makes everyone in the room stop and gasp. I try to sit up, to see what's going on, but I can't manage it. My face is on fire, and my head is still spinning. Henry hit me hard enough to nearly snap my neck. I definitely have a concussion, and I wouldn't be surprised if my cheekbone is broken.

A gurgling cough catches my attention. I turn my head just in time to watch Henry fall to the ground. Parker rushes to his side and yanks the bloody stake from his chest. He clamps a hand over the gushing wound. "Bring Nora to me," Henry rasps.

I staked the bastard, and he can still talk? He's like a damn cockroach. "Bring Nora to me!" he demands again, his voice already growing stronger. Damn him and his vampiric healing.

Terrance and Wulf sure as hell aren't going to obey Henry, so Parker reluctantly removes his hands from Henry's chest and rises to his feet. The second he turns my direction, Terrance snarls. I can't see his face because he's crouching protectively in front of me as if guarding me from everyone in the room, but whatever scowl he's sporting, it's enough to make Parker freeze.

The silence stretches out so long I start to wonder what's going on.

"Impossible," Wulf mutters, gaping with wide eyes at Terrance.

Parker is still frozen with shock and looks paler than normal.

"What's going on?" I ask. My words come out in a slurred moan.

Terrance whirls around when I speak, and I nearly shriek at what I see. His eyes are black—all black—as if a demon has taken possession of his body. They look soulless.

"Terrance?" I whisper. I can't help the fear in my voice.

He lifts his big, meaty hand to my face with a touch so soft I wouldn't have thought him capable of it. The gentleness he's showing doesn't match the rage he seems locked in. I've heard of trolls losing their temper and going crazy on everyone and everything in sight, but this is different.

"Easy, Nora," Parker whispers. "Don't make any sudden movements. Terrance won't hurt you, but if you startle him, he might come after the rest of us."

"What's going on?" Henry demands.

He sits up slowly. The gaping wound in his chest is already starting to heal. The second he moves, Terrance growls. The sound comes from deep in his belly, sending a shock of fear into me. I've never heard anything more menacing. Combine that with those eyes, and Terrance is the most frightening thing I've ever seen.

Wulf immediately lifts his hands up. "Easy, big guy. You've got Nora. She's safe. We won't let Henry near her."

Henry's mouth falls slack. "No," he whispers, shaking his head in disbelief. "She's human. It's not possible."

"She's not a normal human, though, is she?" Parker says.

"She's not a *troll!*" Henry shouts. "Trolls' instincts only kick in for their family and their mates! She's neither!"

Terrance roars again, and Wulf scrambles over next to

Parker to try and block Henry from his view. Nobody moves after that. I don't even think they breathe. Everyone looks a combination of completely shocked and terrified enough to piss themselves. I guess pushing a troll to his breaking point is serious business and doesn't happen often.

We all stay frozen in silence, waiting to see what Terrance does. Terrance is not acting like himself. He's clearly protecting me, but I think he's lost his sanity. He seems like a caged animal about to break loose.

The stillness is shattered when the sound of a motorcycle cuts through the air and purrs to a stop outside. Moments later, the front door bursts open and in strolls—and I do mean strolls—a tall, black-haired, chocolate-eyed, dimple-faced, mocha-skinned stranger dressed in cowboy boots, tight jeans, and a tight gray Nirvana T-shirt under a black leather jacket.

The stranger stops walking when Terrance snarls a warning at him. He takes one look at the troll, and his mouth pops open and his eyebrows climb his forehead. His eyes rake curiously over me, stopping on my face. I'm sure it's bruised and swollen all to hell and a trickle of blood is streaking from my nose.

The man looks at Terrance again and smirks. "Interesting."

I snort a laugh at the casual understatement and then curse when my face explodes in more pain.

The stranger's lips twitch, and his eyes spark with humor. I'm torn between laughing again and flipping the man off. I settle for giving him the finger because it hurts less. The man bursts into laughter and heads for the bar. "I like her, Terrance."

The endless pools of nothingness that used to be Terrance's eyes track the new guy's movement across the room. The troll growls again and hovers on his toes as if readying to pounce. Terrance is on the brink of ripping the stranger apart limb by limb, but the guy does nothing more than grin at him and grab one of the few bottles still intact behind the bar. No one else has dared to move yet.

I stare, bewildered, as the man pours himself a shot of something with a bluish glow, and kicks it back in one gulp. I can't look away. I mean, a scary-looking black cowboy-rock star with a baby face and dimples? Really? Strangely enough, it works for him. Though, with the amount of confidence he's radiating, I'd bet anything would work for him. But who the hell is this guy that he can walk in like he owns the place and pour himself a drink while Henry's a bloody mess on the floor and Terrance is...whatever he is.

The man scans the room again, taking in every detail this time, and cocks his eyebrow when he notices Henry. He reaches for the bloody stake and looks at me. "I take it this was your handiwork?"

I slowly pull myself into a sit. If this guy can move around without Terrance going berserk, then so can I. Once I'm upright and the room has stopped spinning, I shrug at the new guy. "He was going to turn me."

The stranger grins. "Nice aim, but a word to the wise. Next time use an ash-wood stake. It's the only kind that'll get the job done. That, or cut off his head. Fire works with vamps, too. That's about it."

I smirk, even though it hurts my face. "Good to know."

The man winks at me, then turns his playful smile on Terrance. "How you doing, buddy? Calming down yet? Your little charge there looks like she's not feeling too good. Enzo's on call right now. You rein it in a bit, and we can meet him over at the Agency and get her all patched up."

"Stay out of this, Gorgeous," Henry snaps suddenly. Parker helps him sit up and Terrance growls again, but it's not quite as menacing as before. He must be calming down a little.

"Nora is my responsibility. I'll take her to my own healer—"

Henry's cut off by another vicious snarl, and I'm scooped up into Terrance's arms so fast I lose my breath.

"Yeah..." Gorgeous says to Henry. "Doesn't look to me like that's happening." If his smugness wasn't directed at Henry, I might find his arrogance annoying. Instead, the guy is my hero.

"She's still mine. I've claimed her for a mate."

Gorgeous chews on this new bit of information. He holds up the blood-soaked stake to examine it in the light and then points the tip at Henry. "Seems to me she's not too interested in becoming your mate."

"Not at all," I clarify cheerfully. "He's holding me against my will."

Henry glares at me, then scowls so hard at Gorgeous his eyes start to turn red again. Whether he doesn't like what Gorgeous said or he simply doesn't like the man himself, I can't tell. But it's clear Mr. Gorgeous loves to irk Henry.

"She's human," Henry says indignantly. "Claiming her is my right. I don't care if she triggered Terrance's protective instincts. He can't just take what is mine."

"Well, *I'm* sure as hell not going to argue with him while he's in that state, so why don't we all head down to the Agency, get the pretty human all healed up, and sort this mess out with the director?"

"What agency?" I ask. "Director of what? Who are you? And...is your name seriously Gorgeous?"

Gorgeous grins at me like I've just made his entire day. "Can you think of a more appropriate name?"

I snort again and then wince. The guy needs to stop making me laugh. "Conceited much?"

"And proud of it." He pulls a leather ID wallet from his pocket and tosses it to me. I'm still cradled like a baby in Terrance's arms, but I manage to catch the ID.

"Nick Gorgeous, at your service. I work for the Federal Underworld Agency. The F U Agency for short."

I roll my eyes at his stupid acronym—though it's admittedly more entertaining than S.H.I.E.L.D.—and focus on the more important fact. This guy's a cop. An *underworld* cop. Like an FBI agent or something. I didn't even know that existed.

And, I'll be damned, his name really is Nick Gorgeous.

"And you are?" he asks when I toss his badge back to him.

"Nora Jacobs. Psychic human kidnapped by that asshole"—I point to Henry—"and now a major witness in your missing underworlders case. Get me out of here, and I'll tell you everything I know."

The cool and calm federal agent raises his eyebrows in surprise again. "A witness, you say? In my missing persons investigation?"

"A strong eyewitness," I tell him. "I saw Shandra get abducted. I can describe the men involved and the car, and I'm the one who got the license plate."

Slowly, a shit-eating grin spreads across his face. "Well, well, well. It sounds like I need to take you in for questioning."

I can't help matching his grin. "Definitely."

"And maybe some protective custody is in order, too."

"Sounds fabulous."

"Well then, Miss Jacobs, follow me."

"Gorgeous!" Henry snaps. "You can't just take her!"

Nick—I refuse to call him Gorgeous—whirls on Henry, and for the first time tonight I understand how he might not be afraid of a pissed off troll. He pulls his shoulders back, and when he stands up straight, something about him changes. It's almost as if the air around him somehow shifts. The man radiates a frightening power. It's like he has an aura made of fear and anyone in its radius will be brought to their knees. The pupils of his eyes transform into long, thin slits and a wave of heat sweeps through the room. When he speaks, it's terrifying. "Try and stop me, Henry. I would love an excuse to end you."

Henry glowers but wisely shuts up. Parker places a hand on Henry's shoulder and softly says, "We'll follow you to the Agency."

What in the world is Nick Gorgeous? I've never seen anything like that. Never even heard of anything like that. I don't really know what just happened. Whatever it is, I do know one thing. You do not mess with that man.

CHAPTER SEVEN

The Detroit Division of the FUA is right downtown on the riverfront a few blocks East of the Renaissance Center. It sits directly across the street from a plaza that was renovated a few years back. Over the last decade or two, the city of Detroit has done a lot to try and revitalize its life, but the results on that have been bleak at best. I'm rooting for the turnaround, but I don't really have any faith that it'll succeed. The city as a whole is a big cesspit that sucks away your soul if you stay long enough. A few pockets of cleaned up landscape isn't going to change enough.

As I climb out of Terrance's beautiful fully-loaded candy-apple red Cadillac, I glance across the street toward the park. I can hear the river and see the dark outline of the Cullen Family Carousel. It makes me shudder. In the day, the plaza is a little sad—a city revitalization project that just doesn't get a lot of traffic, because as much as you pretty up an area, if you have to travel through a war zone to get to it, you're not going to bother. This time of night, the empty park with the carousel down on the water's edge is downright creepy.

Nick rolls into the parking spot beside Terrance's car and

climbs off his beautiful, expensive motorcycle. "I know the feeling," he says, having seen my shiver of unease. "I'm not a big fan of the fae folk, either."

"Fae folk?"

Nick glances toward the riverfront. "Do yourself a favor. Stay away from the park after dark. The Riverfront Conservancy is owned by Giselle, and she lets the fae have their fun in the park without much supervision."

I shudder again. The fae folk like to have the kind of fun that is never actually fun for the people they're playing with. They should definitely be supervised. Or sent back to Faerie permanently. Who in their right mind would let them run wild? "And Giselle would be...?"

"The Detroit River mermaid."

This is news to me. "We have a *mermaid?*"

"Oh yeah. She's smokin' hot but quite the temperamental fish. Bit of an unstable clinger, too. Really doesn't like to be dumped." A small flicker of a smile washes over Nick's handsome face, as if he's remembering a private joke. No doubt he's speaking from personal experience. The man seriously hooked up with a *mermaid?* How is that even possible? Wasn't the legs-on-land thing just a myth? I thought merpeople were completely waterlocked.

I shake away a rather disturbing image of Nick getting it on with a cracked-out fae version of Disney's Ariel, and head toward the FUA building. The sign on the door says Paxton Shipping. Makes sense. Can't exactly label it Federal Underworld Agency. That wouldn't raise a few eyebrows or anything. "So, tell me about this agency. I didn't realize the underworld had its own police/government/structural system."

"We didn't always. The system's fairly new. It's still a little like the Wild West. We only step in when things get out of hand, and not all underworlders recognize our authority, but it keeps the U.S. government appeased enough that they aren't trying to exterminate all us monsters."

Nick gives me a dry smirk as he holds the door open for me. I don't know what to say to that, so I just nod and walk inside with Terrance and Wulf following close behind me.

The FUA reminds me a lot of the DMV. It has this overall depressing feeling that only the U.S. government can accomplish. It's a large room with dim, fluorescent lighting and tacky linoleum flooring. There are only half a dozen desks or so, with a conference room in the back and a few doors with nameplates next to them, which I suspect are private offices.

There are only two people in the room—a middle-aged black woman a little on the heavy side and a gorgeous Asian man. The man is one of the hottest people I've ever seen. He's... he's...beautiful. Breathtaking. Mesmerizing. There's just no other way to describe him. "How you doing, Gorgeous?" Damn, his voice is perfection, too. I let out a dreamy sigh. "Haven't seen you in the office in a while."

"I wonder why," Nick says with a grunt as he drops his keys and badge onto a messy desk piled high with paperwork. For some reason, he's scowling and avoiding eye contact with the beautiful man. It's strange, considering he's been over confident with everyone else so far.

The man laughs heartily and steps up to me with a beautiful smile and an extended hand. "And who do we have here?"

I blink at the extended hand. It looks so soft and smooth, and his fingernails are perfectly manicured. My policy has always been the less physical contact the better, but I can't help taking what's being offered. His grip is delicate but not flimsy, and his skin is warm and tingly. I shiver at his touch, and goose bumps rise on my arms. Holy shit, what's *with* this guy?

His grin says he knows exactly what kind of reaction I'm having to him, and he likes it. Since I can currently hear his thoughts, I know he finds his attraction to me strange because I'm not his normal type. But he can't deny the appeal of my lust. He brings my hand to his lips, and I totally let him.

"Cut that shit out, Ren," Nick growls. "It's not going to work on me, and you're suffocating Nora."

"Oh, all right, fine." Ren sighs dramatically and gives Nick a very sexy pout. "But you really can't blame a man for trying."

An invisible weight lifts off me, clearing my head and making it easier to think straight. I stumble back a step and have to catch my breath. "What the hell?"

"Ren's an incubus," Henry says, glaring at the guy.

I'd been so enthralled with Ren I hadn't even realized Henry and Parker had come inside. So not good. "Incubus?" Stomach dropping to the floor, I place myself safely behind Terrance.

Ren's smile falls at my reaction. I feel bad for hurting his feelings and insulting him, but I can't help my fear. I have enough problems with men lusting after me. I don't need to be around one that exudes lust and feeds off of it. Though, I'm glad to have an explanation for my crazy-intense attraction to him.

"He's *gay*, Henry," Nick drones in a bored voice. "You don't have to worry about him going after Nora. That was for my benefit." Shooting Ren another dark look, he adds, "It's never going to work."

Ren winks at him. "You never know. One of these days you might change your mind, Gorgeous honey."

Startled, I glance at Nick and then at Ren. He's watching me with a pouty expression. "Sorry." I cringe. Way to make a great impression.

"You've got to forgive Nora," Wulf says. "Henry kidnapped her and tried to claim her as a mate. I think she's already had more than enough seduction for one night."

More like for a lifetime, but I don't bother explaining my

unique effect on people. Ren's eyebrows hit the ceiling, and his smile comes back. "Ah. Henry was trying to woo you, was he?"

I force a nod. "Something like that."

"Well, I suppose I can understand your distress being kidnapped and all, but honey, how on Earth did you resist that man?"

Henry gives me a smug smile until Ren says, "Mmm. I'd love to get my hands on that body just once." He closes his eyes and shudders. It's not the same shiver I get when I think of the master vampire. Not at all.

When Henry hisses, Ren rolls his eyes and flashes me another bright smile. "Anyway. It's wonderful to meet you, Nora. And yes, the gorgeous Mr. Gorgeous here is correct. You don't have to worry about me coming after you. We can just skip all that awkwardness and be great friends from the start."

He's kind of funny. And he's gay. Which works for me. "Sure. Besties from the get-go." I shake my head. "A gay incubus. That's...interesting."

"I like to think so. It's fun, too, because great gaydar seems to come with the package. I like to find the ones who are unsure and teetering on the edge or conflicted about it, you know? The denial cases. Then I pull 'em right over that fence and rock their gay worlds so hard. First timers are *yummy*. All those suppressed hormones finally getting set free..." He takes a deep, sensual breath and licks his lips.

I snort. "So, then, you're telling me *Nick* is on the fence with his sexuality?"

Nick cocks an eyebrow at me and folds his arms across his chest. Ren flashes me a smile so pretty my heart skips a beat. Honestly, gay or not, I just don't think the man can help himself. "Well, no," he admits. "I might have a little bit of a crush where he's concerned."

I glance back at Nick just in time to catch his annoyed eye

roll, and can't help smirking. "I guess I can't blame you there. He's a hottie and seems like an all right guy—he was definitely *my* hero tonight." Nick's lips start to twitch up into a smile, until I grin at Ren and say, "I'm pulling for you, friend. Really hope it works out for you guys one day. You'd make one hell of a sexy duo."

Ren's face lights up at the prospect. "I know, right?"

Nick clears his throat, giving us such a dry look we both snicker. The moment is broken when a short man with dark, wavy hair and brown eyes walks in the front door. "Oh good, the party's all here," Nick says, clapping his hands together once. "Everybody in the conference room. Ren, go get Director West. We've got a situation to get worked out."

We file into the small room, each taking chairs around a long, rectangular table. I snag a chair on the end, and when Henry moves to take the seat beside mine, Terrance yanks him away by the collar of his expensive suit. Henry whirls on Terrance, and the two are snarling at each other before I can blink. "Stay away from her!" Terrance roars.

"She is *mine!*" Henry shouts.

Nick moves to the head of the table and does that scary badass thing again. There's definitely some kind of power rolling off of him in waves. It's a neat trick. I totally wish I could do it. "Shut it! Both of you!" he snaps.

Terrance and Henry glare at each other a moment longer, but they both calm down and fall into empty chairs. Wulf decides to take the seat beside me. Both Henry and Terrance narrow their eyes at him, but neither complains.

"Now that that's settled," Nick grumbles, "first item of business. Enzo?"

"Of course." The shorty with the wavy hair squats down beside me. He holds a hand toward my face and offers me a sympathetic smile. His fingers pause an inch away, and he locks eyes with me. "With your permission?" he asks softly.

This must be the healer Nick mentioned back at the club. I don't know anything about magic healing, and I'm a little freaked by the idea of him using it on me. But my head is still pounding and my face is throbbing.

At my small nod, Enzo gently cups my face in his hand. His thoughts fill my mind. He's livid. He knows my injury came from being hit in the face and realized that it had to have been one of the men in the room. He figures it was Henry, from the way Terrance got after him, and wishes he could put an ash-wood stake through the bastard's heart. Henry is not Enzo's favorite person. This endears me to him just as much as the fact that he's getting rid of the pain in my face. Again, I'm surprised. Like Terrance, Enzo seems less of a monster and more of a person who is genuinely concerned for me. Every belief I've had of underworlders is being proved wrong tonight.

As I sit there reading his thoughts, tingling warmth spreads through my face, dulling the throbbing in my cheek. In less than a minute, the pain and swelling are both gone. I gasp when I realize I'm fully healed.

Enzo grins. His chocolate eyes twinkle with amusement and pride. "Better?"

I nod, dumbfounded, and manage a very breathy, "Thank you."

"You're welcome. Is there anything else?"

"My head. I think I have a concussion."

Terrance growls at this, and Henry grimaces. At least the jackass feels a little bad for almost knocking my head clean off.

Enzo moves his hand to the top of my head, and seconds later my vision clears and the headache disappears. I sigh in relief.

He releases my head and offers me a sweet smile. "Good as new, miss."

He's not lying. There's *zero* pain in my head or my face. Whatever their faults, underworlders have some sweet medical practices. I smile a big, toothy grin at my healer. "Thank you, Enzo. That was amazing."

Enzo ducks his head. A light blush rises on his cheeks at my praise. "Thank you, miss. Glad I could be of assistance."

He steps away just as two people enter the room behind Ren. The first is an older woman—maybe in her fifties. She's got a military no-nonsense vibe about her. Sharp, intelligent eyes and pinched face as if she's used to scowling, and her silver hair is pulled back in a severe bun. She's wearing a power suit with a pencil skirt and practical black pumps. No doubt all personality, this one.

The second is a younger man. Though he's dressed nicely in an expensive suit, making him look much more handsome than I'd first given him credit for, I recognize my sweet bus companion instantly. I'm so shocked to see him that my mouth falls open. *"Oliver?"*

CHAPTER EIGHT

My **library/bus companion's** eyes widen. "Nora? What are you doing here?"

"What are *you* doing here?" I repeat.

He ducks his head at all the incredulous looks being thrown his way and mumbles a soft, "I work here."

My eyes bulge. Oliver is an underworlder.

Before I can ask him any more questions, the woman in the pencil skirt moves to the head of the table closest to me, where Nick is standing. He gives her a nod and moves to take an empty seat near the other end of the table. "Well," the woman says, eyeing first me, then the random group of underworlders that have been assembled, "this is interesting."

"My thoughts exactly," Nick says, smirking.

The woman's eyes circle the table again. "So who would like to tell me what's going on?"

"I say we let the pretty human explain," Ren chirps.

"Sounds good to me," Nick agrees. "She seems to be both the victim and the witness here."

"What happened?" Oliver asks. His question is directed at me and oozing with concern.

I still can't believe he's here. He's an underworlder. The quiet geeky guy that had offered to walk me home when I looked sick is part of the world I've always been terrified of. I just can't believe it. I can't form any words to answer his question.

"You weren't at the library or on the bus yesterday," he says. "After you looked so ill, when you didn't show up the next day, I was worried about you."

He's so sweet. My face melts into a smile, and I finally find my voice. "Well, I missed an entire day because stupid Parker kidnapped me, compelled me to sleep for a whole day—for which I'm probably fired from my job, thank you very much." I scowl at Parker, who sighs in return and mouths *Sorry*. "Then, his asshole master decided I'd make a good tool and kept me against my will until Nick rescued me. Oh, and for some reason, Henry thinks he can claim me as his mate."

Director West's eyes widen, and Nick grins. "See? Told you you'd want to hear this," he says to her. "Only it gets better. The little spitfire impaled him with a barstool leg when he attempted to turn her against her will."

"She is human, and she knows of the underworld," Henry sputters when Director West frowns. "It is my right to deal with her as I see fit."

"But claim a woman to be your mate against her will? *Change* her?" Wulf growls a low, rumbly growl that makes me shiver. "It's despicable."

This comment seems to offend Henry on some deep level, because he shoots to his feet and starts yelling at Wulf. Wulf, of course, does the same, unleashing the fullness of his werewolf temper. Terrance and Parker join in the chaos, and suddenly I can't make out any words among all the shouting.

"ENOUGH!" Director West shouts. She doesn't have Nick's

badassery, but the command still has punch. Everyone returns to their seats and closes their mouths. Director West's eyes return to me. "It seems you are the center of the squabble, so why don't you start by telling us your side of things, miss...?"

"Nora Jacobs." I shoot a nasty glare at Henry and Parker, then shrug. "What's there to say? I got abducted at knifepoint by my psycho neighbor last night, and rather than let him assault me like he was planning to do, I passed him off to someone I knew could handle him."

"Cecile," Parker clarifies when Director West frowns.

"Is that the succubus?" I ask. Parker nods. "Okay, yeah. I handed him over to Cecile. Trust me, the guy deserved whatever she did to him, and then some."

Director West nods. "Okay. And then what happened?"

I continue on explaining how handing my neighbor over to a succubus tipped Parker off that I knew about his world. Once I finish with the entire story—where Nick helpfully reminds her again about the improv wooden stake—all eyes turn to Henry. He sits up straight, defiant and prideful as ever.

"Henry?" Director West demands.

"She is *human*, Madison."

"Gifted."

"Still human."

Director West pinches up her face as if Henry's argument tastes sour, and looks at Parker. "You compelled her and brought her to Henry. Why?"

Parker, unlike Henry, doesn't look defiant. He looks... resigned. "I didn't know she was gifted. She was human, she knew about our world, she knew that I was a vampire, and she was associated with my main suspect."

"Are you a cop, too, then?" I ask. "How come you didn't bring me here instead of taking me to Henry?"

Parker shakes his head. "I don't work for the Agency."

"Though we've tried to recruit him many times," Director West says with a sigh.

Parker shrugs helplessly to the director—who is actually smiling for once—like they're buddies sharing a tired joke. "I'm Henry's chief enforcer," Parker explains to me. "Head of security for the clan."

Okay. I can see that.

"I've been trying to find Nadine all week. Xavier, your neighbor, was my main suspect. I was undercover last night. I thought Xavier was going to try to take another underworlder, but instead he picked up you."

I shiver. Xavier is a creep above creeps. What the hell is he doing that he's involved with underworlders disappearing? I quickly shake off the thought. Xavier is a psycho pervert, but he's also a moron. He can't possibly know that the underworld exists. If he did, he would definitely do something stupid and get himself killed.

As I digest this news and mentally argue the possibilities, Parker turns his attention back to Director West. "It was my job to be suspicious of Xavier and all of his associates. While Nora clearly wasn't friendly with Xavier, she *was* out with him. I didn't know he'd forced her to come, and she obviously knew of the underworld. I hadn't been sure Xavier knew what he was dealing with, but Nora was different. She knew about it. It would have been irresponsible of me not to look into it further."

As much as it grinds, I can see his point. I hate that his argument makes sense. "But why bring me to Henry?"

He shrugs. "Clan rules."

When he says that, it rings familiar. I remember hearing that in his thoughts last night. He'd been conflicted about bringing me to his master but felt he had no choice. It was the rules.

"Henry has special gifts with his compulsion. If we find a human who knows about us or we accidentally expose ourselves to them, we are to bring them to him and let him decide how to proceed. I didn't know you had any gifts. And though I didn't believe it, there was a chance you were involved in Nadine's kidnapping. I'm sorry, Nora."

Damn him for sounding sincere. He's telling the truth, and it makes sense. From his perspective, I can sort of believe he did the right thing. Director West must feel the same as me, because she smiles affectionately at him again and then raises an eyebrow at Henry. "When you looked into her memories, did you find evidence that she was involved in Nadine's disappearance?"

Henry shakes his head. "No. She was merely an innocent victim of her neighbor."

"And do you consider her a threat to the underworld? Do you feel she will expose us to humans?"

Henry's headshake becomes emphatic, and his voice turns prideful. "No. She would never try to harm us that way. Nora is much smarter than that."

Director West levels Henry with a heated glare. "And after discovering that this woman was no ordinary human, that she has gifts of her own, and was not a danger to the underworld, you still felt it necessary to keep her hostage? You forced her to use her gifts to your own benefit, you compelled her to do your bidding, and you attempted to *turn* her without her permission?"

It warms my heart that the woman is pissed on my behalf. It's the first sign of her opinion where I'm concerned. I'm glad it seems to be in my favor. Henry, on the other hand, is pissed. I don't think the master vampire is used to having his authority questioned. "I did what I felt was necessary," he growls. "Nora's is a unique situation. I had her best interests at heart."

Madison turns her angry glare on Parker. "And you? Do you feel your sire was acting in Nora's best interest? Did you have no problems with what was going on?"

Parker is startled to be addressed so directly like this. His eyes bounce back and forth between Madison and Henry, then finally turn my direction. It's clear he doesn't want to answer, but the director is waiting. Finally, his shoulders slump, and he says, "I was conflicted. For the first time in my life, I did not agree with Henry's choices."

The poor bastard sounds devastated by that.

Henry roars. "You *doubted* me?"

Parker pulls himself together and answers with confidence. "I acted loyally, Sire. I never went against a single command. I tried to have faith in your judgment."

Henry's face flushes red with anger. "But you doubted me. You believed I was in the wrong."

It's not a question, but he's waiting for an answer. "No."

Wulf clears his throat. "Some of us in this room can smell lies, Parker."

Henry snarls at this, either angry that Parker lied to him or that he sincerely doubted his master. Parker holds up his hands. "Forgive me, Sire, I did not mean to lie. It is more complicated than a yes or no. It wasn't *you* I doubted. I believed you weren't acting like yourself. I was worried about you."

Henry sputters. "I beg your pardon?"

"Nora got to you, Sire. She got under your skin. She bewitched you."

"I didn't!" I gasp at the outrageous accusation. "I can't do that. And why would I? I didn't want his attention!"

"I don't mean literally, Nora. There's just something captivating about you. Henry fell victim to your charm." He looks back at Henry, who's still seething. "Perhaps it was seeing her memories the way you did. She's had an exceptionally difficult life. You wanted so much to take away her pain and suffering, to help the broken woman who needed your protection. I believe you were trying to be noble. You were doing what you felt was right. But instead of helping Nora, you were hurting her. That's why I suggested you let her go back at the club."

It's true; Parker had sided with me when I'd tried to bargain for my release. Everything he's said tonight has made all of his actions seem justified, noble even. He's making it impossible to hate him. It's really annoying.

Henry's eyes grow wide, as if he's only just considering the possibility that he was making me suffer. Parker's confession shocks him. He's stunned that Parker believed he was hurting me. Pompous jackass.

Parker turns his plea to Madison. "Henry's intent was neither malicious nor selfish."

When I snort, Parker cringes a little, and Henry glares at me. I glare right back. Henry was being a selfish bastard, and he knows it.

"Henry's right," Parker says, clearing his throat to break the hostility between Henry and me. "Nora's case is unique. It was difficult to know what the right answer was. I believe Henry did his best. I wanted to help them both, but I couldn't betray my sire, and I wanted Nora's safety and well-being, too. I wasn't sure what to do."

He meets my gaze then, and his deep azure eyes pierce mine. When he silently begs for understanding and forgiveness, my heart softens against my will. I actually kind of feel bad for him, as sick as that is. Not that I'm suffering from Stockholm Syndrome or anything. But Parker seems caught between his own morals and his loyalty to his sire.

It's crazy, because Parker doesn't seem like the type of man scared to speak up for himself or defy someone if he feels it necessary. The way he defers to Henry doesn't make sense. The sire bond must be stronger than I thought. And I was so close to being stuck with one myself. I shudder. I'm so glad Nick Gorgeous brought me to the Agency.

Our stare is broken when Director West once again takes over the conversation. "Very well," she says. "Parker, if you truly believe Henry's intents were honorable..."

"I do."

I scoff, but everyone ignores me.

"And technically the girl is human, so *technically* no underworld laws were broken..."

I fold my arms over my chest and grit my teeth, but I manage to refrain from calling out bullshit.

"Henry, consider this a warning. I would advise you to make better choices in the future. Perhaps listen to the council of your advisors more often." Her eyes flick to Parker, and she smiles.

"A slap on the wrist?" I nearly jump to my feet. "That's it? Are you kidding me?"

Ren flashes me a smile from across the table. His eyes are sparkling as if he's amused by my temper. "A warning from the Agency is serious business, honey. It'll put him in check. Don't worry."

I have my doubts about that, but there's no point in arguing.

"What about Nora?" Terrance demands, earning the room's full attention. He meets my gaze, then narrows his eyes on Director West. "She knows about our world, and she has her own gifts. She probably has underworlder blood in her somewhere. She should be able to interact freely within our world and learn what she needs to keep herself safe. She should be considered one of us and protected by our laws so that a *misun-*

derstanding like this won't happen again. Are we allowed to help her even though she's human?"

Director West gives me a long, searching look, then slowly nods to Terrance. "That is probably the best thing to do in this case. Yes, you may bring her into the fold." Her eyes turn to me, and she smiles a sincere smile. "Welcome to the underworld, Miss Jacobs. You are free to go."

CHAPTER NINE

I **can leave**. And Henry's not allowed to stop me. It takes a moment to sink in.

"Congrats, Trouble."

A giant grin spreads across my face as I stand up and spin around to face my new friend. "I don't care what anyone says about trolls, Terrance; you are one stand-up man." As he laughs, I lightly punch his shoulder. It's the closest I can manage to a physical gesture of appreciation—I am so not a hugger. "Thank you. Seriously. For trying to stop him at the club earlier. For coming to the Agency. Being here right now. No one's ever stuck up for me like that before."

"It was my pleasure. You're welcome in my club anytime. Wulf and I'll look out for you."

I smile, but before I can tell him thanks-but-no-thanks, Wulf approaches us. "A word of caution for you, Nora." His low voice is surprisingly soft with compassion. "The underworld can be a harsh and dangerous place."

"Buddy, I live in *Detroit*."

I kick myself for that lovely bit of sarcasm. Mouthing off to a werewolf can't be smart. Luckily, he just smirks and says, "A fitting training ground. However, the more you interact with our world, the more you will face new dangers. You are still human. It won't be easy for you."

I'm grateful for the warning, but he's preaching to the choir. "You don't have to worry about me. I don't plan to jump in headfirst or anything. I'd rather not jump in at all." I give Terrance a sheepish smile. "Thanks for the offer, T. Your club is kickass, but I'm not sure it should really be my playground, if you know what I mean."

Terrance sighs at the truth in my statement.

"What do you plan to do?" Ren asks. He and Director West have come over, looking politely inquisitive.

I blow out a long breath, wishing I had a solid answer. "I'm not sure exactly, other than get out of town. I've got a little money saved up. It's not much, but it'll get me a bus ticket and an apartment somewhere."

"You're going to leave Detroit?" Parker asks, coming over to join the conversation.

Henry is behind him, but he's keeping a little distance. I ignore the pout on his face and nod to the entire group. "That's been the goal since I was a kid. I've been stalling trying to save money, but Xavier has made for some pretty good incentive to leave. I've got to help Terrance find his sister's friend if I can first, but then, yeah, I'm gone."

Terrance's eyes snap wide. "You still want to help me find Shandra?"

I don't understand why he's so shocked. After what he's just done for me, the least I can do is try to help him. "Of course I still want to help. Not that there'll be much I can do unless we get a lead on that car."

"Nora." Terrance swallows back a lump of emotion. "You don't have to do that. It's dangerous, and you want to leave. You've done enough to help already."

He's saying no, but there's hope in his eyes. It makes me smile. I've never told anyone about my gifts before, much less used them to help someone. It's a nice feeling, and Terrance deserves the help. "Don't be ridiculous, Terrance; of course I'm going to help you. I don't make friends easily, but when I've got your back, I've got it. And T-Man, I've got your back. From now on. You feel me?"

Now I'm being absurd, holding my fist out to Terrance for a fist bump. Terrance grins and crashes his huge, meaty hand against my knuckles. "Right back atcha, Trouble. No matter where you end up after this, you need me, I'm there."

"You're welcome to stay," Director West says. "If you need a job, you could come work for the Agency—gifts like yours could prove very useful."

I shake my head automatically. "Thanks, but I just want to keep my head down and my nose out of trouble. Your world isn't exactly safe for humans. Besides, I could use the change. I've got a lot of bad memories here that I'd like to escape...and certain asshole vampires to avoid."

Director West lifts an arched brow at me, but the corner of her mouth tips up into a small smile. "Very well. Stay safe, Nora, and good luck in your next venture."

After saying good-bye and giving my thanks to everyone, I make my way to the back of the room, where Oliver is still sitting at the table. He starts to fidget when I approach, but he stays put knowing I've got questions. "Oliver, hey."

"Hi, Nora."

I sit down next to him and offer a smile to put him at ease. He runs his fingers through his hair and then tucks both of his hands in his lap.

"So..." I ask the million-dollar question. "You work here?"

He meets my gaze and gives me a small, almost cocky smile as he shrugs a shoulder. "I'm the assistant director."

"Seriously?" My eyes bulge. That title sounds important. Like...is he *Nick's* boss? Sweet, cute Oliver? He certainly looks the part now. He's handsome in his suit and seems to have more confidence than he had on the bus yesterday. "If you have a good job here, what in the world are you doing hanging at the library and taking the bus out in my neighborhood every night?"

Oliver's cheeks blush. "I was keeping an eye on you."

My jaw falls slack, and I quickly pop my mouth shut. My mind starts racing. What did he mean by that? Why would he be looking out for me? How did he even know who I am? It was sweet that he was worried about me, but it was a little creepy at the same time. Was he *stalking* me?

Oliver grimaces, as if he knows exactly what I'm thinking. "You don't remember, but we've met before. Years ago. I've been looking out for you ever since."

I'm shocked. Had we met before last night? Sure, I'd seen him around the library over the last few months, but I didn't think we'd ever talked. Had we? I think really hard and come up blank. "Um...no...?"

He shakes his head. "No. You *don't* remember, because I spelled you to forget. A long time ago. About nine years ago."

It only takes me a second to realize what he's talking about, and then I gasp so loud I gain the attention of everyone in the entire room. "That was *you?*"

Oliver flinches, startled, and his face drains of color. "You *do* remember?"

A shadow closes over me, and I glance up to find a giant, overprotective troll giving Oliver a stink eye. Everyone else gathers in behind him. "Everything okay over here?"

"Yeah, sorry, I just..." I look back at Oliver, my mouth flapping like a fish's. "The park that night? Those men... That was really you?"

He nods, face ashen, and mumbles, "I didn't mean to kill them."

"*What?*" Nick asks. He sounds morbidly curious.

Director West, on the other hand, seems much more concerned when she says, "You *killed* people?"

I want to slap my hand over my face. Wrong thing for him to say in front of a whole group of people that happen to be the underworld police. No wonder he seems so distressed. His face goes green as he glances up at his boss. "I didn't mean to."

Poor guy. There's no way I'm going to let him get in trouble for that. "I'm glad he did. Those bastards deserved a lot worse than they got."

There's silence for a few moments, until Director West says, "Would you two care to explain?"

I really don't want to explain, but it sounds more like a gentle command than a request, so I take a deep breath before launching into one of the most horrific memories of my life. "I was thirteen, living with a foster family up in Chaldean Town. Sometimes my foster dad would drink, and when that happened, it was better for me to not be around, so I'd duck out of the house and wait him out in the park nearby."

"A thirteen-year-old girl wandering alone in Chaldean Town after dark?" Nick mutters. "Were you *crazy?*"

"It was usually the safer option," I murmur as I fall, unavoidably, into the memory. "Just not that night."

Several people in the room curse under their breath.

"What happened?" someone asks gently. I don't know who, because I've got my eyes closed, and I'm fighting to stave off the PTSD panic attack.

When I can't answer the question, Oliver speaks up. "It was late in the evening, and I was out in the park practicing my control of my magic. I had a hard time containing my power back then. But anyway, I was on my way home cutting through the playground when I saw two human men...um..."

"Attacking me," I finish, my voice a ghost of a whisper.

The energy in the room grows heavy with friction. A low snarl breaks the silence that's so menacing the hairs on my arms stand up. I've heard that growl before. Terrance's eyes have gone black, like they did back at the club. The entire group seems just as shocked by his change as those at the club had the first time.

I understand this is some kind of reaction to the news that I was hurt like that, because Terrance feels protective of me. I'm a little baffled that the troll cares so much, but it punches me in the gut at the same time. I've never had a true friend before. Never had anyone to watch my back. My chest burns at the thought of the treasure I've acquired in my acquaintance with Terrance.

I hate touching people, but I place my hand on his arm anyway. I'm plunged straight into his thoughts because they're so close to the surface. He's so beside himself with rage that he's having a hard time not tearing apart the people in this room. The only thing keeping him from rampaging is the thought of figuring out who those men are. When he does, they'll be dead for what they did to me.

"They *are* dead," I assure him. "Oliver took care of them that very night. I've been safe from them for years now. It's okay, Terrance."

Terrance takes a deep breath. His eyes morph back to their normal brown, but he's still trembling slightly. "It's okay," I promise him again. "It was a long time ago, and Oliver saved me."

It hasn't been long enough—will probably never be long enough—but I'm not going to admit that to Terrance right now.

"I didn't mean to kill them," Oliver whispers. His voice

sounds as haunted as mine. "I was just so angry and scared. And I didn't have control of my magic yet. One minute they were terrorizing Nora, and the next they were on the ground, charred beyond recognition. Nora was still conscious, and I was afraid she would tell people what happened, so I spelled her to forget what she'd seen and took her to the hospital."

I don't realize I'm shaking my head until Director West questions me. "His spell didn't take?"

I glance up at her, startled. "Sorry. No, it did. I did forget how they died, but..." I meet Oliver's gaze. My eyes start to glisten, and I take a deep breath to keep from crying. "But when you took me to the hospital, you carried me in your arms. We were touching, so I could hear your thoughts."

Everyone in the room except Parker and Henry gasps, but I barely notice. My gaze is locked on the man I'd remembered as my savior for the last nine years. The scared but brave boy who made the horror stop and got me help. "You thought about it all the way there. I could see what had happened in your mind, and I felt your fear that you'd be in trouble for killing them."

Seeing his fear even now, I offer him my sincerest smile. "I would never have told anyone on you, Oliver. You saved my life that night. You were a hero."

Oliver swallows hard and then gives me the faintest smile. When he looks away, I glance up at Nick and Director West. "He saved me. You can't punish him for that."

Director West gives me a gentle smile. "Oh, don't worry. It sounds like there's no need to look into that. We know Oliver's character, and we know he's got control of his magic now."

"Of course, now we understand why he won't *use* it," Nick grumbles.

My head snaps toward Oliver. "You don't use your magic? Because of that night? Those men were evil, Oliver. Your magic saved me. It's a *gift*. And you must be powerful to have done that kind of damage accidentally at such a young age."

"Extremely powerful," Nick says. "There's only one other sorcerer with as much power as him in all of the Midwest."

"But he's always refused to use his magic," Director West adds. "We originally hired him hoping we could eventually teach him to trust himself. We could really use a sorcerer like him."

He's the most powerful sorcerer in Detroit? Suddenly, something in my mind clicks. "Wait!" Oliver's eyes snap to mine. He knows what I've just figured out. "You're *SorcererX?*"

He meets my eyes and gives me a crooked grin. It's so adorable I find myself grinning back.

"Who's SorcererX?" Nick asks.

"He's the closest thing I've ever had to a real friend. SorcererX is a guy I met in a paranormal chat room when I was desperate for answers about the underworld. Once I decided he was legit, I started asking him questions. He's been feeding me bits of information ever since."

"Nothing illegal," Oliver says quickly at all the raised eyebrows. "I never outright gave up our secrets. I only ever cleared up some of her confusion when she learned something new, or corrected her misconceptions. I cautioned her about things, but I never told her anything she didn't already know."

I slump against my seat. My mind is so blown right now. "You're *SorcererX*. The closest person I've ever had to a real friend is also the boy who once saved my life. I can't even..."

Oliver lets out a long breath. "I've wanted to introduce myself to you for so long, but you're so skittish."

I cringe, remembering the way I'd blown him off when he tried to help me on the bus. "Sorry about on the bus last night. It wasn't personal."

Oliver shrugs. "It's okay. I didn't blame you. I know you've had a rough life. I'd be wary of strangers, too."

I start to tell him he's not a stranger anymore, but another question rises. "Wait. How did you know it was me online? And how did you know I had powers? Have you really been watching me all these years?"

Oliver sighs. "Your story was in the newspaper the morning after I took you to the hospital, so I learned your name. I couldn't help keeping an eye on you after that. It was a bad neighborhood, and it didn't take a genius to figure out your home life was rough. It also didn't take me long to realize you knew about the underworld. I didn't mean to stalk you or anything; I was just worried that you'd somehow remembered me using magic.

"But then I realized you were different, too. Human, but hiding a secret of your own. I knew you knew of the underworld, knew you were researching it. But you only seemed to want to know more so that you could keep yourself safe. After the system bounced you through a couple foster homes, I lost track of you, but I still worried so I reached out online. I knew the screen name and the chat room you used. Anyway." He clears his throat again. "Sorry if that freaks you out. I swear I only ever wanted to help keep you safe."

He's so sweet. He's totally forgiven for the stalking. I pat his hand and smile so that he knows I understand. "I'm sure you did. Thanks for looking out for me. Just please don't be a stalker about it anymore, okay? Friends?"

He's staring down at my hand covering his, but glances up when I say *friends.* His eyes alight with hope. He can't believe I don't hate him right now. He's wanted me to know him for so long, but he was afraid I'd remember him or figure out the truth, and he was sure I'd never speak to him again. He thinks I'm an angel. Perfect.

I pull my hand away, not wanting to hear any more of his thoughts.

"You're really not mad?" he asks.

"That you saved my life when I was thirteen and have looked out for me ever since? That you've been helping me navigate the underworld? That you happen to be the closest friend I have in the world, even if we only know each other online? No. I'm really not mad."

He grins at me, eyes wide in wonderment, as if he can't believe this is really happening. I know the feeling.

Nick breaks up the moment. "Well." He claps his hands together loudly, startling poor Oliver out of his skin. "This little reunion has been very sweet, but unlike the vamps, I'm not nocturnal, and it's starting to get late. Come on, Spitfire. Let's get you home."

Home. Even with the possibility of Xavier lurking nearby, the idea of sleeping in my own bed away from any vampires is heavenly.

It's not until we're in the parking lot out front of the Agency that Henry approaches me. I give him a flat look, and Nick crosses his arms over his chest. Nick's not nearly the size of my troll bouncer friend—he has the build more of a UFC fighter—but he's every bit as scary. Again, I wonder what kind of underworlder he is. I bet it's something totally badass.

Henry puffs out a breath. "Nora—"

"Do I need to get a restraining order before I leave?"

Henry ignores my threat. "Are you really going home?"

"I'm sure as hell not going back with you."

"I understand you're upset with me, but your home isn't safe. Come back to the estate. At least for the night." When I roll my eyes, he grudgingly adds, "I won't come near you. I just want you safe."

Yeah. Not buying that.

"Hang on," Nick says. "He has a point. That creep still lives next door to you."

"Yes," Terrance adds, abandoning his own car to join our conversation. "You can't go home."

One look at Terrance's face, and I know I won't be living in my apartment anymore. I give it my best shot anyway. "Xavier is a perverted psychopath, and he's got an obsession with me. But I'll be fine. I've been dodging him for months already. He's probably still feeling the effects of his encounter with Cecile, and I only need a day or two to pack my stuff and figure out a plan."

Terrance's jaw clenches. When his pupils start to dilate to all black again, Nick places a hand on his arm. "Easy, friend. We won't let any harm come to your young one. The Agency has a few housing capabilities. We'll figure something out for her."

I'm as surprised by Nick's serious-but-gentle tone as I am by his choice of words. He's talking to Terrance as if Terrance has a claim over me. "What do you mean *his* young one?"

"Nothing," Terrance says quickly. His voice is gruff, and he rubs the back of his neck as if a flush is creeping up it. "It's nothing. I'm sorry. Trolls have...very strong protective instincts. Sometimes those instincts take over."

I let out a relieved breath. For a moment there, I thought he was going to go all crazy like Henry and try to claim I'm his mate or something. "Right." I force a laugh. "I could have guessed that. Hey, it's okay. I think it's cool that I'm friends with The Hulk."

Terrance's nerves disappear, and he bursts out with a huge belly laugh. "The Hulk. It's an apt comparison," he says. "But I don't like the idea of you going home to live next to that pervert. I have a couple spare rooms. You're welcome to take your pick, if you'd consider bunking down at my place until you figure out where you want to go."

Normally, I'd turn down the offer without hesitation. Stay at a single man's place? No way in hell. But Terrance isn't putting out any lusty vibes. He wants to protect me. It's his troll instincts. I can't deny I'd feel safer at his place than I would staying at home with Xavier close by. "Yeah, okay," I say slowly, testing it out to make sure I'm really okay with it. "If you're sure."

"I'm sure." Terrance grins. "It's no trouble, Trouble."

I roll my eyes, but my smile stretches wide. "All right. Sure. That would be nice. Thank you."

"Awesome." Nick claps again and starts up his motorcycle. "If that's all taken care of, I'm out. I'll see you around, Spitfire. Take care, and try to stay out of trouble."

After he roars out of the parking lot, Terrance opens the passenger door of his red Caddy.

It fits him perfectly. "I like your ride, T-man. Very pimp."

"Well, I *am* a nightclub owner."

"I thought you were the bouncer." I'm teasing. I'd already figured out he owned the place.

He gives me a terrifying grin. "That's just a hobby."

"And that's why I like you."

When he waves me forward, Henry hisses.

"Are you still here?" I snap. He's seriously grating on my last nerve.

"You refuse my offer, but you'll go home with him?"

"Oh. In a heartbeat. And I won't lose a wink of sleep over it. Have a nice life, Henry."

I flip him off and climb into Terrance's car. Driving away from him seconds later is the most satisfying feeling in the world.

CHAPTER TEN

Terrance and I are quiet as we leave my apartment with a few of my meager belongings. I don't have to read his thoughts to know he's thinking of his missing potential mate. I want to tell him everything will be okay. That we'll find Shandra, and everything will end happily. But I can't bring myself to promise that. I know things don't always have happy endings. In fact, in my experience, they rarely do. Even if we do find her, chances are we'll be too late to help her. We probably already are.

I try to lighten the mood and distract him. "I may have had a hell of a last twenty-four hours, but I got you and Oliver out of the ordeal. I've never had real friends before. Thank you, Terrance."

Terrance slides me a quick glance, and answers me with a grunt and a shrug of his shoulders. Then he flips the radio on. I turn my head toward my window so that he doesn't see me smile. Note to self: trolls don't do sappy, sentimental stuff. At least not my troll. I grin again. *My* troll.

We let the peace ride for a while as we head toward downtown. It makes sense. I can see Terrance living in one of the nicer apartment towers. But when we hit the heart of the city, we keep driving, zooming past the Cobo Center and Joe Louis Arena into the westside industrial area. I might fear for my life if it were anyone but Terrance behind the wheel. But I know he'll keep me safe, so I don't say anything when the city center high-rises give way to dilapidated warehouses.

We're not too far from the water's edge, driving on a street parallel to the river, and after a few minutes, the Ambassador Bridge looms in the air above me. The Ambassador Bridge is the only bridge in the city that crosses the Detroit River connecting it with its neighbor Windsor, Canada. I'm not worried that I don't have a passport, because Terrance isn't getting on the bridge; he's taking us under it. *"Under the bridge?"* I blurt when I get it. I can't help my disbelief. "You actually live *under* a bridge?"

Terrance slides me a glance. "You've never heard of a troll living under a bridge?"

"Of course; in scary stories or children's fables. But I didn't think you guys *actually* lived under bridges."

He shrugs. "Stories have to come from somewhere."

We reach a large cement bridge support closed off by a high chain-link fence. When Terrance stops in front of the closed gate, I assume he's going to get out and unlock it. He looks up at the bridge and smiles. "Beautiful, isn't it?"

It's no Golden Gate, but I have to admit it's pretty cool.

Terrance suddenly hits the gas and, without warning, drives right through the fence. I start to gasp, but I feel the tingle of magic right before we hit, and realize it's merely a glamour to keep people away.

Terrance pulls to a stop in front of the bridge support and watches me as I force myself to relax. "You took that pretty well. You're one brave little human."

"It helps that I understand glamours and can feel the magic. A warning would have been nice, though."

"You can *feel* the magic?"

"Sort of. A little. It's hard to explain. Why, can't you?"

"Yes, but I'm a magical being. All magical beings can feel magic's presence."

I shrug. "Well, maybe your theory of my having underworld blood in me is right. Who knows?"

"It's definitely curious. Come on, I'll show you around."

After exiting the car, Terrance snatches my bag from the backseat before I can and heads for the cement structure in front of us. There's a dimly lit steel door in the base of the bridge support with a large sign warning people to *keep out* and that *trespassers will be prosecuted*. I snort. "Nice welcome mat."

Terrance grins at the sign. "I think so. No one's welcome here, Trouble. 'Cept you, now."

This startles me. "No one?"

He stops unlocking the door and glances at me with unease. "I guess, uh, if you have friends or, um, lovers, as long as they already know of the underworld, they are welcome here, too."

He rubs the back of his neck and starts fiddling with the door lock again. His shyness is cute. Adorable, even. For such a big, formidable-looking man, I'm amazed he can accomplish such a feat. Suppressing a grin, I ask, "What about *your* friends and lovers?"

His discomfort finally passes, and he manages a surly grunt as he leads me inside and down a steep set of stairs. The door behind us closes, plunging us into the dark. Terrance doesn't seem to have a problem with this. Thank heavens there's a railing. It's the only reason I don't tumble down the stairs.

"Trolls don't mingle much outside their clans," Terrance answers as I follow him into what feels like an endless abyss. "My clan is up North."

"Are you saying you don't have *any* friends? No lovers?"

I frown when I get no vocal response from Terrance. He probably shrugged again. Not that I can tell in the dark. I'll have to point out my human lack of night vision and invest in a good flashlight.

"None?" I press. Not that it's such an impossible thought—I don't have any friends or lovers, either—but Terrance doesn't strike me as the loner type. Plus, he's been so good to me. I don't like the idea of him being lonely. "I find that hard to believe, T-Man. Your employees seem to like you, and you've been nothing but friendly with me from the moment we met."

It takes him a minute to answer, and when he does, he grumbles as if he doesn't like the focus of this conversation. "My temper is mild for a troll, and I'm used to being in the city around others. I also pay well and provide a good benefits package."

He obviously wants to drop the subject, but I can't let it go. "I suppose that explains the employees, but not why you've decided to take me in."

He grunts his dissatisfaction, but answers me anyway. "You're different."

It's all the answer I'm going to get, but that's okay because I'd rather avoid that subject. I *am* different. Not that I know why. My inexplicable allure has always bothered me. It's much worse with some than others. Terrance falls on the not-as-affected side. Perhaps because he's telling the truth, and trolls generally don't like anyone outside of their clans.

We reach the bottom of the staircase and, thankfully, Terrance flips a light switch. He turns his head away, to hide his pink cheeks, and waves his hand around the main living area. The space is shockingly large. It has a ten-foot high ceiling at least, and the doors and hallways that break off from it are all at least double, maybe triple the width of a normal human house.

I'm grateful to see painted drywall and not the carved-out dirt cavern I expected. It looks like a normal house minus any windows. A really nice house.

It's tastefully decorated despite its clear bachelor pad/man cave feel. There's a large television mounted on the wall that has to be seventy-two inches at least, several huge leather sectional sofas, and a couple of recliners. In the far corner there is a pool table near a large built-in wet bar that looks like a smaller scale of the bar in his club.

"There's a bathroom over there, but each bedroom has a private bathroom as well." Terrance points to a door on the other side of the room, then heads into a large arched entryway that brings us into a massive kitchen and dining area. The kitchen could cater to a large restaurant and the dining table could seat at least twenty. "I keep the fridge well stocked. You're welcome to anything you can find, and if you have any special requests, just let me know."

I'm still gawking at the kitchen when he leads me through another archway into a long hallway with a number of doors. He walks to the second door on the left and leads me into a modest bedroom. It's nothing like the suite Henry kept me in, but it's the largest room that I've ever stayed in by at least double. There's a king-size bed, a large dresser, a walk-in closet, and a private bathroom. The room is decorated in warm browns and greens—earthy colors.

Terrance drops my bag on the large bed and can't quite meet my eyes as he says, "My room is next door. I figured you'd want to be close. But if you don't like this one, there are several other rooms to choose from."

I'm surprised by the hint of vulnerability he's showing. I'm not sure what has him so nervous. "Are you kidding?" I say, wanting to put him at ease. "It's fantastic. This is by far the nicest room I've ever been offered. I can't thank you enough."

He relaxes at my enthusiasm and finally looks me in the eyes. He doesn't smile exactly, but there's pride and satisfaction in his expression. He covers it with clearing his throat and a gruff, "I will install a light at the top of the stairs tomorrow."

The statement startles me. "Can you read minds?"

"No. But I know humans don't have a troll's night vision."

"So you *do* have night vision?"

Now he grins. "Aye, little lady. It's one of my many talents. Sorry if the place isn't lit very well. Bright light is hard on our eyes, and I wasn't prepared for a roommate. Especially not a human one. That's probably a first in troll history." He shakes his head as if he still can't believe it's happening, then looks at me again. "I can make whatever adjustments you need. Just let me know. For now, let's eat. I'm starving, and I can hear your stomach rumbling."

He's all smiles as he heads back toward the kitchen, but I can't quite share his good mood. His normal need for complete privacy is disconcerting. I feel terrible for putting him out and don't want to overstay my welcome. He's like, the second friend I've ever had. I don't want to ruin that by making him uncomfortable in his own home. "You don't have to trouble yourself with changing anything. I won't be here that long. I can manage in the mood lighting."

Terrance points to a tall barstool on the far side of the kitchen island, frowning. I sit as instructed and try to keep the atmosphere light while he heads to the fridge. "I'll just go topside when I need a little vitamin D boost. No biggie. As long as me being here really isn't going to be hard for you."

Terrance folds his arms across his wide chest, and I get another frown with a no-nonsense stare. "I told you, you're welcome here as long as you want to stay. You don't need to rush away on my account."

It's a kind offer, but I can't help feeling self-conscious. "Are you sure? I know you value your privacy and...well...not that I'm worried about you attacking me or anything, but, don't trolls sometimes...*eat* humans? I'm not going to be some kind of tasty temptation that tortures you day and night, am I?"

Terrance blinks at me a couple of times in a stupor and then throws his head back and laughs so loudly the walls shake. "A few of the savage ones may snack on a human every now and then, but it's not the norm." He pulls out a package of ground beef from the fridge and winks. "We prefer red meat. I hear you all taste like chicken. Nothing especially tempting about that. Burger?"

I blush despite myself. I feel stupid for asking, but I'm relieved by his answer at the same time. I give him a sheepish nod. "A burger would be great."

He goes to work forming a couple of big meat patties. His enormous state-of-the-art stove has a built-in gas grill where he can cook the burgers over an open flame. As he cooks—and he looks very comfortable in the kitchen, which I find oddly fascinating—he continues his explanation of his kind. "Eating people would bring the humans into our business, and that's the last thing any troll ever wants. For the most part, we're not a threat; just a big, ugly, grumpy lot that stays away from humans and keeps to ourselves."

I grin at him, thankful he's able to put me at ease. "Well, you've got the big part right, T-Man, but I don't know about ugly. You're at *least* average-looking."

He snorts a laugh at the playful taunt.

"And you laugh way too much to be considered a grump."

He slides me a glance over his shoulder as he tends to our burgers. The smell is tantalizing and makes me realize it's been well over a day since I've eaten anything. "That's why I was chosen to come to the city. My clan is small and extremely standoffish. They don't blend well in the human world. They live up north on Mackinac Island and stay out of the way of humans as much as possible. They needed a steady source of income and wanted a voice among the underworld. I was sent here to be our representative because I was the most sociable in the clan." When I grin, he matches my smile and adds, "I'm also a bit of a runt. I fit in better among humans."

Eyeing his seven-plus feet and mountainous pecs, I say, "I've got news for you, dude; if you didn't work at Underworld, you would fail epically at the blending thing."

Terrance pulls his shoulders back and stands tall, as if I've just complimented him. "Good." I raise an eyebrow, and he shrugs before reaching for a couple of plates from a cupboard. "I've been here long enough, and I do well controlling my instincts, but all trolls have horrible tempers. I'm no exception. That's my main reason for keeping to myself so much."

I believe him. After seeing him almost lose it on Henry several times tonight, and seeing how seriously everyone responded to his lapse in control, I don't think I ever want to see him lose his temper. I can understand his fear of hurting his friends if his rage is really that hard to control. It makes him offering me a place to stay that much more baffling, though.

"So I don't annoy you?" I laugh, but I'm genuinely asking. "I've been known to piss off my fair share of people. Are you sure I'm not going to send you into a rampage?"

"I'm sure." Terrance grabs a package of hamburger buns and, while avoiding eye contact, points to the fridge. "Would you gather all the fixings?"

I hop off my stool and start rummaging through the fridge without complaint, but I don't let the conversation drop. I hand him a couple slices of cheese. "*How* are you sure?"

He places the cheese on the sizzling burgers and sighs. "I told you, you're different. You have nothing to fear from me.

Even if I were to become angry with you, I could never hurt you. My instincts would not allow it."

"But *why?*"

Pressing the topic is making him uncomfortable, but I have to know. I hadn't thought him to be under my whacked out spell, but if he is, I need to know. I can't stay here if he's infatuated with me.

Terrance slathers some mayo on his burger, and I drench mine in mustard. While we both add lettuce, tomato, and onion, he purposefully focuses on his burger and says, "Even after I refused to help you, you stood up to a master vampire on my behalf and offered to help me find Shandra, no questions asked. You went against your master's wishes at a sacrifice to your own personal health and safety, and you didn't even ask for compensation afterward."

"A) that bastard was not my master, B) I told you—I understood why you couldn't help me. And C) you were kind, and Shandra was innocent. You both deserved my help. I was more than happy to give it."

As he grabs a couple cans of soda from the fridge, his quiet reply catches my attention. "Yes. And for that, you have earned my trust and my loyalty." Handing me a drink, he finally meets my gaze and sits at one of the counter stools. "That is rare among my kind, especially outside one's clan. It is *unheard of* outside our species. I don't understand it, but tonight you invoked my protective instincts."

He uses the phrase like *protective instincts* are some kind of official troll thing, and he's staring at me as if he's dumbfounded by the possibility that I invoked them. The attention makes me uncomfortable. "Is it really such a big deal to feel protective?" I ask. "I mean, I'd have your back in a fight, too."

"I—" He pauses and seems to change his mind from whatever he was about to say. "You're right. It's not that big a deal.

It's just surprising. Like I said, it's a rare thing for a troll to befriend someone outside his clan. You can trust me, though; you're safe with me. I snore like a troll, and my feet smell like troll's feet, but if you can handle it, I don't mind the roommate."

He brushed off my question, and I hate that I feel like he's hiding something, but I do. I want to trust him, but I've had too many bad experiences, especially with men. I need to clear the air in this department or I'll never relax around him, so I drop onto the stool next to his and spit out what has me so bothered.

"Um, Terrance...?" His brows draw low over his eyes at my sudden nerves. "I just, um...I don't date. Anyone. Like, at all. Ever. I mean, I doubt you were thinking that direction, but if I'm going to crash here, I figure it's better to just lay the ground rules now, you know?"

I place my hand on his forearm with a grain of guilt. I hate reading people's minds, but I need his honest reaction this time. And though I'm afraid of what I might hear, I have to know. I like Terrance. I want this new friendship to work.

His thoughts surprise me. He's relieved. *Really* relieved. Having someone to take care of and protect is so new to him. He's still reeling from the intensity of his instincts earlier. I guess that was the first time it's ever happened to him. He thinks it's going to take him some time to learn to control himself. He's afraid having to deal with any possible suitors of mine might throw him over the edge. He was certainly ready enough to kill Henry, and likely would have gone into a full rampage at the club earlier had Wulf not stopped him.

Nowhere in his mind is there any disappointment. His interest in me is purely platonic. He's right about his protective instincts. He only means to look out for me and help me when I need it. He wants to take care of me, and he's excited by the thought of having a friend—a companion that he doesn't have to feel pressured to date. It's been a lonely seventy years away from his family.

He's been here on his own for *seventy years?* How sad.

I'm pulled from my mental eavesdropping when Terrance chuckles and pats my hand. "You're breaking my heart right now, Trouble," he teases, "but I'm sure it's for the best." Eyeing me critically, he adds, "I doubt a little thing like you could handle all of this."

He gestures to his enormous body, the motions thick with innuendo. I laugh, grateful he's broken the awkward tension I created. "I'm sure you're right. I'd be terrified to even try."

He unleashes his booming laugh again. "I like you, Trouble." Elbowing me lightly, he tries—and fails—to sound serious when he adds, "Strictly platonic, of course."

"Of course."

I finally take a large bite of the amazing burger Terrance grilled up for me. For a moment, I almost regret the platonic thing. He's an amazing cook. Moaning with pleasure, I quickly finish off the burger. Terrance grins at me as I suck the grease off my fingers. "You keep feeding me like this, and you may never get me to leave."

I'm teasing, but the jaunt seems to please him. Judging from his thoughts I'd overheard a minute ago, I'm not sure he'd mind this situation being permanent. If I weren't so desperate to leave this shithole city, I don't know that I'd mind, either. I've never felt like that about anyone before. It's crazy how quickly my life has changed.

As I take my plate to the sink, I look around the room again and am hit by a sudden lump of emotion. I feel safer right now than I have in my entire life. No one has ever been so kind to me, either. Swallowing back the threat of tears, I force myself to smile at my new roommate. "Thank you, Terrance."

"No thanks necessary." Terrance joins me at the sink with his empty plate. "I'm happy to have you."

An awkward silence falls on us that's broken when I yawn. "It's late," Terrance says. "You need anything before you go to bed?"

"Nope. I should be good."

When he reaches for his wallet and keys again, I give him a curious glance. "You going back out?"

He shucks a thumb toward the front door. "I'm going to head back to the club and help finish with the cleanup."

On closer inspection, I realize he doesn't look the least bit tired, while I'm practically dead on my feet. "Are you nocturnal?"

He bobs his head up and down. "Mostly. Not that I can't be up during the day, but I get even grumpier than normal when I have to be." He frowns at me and adds, "I didn't think about that. We'll be on different schedules. Is that going to be a problem for you?"

I smile at his concern. "I'm a big girl, T-man. I can amuse myself when you're sleeping. And I'm a bit of a night owl anyway, so we'll see each other plenty. You'll be ready to kick me out in no time."

His frown melts into a grin. "All right." He glances around the room and sighs. "Well, as long as you're here, make yourself at home. I'll get a key made while I'm out tonight. It'll be waiting for you on the table when you wake up. Feel free to come and go, and help yourself to whatever. *Mi casa es su casa*, and all that. You going to be okay here all by yourself? If you aren't comfortable here alone yet, you're welcome to come to the club with me, but you look exhausted."

"I am exhausted. And now that I'm fed, that bedroom is calling my name."

"So you'll be good?"

I smile at his concern. "I'm probably safer here than I ever have been in my life."

"That's true. I had this place warded by a sorceress along with my own protection charms. No one who isn't expressly invited can get in." He stands up a bit straighter and gives me a cocky smile while puffing up his chest. "Not that anyone would try. Breaking into a troll's den is suicide."

I laugh. His cockiness is adorable because it's not natural. "I have no doubt, T-man. Go back to work, and don't worry about me. I'm going to sleep better tonight than I have in months."

The declaration pleases him so much that he gives me a wide grin. The man keeps claiming to be a grump, but so far I'm not convinced. "All right. See you tomorrow, then. Stay out of trouble, Trouble."

"No promises."

As he walks out of the kitchen, chuckling to himself and shaking his head, I call after him. "Hey, Terrance..." When he looks back, I flash him a grin. "About those stinky feet...are we talking air freshener, or should I start looking for my own place now?"

Like I'd hoped, Terrance breaks out into his deep, roaring laughter that shakes the whole room.

CHAPTER
ELEVEN

When I wake up, it's after three p.m. I've never slept in that late, but the last two days had been very taxing, and I haven't had a good night's sleep where I felt completely safe in years, if ever. I feel more rested than I've ever been.

As soon as I shake the sleep off, I smirk. Terrance wasn't kidding about his snoring. Like his laugh, it's loud, deep, and rattles the whole house. I'd been so exhausted it hadn't wakened me, but I'll be investing in some earplugs.

After a nice, hot shower where I'm not worried about hidden cameras or perverted neighbors breaking in on me, I get dressed and make my way into the kitchen, wondering what a troll keeps in his pantry. I don't make it to the cupboards, because there's more than a key waiting for me on the kitchen table. Terrance has left me a laptop, and on the same ring as the house key, there's a fob for a car sporting a Cadillac logo. *He gave me a key to his car?*

Along with the computer and keys, there's a note. It simply says *NO ARGUMENTS* and lists five contact numbers. The handwriting is strong, slanted, and all caps. And it's dark, as if he bolded the letters to emphasize his point. *Point?* I snort. It's not a point. It's a *threat.*

I don't take charity. In my experience, when guys give you stuff, they expect too much in return for it. But somehow I feel safe accepting this loaner. I know Terrance is only trying to be nice. He's trying to take care of me. And he's doing it because he wants to. Not because the state is paying him to. I've never had someone look out for me like that. It's overwhelming.

After scrounging up a bowl of cereal, I sit down at the table and open the laptop as I eat. Terrance has already set it up and connected it to his Wi-Fi. While I connect to the Internet, I look over the list of phone numbers and add them to my contacts. The five numbers he gave me are for himself, his bartender Wulf, Nick Gorgeous, Parker, and Oliver. The list makes me grin. It's like he's telling me these are people I can count on. People I can trust. The irony of it is that they're all underworlders. Who'd have ever thought I'd find more friends among monsters than humans?

I'm surprised Parker's number made the list. As angry as Terrance was at him and Henry last night, I'm shocked he'd trust Parker enough to give me his number. Still. It's a good thing he did since he's the person I need to talk to right now. My thumb hovers over his name, but I can't make the call. I shake off my nerves and take a deep breath. "Get over it, Nora. Parker's not Henry, and you need his help."

The personal pep talk does the trick. I dial his number before I can think better of it.

"Hello?" His voice sounds sleepy. It's cute. That thought shocks me almost as much as the small smile currently on my face. What the hell is wrong with me?

"Hello?" he asks again, because I haven't said anything yet.

"Hey, Parker. It's uh...Nora."

"Nora?"

His surprise sucks away the little confidence I had. "Um, yeah, it's me. Terrance gave me your number. I hope it's okay that I called."

"Of course. I'm glad you did." He doesn't sound groggy anymore. "Listen, Nora, I—"

"Don't bother with the explanations or apologies. I don't want them. It happened. It's done. End of story. I'm just calling to see if you found out anything about that license plate number I gave you."

There's a long pause, and then Parker says, "Let me take you to dinner, and we can discuss it."

My heart jumps up into my throat. I go with my initial knee-jerk reaction to being asked out, even though something akin to butterflies flutters in my stomach at the offer. "No. Hell no."

"I don't mean you harm, Nora. I'd just like to see you again. Under normal circumstances this time."

I'm tempted to accept, and that scares me. "I don't date," I whisper. "Ever."

"Not a date, then," Parker persists. "Consider it a business meeting. We're both working on the same case, and we can help each other."

Tempting. Very tempting. I almost say yes. But I just can't disregard years of bad experiences and gut instinct. "*Or*...you could just tell me what you know now, and I won't have to wait for dark to get to work."

Parker sighs. "The plates were fake," he says.

"What?"

"The license number you gave me belongs to the minivan of a soccer mom in Plymouth."

My heart sinks. That was our only lead. "You're certain?"

"100 percent. It was most likely an illusion spell."

"Magic?"

"Yes. The club's cameras and the street cameras were all spelled out of commission that night, too."

I leave the kitchen and start pacing in the living room. This doesn't make any sense. But it does go along with the vision I had of the guy who took Shandra. He'd breathed something in her face that knocked her out. I'd assumed drugs of some kind, but maybe he was using magic. "So we're looking for a sorcerer."

"One who's stealing underworlders," Parker says. "Though I can't imagine why."

I thought about the two guys in my vision, and their conversation. "It was like they were collecting them—different kinds of underworlders, I mean. They were really excited to have a troll. I guess that's pretty uncommon."

"And dangerous. Trolls have unbelievable strength and stamina. And they're fiercely loyal to each other. Mess with one troll, mess with their whole clan."

"Then why risk it? Why do they want them? For what?"

"I don't know."

Parker yawns, and I realize the wariness in his voice is probably just fatigue. It's the middle of the night for him, and the fact that he can be awake at all while the sun is up means he's a very powerful vampire. I feel bad for disturbing his sleep. "Sorry. I know you're tired."

"I am. It's very hard for vampires to be awake in the daytime. I won't last much longer. But if you would just meet me tonight, we could go over all of this together."

I still don't want to, but he has a point. If I can't find anything else out today, I might have to. "Call me when you wake up, and we'll see."

Parker chuckles. The sound gives me shivers. "Strictly professional. You have my word."

"We'll see," I say again. "No promises. And *no* Henry. Don't you dare give him this number. Don't even tell him I called. Or any other vampire, either. At all. Just you. I mean it."

"You have my word, Nora. I'll call you around eight."

I swallow back dread as I hang up the phone. What did I just do? Did I just make a date with the devil? *It's not a date. I didn't even promise to meet him.*

I continue to rage a war with my inner thoughts as I google *Greek life* and start sifting through different fraternity images. If the license plate number on the car was a fake, the only other lead I have is the sticker that was on the back windshield. I can't exactly remember the symbols, but I'd know them if I saw them.

I look through photo after photo and don't see what I'm looking for. I look on several sites that list all the Greek fraternities and sororities and still can't find the image I remember. But I would swear that's what that window decal was for.

Before giving up, I have one last idea. I turn on my chat and smile when I see that my only contact is online. Knowing the face behind the screen name is still surreal. It makes me feel shy as I send a message to my longtime guardian angel.

PsychoPsychic: Hey...Oliver.

I immediately get a reply.

SorcererX: Nora! I'm glad to hear from you. I was worried about you going home with your neighbor after you and all...is everything okay?

His concern warms me. I might have five contacts in my phone, but at the moment there are only two people in the world I trust—Oliver and Terrance.

PsychoPsychic: Actually, I'm pretty great. Terrance wouldn't let me stay there anymore. He's putting me up at his place until I decide where I'm headed.

SorcererX: TERRANCE??????? The TROLL took you in?

PsychoPsychic: It's okay. I know he's a troll, and I know they're dangerous, but I swear he won't hurt me. I don't know how I know, I just do. I actually slept better last night than I ever have. I'm safe here, Oliver. I promise.

SorcererX: Of course you're safe. Terrance took you in. That's not what I meant. I'm just surprised. Nora, him bringing you home is a BIG deal. You're under his protection now. You're probably safer than most underworlders in this city. I can't believe he took you in. That's CRAZY. I'm glad, though. I'm glad you're safe now.

I laugh at his shock. I guess it really is unusual for Terrance to bring home guests.

PsychoPsychic: Thanks. Me too, though I'm still trying to wrap my head around the concept. Anyway, listen, you said you were taking criminal justice classes. Does that mean you go to Wayne State U?

SorcererX: Yeah. Finishing up my master's here. Not my school of choice, but my budget disagrees.

I laugh. I know how it feels to settle for less than what you want because you're strapped for cash.

PsychoPsychic: Are you on campus now?

SorcererX: Yeah, my last class just ended. I usually head to the library by your place to do my homework right about now, but I guess I don't need to go all the way over there, since you won't be there. Why? You need something?

I hesitate before I respond, my heart speeding up at what I'm about to ask him. The idea of hanging out with Oliver in person is both exciting and terrifying. Right now, as things are, we could still continue to be just random Internet buddies. He can keep feeding me info about the underworld and answering my questions, but things would stay the same. If I ask him to meet me, that changes things. Then, I'm acknowledging our friendship as something more. Something real. I've never had a real friend before. He would be my first.

"Suck it up, Nora," I whisper to myself. "It'll be fine. He already knows your secret. You don't have to hide from him, so maybe he could be a real friend."

With a deep breath, I reply to his question and try not to have a heart attack.

PsychoPsychic: I need to go over there and check something out. I thought maybe if you're there already, you could give me a tour? Help me find what I'm looking for?

SorcererX: Of course. I'd love to.

I wince. Oliver is going to be hard to have as just a friend. Normally his interest in me would have me running for the hills, but I like Oliver. I want to find a way to be friends without hurting him.

PsychoPsychic: Thanks. I'm on my way. T-man gave me your phone number, so I'll text you when I get there.

Sighing, I close the laptop and grab the set of keys from the counter. I still can't believe Terrance is letting me use his car. I'll try not to make a habit of it, but for now it's my only option. I'm a good seven or eight miles from the college right now, and I don't know the bus routes on this end of town. I doubt there's a stop anywhere near me, anyway. I'm under the bridge, for heaven's sake.

As I leave, I'm shocked to find the stairs to the exit are already lit up with built-in overhead lights that give off a soft glow like the rest of the house. *When the hell did Terrance have time to install a whole lighting system?*

An even bigger shock comes when I get outside and click the lock button on the car key fob Terrance left me. After taking a moment to let my eyes adjust to the harsh afternoon daylight, I realize the key on my ring is not for his candy-apple red Caddie. It belongs to the smaller silver sporty-looking coupe parked next to it. This car is a Cadillac, too, and I happen to know it's an expensive one. Not as expensive as Terrance's, but close.

My stomach drops as suspicion creeps in. I hadn't seen a second car parked out here last night. I scan the temporary license sticker in the back window and curse. He'd bought the car this morning. He'd purchased a whole second car just so that I'd have something to drive, even when I told him I don't plan on sticking around more than a few days. "Damn you, Terrance," I whisper as I walk around to the driver's side.

It was a kind gesture, but I hate feeling beholden to anyone, and how could I possibly not be indebted to Terrance for this?

Oh, well. Nothing to do about it at the moment. I'm not going to wake him up to argue with him when he was awake all night making sure I was taken care of. And he'd probably be insulted if I refused to use the car, so I climb behind the wheel and head over to the college in the nicest car I've ever driven.

I'm in heaven with each acceleration, each stop, and each turn I make. I get to the college way too soon and find the visitor's parking lot. I'm afraid for such a nice car to be parked in Detroit, but as I get out and lock it, I feel the slight zing of magic surrounding it. I smile to myself. It's protected by wards. I'm not sure what they do—do they make people not see it, or zap them if they're not supposed to touch it and do—but I know it's safe to leave it where it is.

I head toward the nearest building, about to text Oliver when he calls my name. He's wearing jeans and a Zelda hoodie. I recognize him instantly. His warm amber eyes are locked on me, sparkling with delight, and his smile is wider than I've ever seen it.

"Oliver!" I wave and close the distance between us quickly. "Hey! How'd you find me so fast?"

He shrugs. "I traced your phone number. I saw you park in this lot."

I cock a brow at him. Tracing phone numbers? So he's a bit of a computer hacker? Honestly, I'm not surprised. "Sorry." He runs his fingers through his hair. "It's just, this isn't the best neighborhood, and now that the underworld knows about you, people are going to be curious. Not all of us are nocturnal."

Sighing, I give him a small smile so he knows I'm not upset. "Looking out for me, as always."

The twinkle in his eyes comes back. "Of course. Always, Nora. I promise."

I have no idea what to say to that, so I clear my throat and shrug toward campus. "Okay, so here's the thing...I need to find a fraternity."

Oliver jerks his head back and gives me a peculiar look. "I think you mean sorority, and *you're* interested in rushing?"

I shake my head, thinking back to my vision and the meatheads who stole Shandra. "Oh, no, I mean a frat." I shoot Oliver a look as dry as my next question. "And do I seem like someone who would rush a sorority to you?"

Oliver grins. "No."

"No is right. We're not here to rush, Oliver, we're looking for clues. The car Shandra was taken in had a decal on the back window. It looked like the Greek letters of a fraternity name, but I couldn't find it on Google. I'm hoping since Wayne State is the only university in the area, the sticker I saw belongs to a fraternity here. If we find the fraternity, we find the car. We find the car, I can do my Sherlock thing and find the clues."

"We?" Oliver asks in a quiet voice as he holds the straps of his backpack.

I can't tell if he's nervous because he doesn't want to get involved, or because I invited him along. "Well, I suppose you don't have to play Watson to my Sherlock, if you don't want to," I say. "It might get dangerous. Powerful underworlders are getting snatched, and Nick Gorgeous mentioned you're crazy-ass strong. These psychos might want you. Maybe you should just point me to the student union and—"

"No, I want to help," Oliver blurts. "I was just surprised you'd include me."

"Why?"

"Don't take this the wrong way, Nora, but...well...you're a loner. You aren't the type to work with a partner or ask for backup."

He's not wrong about that, but what he doesn't know is that I've always been a loner out of necessity. "Only because I've never had anyone I could trust with my secret before."

"You can trust me, Nora," Oliver says quietly.

His declaration makes me feel all kinds of emotions I'm not used to experiencing. *Warm* and *fuzzy* are not words I'd use to describe my life.

Ignoring the heat in my cheeks, I casually bump his shoulder with mine. "I know I can, or I wouldn't have called you." There's a brief, awkward pause, which I break up with a clap of my hands. "Come along, Watson. We've got a troll to find."

CHAPTER TWELVE

Even though Wayne State University is no Notre Dame, it's still fun to be walking around campus with Oliver as if I belong here. It makes me wish this were my life —that I was normal, and had friends, and went to college. I almost see myself graduating, getting a job, having a boyfriend. For the moment, I feel normal. Of course, I'm a psychic strolling across campus with a sorcerer, looking for a group of supernatural kidnappers who've snatched my troll roommate's potential mate, so...normal is relative, I guess.

"You're in luck, because it's Rush Week right now," Oliver says as we move into what seems to be the main quad. It's full of tables and booths all advertising different sororities and fraternities. "Every Greek organization affiliated with Wayne State will have representatives here. We'll just start at one end and work our way around the quad."

"Sounds good to me."

Oliver smiles, lighting up his whole face. When he offers me a hand to hold, as if this were a date, I grimace and shake my head. "Sorry. I've got a no touching policy. Unless you want me to hear every thought in your head."

Oliver's face heats up, and he matches my grimace. "Oh, right. I forgot about that."

I try to smile, but the mood has slipped into awkward territory. Surprisingly, Oliver is the one to drive us back into comfortable conversation. "You can't turn your gift off, then?"

I shake my head, grateful that I have to be paying attention to all of the booth banners so I don't have to maintain eye contact. "I wish. That would make my life a hell of a lot easier."

"What about clothes? Does it work through material, or do long sleeves, gloves, and things stop it?"

"Mostly. But I hate gloves. I hate having my fingers restricted, and I really don't like to draw attention to myself any more than I have to. It's bad enough I'm a small single woman living in the inner city."

Oliver sighs. "That's true. I guess I don't blame you. But... don't you ever crave human touch?"

No way am I answering that question. I stop to look loosely at a yellow banner advertising a fraternity.

"That it?" Oliver asks, following my gaze when I stop walking.

After a moment, I shake my head. "I think it looks similar, but the symbols were different. I'm sure of it."

Oliver heads over to the booth. It's being manned by a couple of tall, well-built guys—one white and one black. Both look like basketball players. They're leaner than the meatheads from my vision, and they seem like they're slightly more intelligent, even though all the pictures at their booth are of raging parties.

They both eye skinny, geeky Oliver warily. "Hey, bro. You looking to join up?" the black guy asks.

He's good looking, but his condescension toward Oliver pisses me off. As if he can feel me seething, he looks my way and then does a double take before smirking at Oliver. "Damn, man, your girl is *fine.*"

I know Oliver is about to correct his assumption that I'm his girlfriend, so I jump into the conversation before that can happen. "Thanks."

The white guy joins the conversation, grinning widely at me. "Hey, beautiful, whatcha doin' with this joker?"

My jaw drops. Are these guys for real? At least Oliver doesn't seem to care about this guy's low opinion. He slides me a sideways glance and gives me an eye roll that makes me smirk. I move close to Oliver and slip my arm around his waist. He glances curiously at me but follows my lead, wrapping his arm around my shoulder. He's so considerate that he's careful to only touch my sleeve. "Haven't you boys heard the news?" I ask. "Geeks are totally in now. And I'll have you know that not only is my man brilliant, fun, and a god between the sheets, he's powerful, too."

Both guys' mouths fall open, and their eyebrows climb up their foreheads. I shoot them a smug smirk and lean in closer to Oliver. "Oh, yeah. He's got his own brand of self-defense. He could kick both your asses to defend me—kill you if he had to."

I give Oliver a knowing wink. He had come to my defense before, and maybe he doesn't use his magic anymore, but I have no doubt he would if my life were in question. My praise makes him squeeze my shoulders. "And it's a good thing, too," he teases me, "as much as you find trouble."

"Very true." I chuckle. Oliver is kind of hot when he's being assertive. Maybe I misread him before. Maybe he's not shy like I thought, but just introverted.

Both frat boys get over their shock and laugh along with us. They're eyeing Oliver differently now, with curiosity and respect. "Okay, okay, shorty," the first guy says to me. "We get you. No offense meant. So..." He turns his attention back to Oliver. "You looking to pledge?"

I give Oliver a questioning look that he snorts at. It makes me laugh. Man, this having a friend thing is awesome. "Actually," I say, and Oliver happily lets me answer for him, "we were looking for a specific fraternity. I thought maybe it was you guys, but I can see now it's not. Do you guys know of another house that has a logo similar to yours? Same yellow color, but the symbols were different. Loopier somehow."

The white guy scoffs, and the black guy glares at nothing in particular. "Are you talking about those punk-ass poser bitches?" he asks.

I perk up at this. "So you *do* know them?"

The white guy shakes his head. "Those jokers made up their own house and walk around like they're all legit, but they aren't even Greek."

"Girl, you don't want nothing to do with them. They ain't right. More like a cult than a frat, and they get rough."

"I've heard their parties get weird. Real freaks, you know?"

"Yeah." I nod at Oliver. "That sounds like our assholes."

He returns my nod, then looks at both our new friends, sighing. "That's them, all right. Do you know where their house is?"

"Do we ever," the first guy says. "Those mutha truckers moved into a house down the street from us and then stole our design. They steal half our crowds whenever we throw parties, and they've scared off a lot of people from wanting to join us." His face turns grave, and he lowers his voice as he pins both Oliver and me with a sincere gaze. "Seriously, you guys should stay away from them. You seem like good people. I'm sure you can take care of yourselves, but those freaks are dangerous. Everybody hates them, but nobody messes with them for a reason."

"*We're* having a party this weekend, though," the other guy says. "You should both come." He hands us flyers advertising their frat house and the party hours. The house address is conveniently written along the bottom of the paper. "And hey, bro..." He holds his hand out to Oliver. "If you're interested in pledging, let us know. We'll introduce you to the other guys and let them know you're cool."

I can see the smile Oliver is trying to hide as he shakes the guy's hand. "I'll think about it. Thanks for the info on those other guys. We'll make sure to steer clear."

"Steer yourselves to our place. Friday night. It's gonna be awesome."

"We will, man, thanks."

With a casual nod, Oliver leads me away toward the next booth. "Huh," he says once we're out of earshot. "So this is what it feels like to be one of the cool kids."

A laugh bursts from me that makes Oliver chuckle. I nudge his shoulder with mine as we walk. "Don't let it go to your head, Ollie. I happen to like you just how you are."

Oliver shrugs his shoulders and smiles at the ground as we walk. "Thanks," he mutters, nudging me back the way I'd bumped him. Then he clears his throat and changes the subject. "So I take it we're on our way to the *punk-ass poser bitches'* house?"

I grin. "Oh, yeah. I'm gonna go all Nora Jacobs psycho psychic chick on those *mutha truckers*."

THE GPS in Terrance's fancy car takes us right to the frat house. From there, our guys aren't hard to find. For one thing, a very familiar yellow hooptie of a car is parked on the street out front. And for another, the entire house has been painted a pale yellow exactly like the frat house. No wonder our new friends at the booth were so bitter. They say copycatting is a form of flattery, but it's still annoying. "Bingo. That's our car."

Oliver follows my gaze and snorts. "Nice ride."

"You should see the tool who drives it. Come on. Be my lookout while I do my thing. When I get sucked into visions, I can't pull myself out."

Oliver gets twitchy as we near the car. He's looking at the large pale yellow house. "Are you sure we should—"

"It's the only way to find Shandra." I glance at the house. "Look at the place. All's quiet. Either the majority of them are in class, or sleeping, or out kidnapping more underworlders. I doubt we'll have a better opportunity. Just keep an eye out, and if someone comes...drag me away. If I let go, it will break the vision. Then we can run."

Oliver doesn't reply to this other than to take a deep breath and stare at the house again. When we reach the car, and the edge of the property, my skin prickles and all the hair on my arms stands up. Oliver gasps, and I let out a long, low whistle. "That's a lot of magic," I say. The tingling sensation is stronger than I felt at Terrance's house. "It feels different, though. It's not normal, is it?"

When I get no reply, I glance at Oliver. He's white as a ghost, and his eyes look like softballs. His jaw is hanging open.

"What is it?"

Oliver snaps out of his shock with a shiver and swallows hard. "It's dark magic," he whispers. "It's banned in the underworld because it's gained through sacrifice and it's really dangerous. It doesn't always do what you want it to. It sort of has a will of its own and will twist the mind of the person using it."

"Let me guess. It turns people evil?"

Oliver frowns at my sarcasm. "Yes, it does." He tugs on my arm. "We need to get out of here."

"What?" I pull away from Oliver's grip. "We can't leave yet."

I reach out for the handle on the driver's side door of the car, but I get nothing. There is no imprint on the handle. Lucky for me, the old, obnoxious car is unlocked. Guess the owner thinks his reputation will keep people from breaking in. Or maybe he just forgot to lock it. I mean, why would he need to? This is only Detroit. It's only one of the top ten crime capitals of the country. Mr. Muscles did seem rather stupid, though.

I hold my breath as I open the car door. I'm *pretty* sure all the magic I feel is coming from the house, but there's a slight possibility the car is warded, too, and I just can't tell. When I pull the door open and nothing happens, I let all the air out of my lungs. So Muscle Guy is just stupid after all. Awesome for me.

As I slide in behind the wheel, I glance over my shoulder at my lookout. Oliver has called someone and is murmuring anxiously into the phone, glancing at the house over and over. Whatever. He can have his freak-out. I need to scope out this car.

As soon as I place my hands on the wheel, I'm pulled into an intense vision. It's night, and the guy from the bar is gone, but the driver of the car who picked him up sits gripping the steering wheel with white knuckles. I'm sitting in the backseat of the car—Shandra is gone. It's nighttime, and the house in front of us is hosting a raging kegger.

Muscle Head sees a guy in the crowd and nods for him to come get in the car. The new guy is a redhead. He's tall and lean, but his shoulders bulge under his T-shirt and his arms show definition. Unlike Muscle Head, the new guy looks intelligent. He slips into the passenger seat with an irritated look on his face. "You were supposed to check in an hour ago. Why didn't you call?"

Muscle Head twists his hands over the steering wheel again, shooting his companion a dark look. "I didn't think we should have this conversation over the phone. You're not going to believe what went down tonight."

Red only cocks an eyebrow and waits for an explanation. Muscle Head sighs. "We have to take Noah."

"Noah?" Red whines. "I hate that idiot. Why would you want him?"

"That idiot bagged us a troll tonight."

Red flinches, his mouth falling wide open. "No shit. A troll? Is he crazy?"

"YES!" Muscle Head shouts. "He snagged her right from under the noses of two other trolls. I had to use up all the last of my powder to cover our tracks."

Red breathes out a small sigh of relief. "You spelled the cameras, then?"

"The cameras, the alley. I cloaked the car. I drove around randomly for over an hour before I helped him take the ugly bitch to the sanctuary. Been looking over my shoulder for angry trolls ever since. I think the bastard got lucky. I think we got away with it."

Red's eyes gleam with excitement. "A troll. We've never had that kind of strength before."

"Yeah, because trying to harness that kind of power is suicide."

Red glares at Muscle Head. "Have I ever lost control? Ever?"

Muscle Head's glare turns to a pout. "No, but it's getting close, and you're starting to lose your power."

"You don't think I've planned for that? The culling will take place before our life forces run out, and hell, I'm a damn mid-level sorcerer. We'll be fine. We'll have to let Noah in. He's the only other option, and he scored a damn troll. Now if Xavier would just hurry his ass up, we'll be all set."

"Xavier! Didn't you hear? That pussy didn't pan out."

"What?" Red yells. "What happened? He was my favorite initi-

ate! He didn't get his vamp? He said the guy was over four hundred years old. Do you know how powerful a vamp that age would be? He didn't get himself killed, did he?"

"Almost. But not from any vamp attack. The idiot went to Underworld the other night, got his ass beat, and OD'd on something no one can identify. He ended up in the hospital, almost dead. He's claiming he was drugged, but the cops are still on his ass about it. We can't have him bringing that kind of shit to us."

"DAMN IT!" Red smashes his fist into the dash in front of him. He rakes a hand through his hair and blows a puff of air out. "Who else is there?"

"No one, Elijah. Only Xavier."

Red—Elijah—shakes his head. "We need Xavier, then. Tell him he has one last chance to bring us an underworlder, or he's out. Let's see if he can really get his 400-year-old vamp like he said he could."

"And if he can't? It doesn't work without twelve," Muscle Head says. "The Blood Moon is on Tuesday. We're cutting it kind of close."

Elijah glares at Muscle Head. "Tell Xavier he's got new competition. That'll motivate him. Tell him to bring his underworlder to the... I don't know. We don't want him to come to our place, just in case he does have problems with cops. Who's having a party tomorrow night?"

"Umm, I think Alpha Gamma Delta's holding a mixer tomorrow night."

"Perfect." Elijah opens his door to exit the car but turns back to Muscle Head with a grimace. "He'd better come through. You're right that we need twelve. I was counting on Xavier."

Muscle Head sighs. "Me too. I'm not crazy about the guy, but at least he has a brain, unlike Noah. I'm not sure how he got so messed up."

"Let's hope he's telling the truth and he really just got drugged or something." Elijah sighs and nods his head toward the lively house. "You coming?"

Muscle Head nods. "Hell yeah. I need a drink after tonight. Something strong."

"How about a little elixir in your whiskey? I've got a little left saved for a rainy day, and I'd say you earned it tonight."

The vision fades before I get Muscle Head's reply, but I'm fairly certain he wasn't going to turn down whatever that elixir was.

I slump back in the seat, groaning. My head is freaking pounding. Those long visions kill me. But at least this vision was informative and not just some quickie Mr. Muscles had in the car.

When I come to enough to take in my surroundings, I hear two voices calling my name. Nick Gorgeous is standing right behind Oliver, a worried expression on his face. "What are you doing here?" I mumble.

His face turns annoyed. "It's *my* case."

Oliver takes my hand as I turn to the side and set my feet on the ground. His look is rueful. "We can't deal with dark magic by ourselves, Nora."

"You shouldn't be dealing with this at all." Nick harrumphs from over Oliver's shoulder.

I ignore him and hold out my hands to Oliver. "Help me out of here. I think I'm gonna hurl."

Oliver jumps to action, helping me to my feet. Nick shuts the car door behind us, then steals me up into his arms. Damn, it's like I'm weightless. If I didn't feel so shitty, I'd enjoy the ride in the hot guy's arms. I'd even enjoy the fact that Mr. Just Call Me Gorgeous is wearing an old school AC/DC shirt and a cowboy hat. But...like I said, I feel too awful to care. Without warning, my breakfast comes back up.

Cursing, Nick holds me out away from him as far as he can so that the splatter of my puke barely misses his nice, shiny cowboy boots. "Easy, woman. Watch the snakeskin!"

"Oh, I'm *so* sorry. I'll just defy the laws of na—" I'm cut off when my stomach heaves again, and I hurl round two. There's a hiss behind me, and then Nick sets me down on the curb behind Terrance's nice loaner. "I'll just defy the laws of nature," I say again once I can breathe, "in order to spare your obnoxious shoes."

"Obnoxious?"

"Yeah. I mean, look at them." I'll never admit how badass I think they are.

"Please. These are sexy."

They totally are. "If you say so."

"I do. Now what the hell are you doing here? And why are you throwing up everywhere?"

While I'm rolling my eyes at Nick, Oliver digs up a water bottle from the bottom of his backpack and hands it to me. I moan with pleasure as I take it from him. "Oh, Ollie, you are my new best friend."

I rinse and spit several times while Oliver sits down on the curb next to me. "Are you okay now? Feeling better yet?"

I nod and wipe at the sheen of sweat on my forehead with the sleeve of my shirt. "I'm good now. I don't normally puke, but that was a particularly strong vision. The stronger the vision, the worse the backlash."

"You just had a *vision?*" Nick asks.

Oliver smirks when I sigh, as if Nick is hopeless. "I'm not here looking to buy a car," I say.

Nick glances back down the street at the yellow monstrosity he found me sitting in and shudders. "Wise decision."

I snort. It really is a hideous car. "I'm here trying to find Shandra, like I promised Terrance I would do. And, hey!" I wave my hand at the pale yellow cult house. "I found our guys!"

Nick glances warily at the house. "The missing underworlders are in there?"

I wish it were that easy. I shake my head. "No. They're keeping them somewhere else. A place they call the sanctuary. I think it's where they perform their rituals. This is just where they sleep and party. But these are definitely our guys, and I think I know how to find our missing underworlders."

"I could just go in there and make them tell me," Nick suggests, pulling a gigantic knife from inside his boot. Awesome. The boots are both sexy and functional. Man, Nick is such a badass.

Badass or not, I shake my head at him. "You don't know who and how many of them are involved. You couldn't possibly grab them all. It would only take one to get away or make a call to whoever's guarding the sanctuary, and then Shandra and all the others are either gone or dead to hide evidence. We need to find the sanctuary before we go busting in anywhere like a couple of cowboys in the Old West."

The cowboy reference was totally for Nick's sake, and he knows it. He can't hold his frown and starts to chuckle. "Ruin all my fun, Spitfire," he jokes. His smile turns proud. "Still. Way to think like a detective. You're not so bad, for a human."

I roll my eyes at the backhanded compliment.

"So what's this plan you have, and what makes you think there are others besides Shandra?" Nick asks.

"And Nadine," Oliver adds. "Henry's missing vampire."

I can't help wrinkling my nose at the mention of vampires —especially Henry. First impressions are a bitch to overcome, and, well, Henry screwed the pooch with that one.

A car drives slowly down the street with a couple of frat looking guys in it. They shoot us suspicious frowns as they pass us by, but luckily they park at the real frat house instead of the evil cult one. "Let's go somewhere else to hash out the details," I say.

"Let's get you back to Terrance's place," Oliver says. When I question his choice, he points at my shirt and the small dots of puke that ended up there. "Figured you'd want to change and brush your teeth."

"You are a wise and thoughtful man, my dear badass sorcerer BFF."

Oliver shakes his head and laughs. He climbs into the passenger seat of T-Man's awesome loaner without word, and as I open the driver's side door, I glance back at Nick. "Come on, cowboy. Follow us to the troll's den." I start to climb in the car and then pause, glancing quickly at Oliver and then back at Nick. "Wait. Terrance isn't going to, like, eat you guys if I bring you inside or anything, is he?"

I expect both of them to laugh; however, they both do the opposite. Oliver's face pales and Nick freezes, whatever quip he'd been forming dying on his tongue. He thinks about it for much too long and then says, "Maybe you should call him first and ask if it's okay."

CHAPTER THIRTEEN

Terrance gives me permission to bring the rodeo back to his place. Our place, I guess. He'd called it my home when I asked if I could bring Nick and Oliver over, and told me that as long as I felt someone was welcome, the magic around the place wouldn't kill them. That had given me pause, and I'd mumbled a sort of mantra that Nick and Oliver were welcome from the time we neared the wards to the time we hit the bottom of the stairs.

Oliver gawks, standing so close to me that our arms brush. I don't begrudge him his lack of space because he looks equal parts fascinated and terrified to be here. Nick seems much more casual. He lets out a low whistle. "Nice digs."

"I know, right?" I laugh. "And to think all of this is under the bridge."

"Well, I'm a troll, Nora," Terrance says, entering the main living room. "We live under bridges."

Oliver stiffens and gulps while I laugh. "Sorry. Nursery rhymes are real. It's going to take me some getting used to."

Terrance shakes his head, but he can't stop the small smile from creeping across his lips. I amuse him. "So, T-Man, I've got some news about Shandra." His eyes bulge, and I quickly hold up a hand before he can spout a bunch of questions. "First of all, I'm sure she's still alive."

He breathes out a huge breath of relief, and his entire body seems to sag as the air leaves him. "What happened? Where is she? Is she okay?"

I hold my hand up again. "I'll tell you everything I know, but first, let me go change. I puked big time after a nasty vision. I could use some new clothes and a toothbrush. I'll hurry, and then we can hash out my plan to get Shandra back. Why don't you make us all some coffee while I go clean myself up?"

Oliver gasps, and Nick makes a choking sound. I'm not sure what that's about, but whatever. I look at Terrance, and his hint of a grin becomes a wide smile. "You got it, Trouble," he says, holding up his fist to me.

I bump his knuckles before heading toward my room. "You're the best, T-man. Be right back."

As I leave, I hear Oliver mutter, "The woman just fist-bumped a troll."

"After she ordered him around like a damn maid and lived," Nick whispers. "Unbelievable."

Terrance's laughter shakes the whole place.

The coffee is in mugs when I come out of my bedroom. I follow the smell to the kitchen, where Terrance is at the counter and Nick and Oliver sit at the table. Terrance looks over his shoulder when I enter the room. "How do you like your coffee?"

"Straight black, thanks."

"Is that how you like your men, too?" Nick asks, grinning roguishly at me. "Straight and black?"

I can't help it; I laugh. I laugh because I can tell he's teasing me more than hitting on me. Oh, I have no doubt he'd have a good romp in the sheets with me if I were down, but I'm not, and I can tell he knows that. He's teasing but not pressing. "Oh,

Gorgeous." I sigh. "You do live up to your name, I'll give you that. But the only way I like my men is as friends. I don't date. Ever. Too much past drama for me."

I pretend not to see the crestfallen look on Oliver's face and sit down at the table next to Terrance. "Okay." I blow on my coffee and take a sip. It's not sludge. Terrance really knows his way around the kitchen. "So...here's what I got from the vision. I think—this is an educated guess, mind you—but I *believe* they're going to attempt to acquire the power from all the underworlders they've collected. Like they're going to siphon out the underworlders' life forces and keep it for themselves in some sort of sacrificial ritual." This earns me a round of gasps and growls. "Can that be done?"

After the outraged shouting and swearing from Nick and Terrance ends, Oliver answers my question. "It would be very difficult, and could only be done through dark magic. Regular magic—good magic—comes from within. That's why only sorcerers can do magic. We are born with it inside us. We don't have to steal it to use it. Dark magic is power stolen by killing magical beings. It's extremely powerful, but also highly unstable, and becomes evil. It's hard to use. In order to perform the kind of thing you're talking about, you'd need..."

"Twelve guys?" I guess. "They said they needed twelve."

All three men at the table groan. Nick curses again and throws his head back, staring at the ceiling. "We're dealing with an entire coven?"

"I don't think so." All eyes come back to me. "I think we're dealing with wannabes. I think they're all humans pretending to be sorcerers. They don't have magic of their own, they get it from their leader—a mid-level sorcerer, he said. I think they're using his magic to perform the ritual so that they can gain underworld power. I don't think it's their first time, either. He said that their power is starting to fade, but that they'd do the ritual before it was all gone."

Oliver nods as if this makes perfect sense. "Yeah, that seems more like it. No way would there ever be an entire coven dumb enough to get mixed up in dark magic. One idiot mid-level sorcerer looking to gain more power by getting humans to do his dirty work? That's much more realistic."

I meet his eyes and smirk. "You know, he said *mid-level* like it was the most badass thing ever."

A ghost of a smile crosses Oliver's face. It's almost cocky, but not quite. "It's not bad if he really is one," he says with a modest shrug. "He can probably do some damage. He'll be tough to defeat if he's using dark magic. We'll have to get backup when we're ready to invade their sanctuary. Two or three sorcerers, at least."

"Or maybe," Nick says, tapping his chin with his finger, as if thinking very hard. "If only the Agency had someone like a high sorcerer to help them out. Dark magic or not, a mid-level sorcerer would be a walk in the park for a guy like that."

When Oliver glares at Nick, I join him, feeling both protective and possessive all of a sudden. *How dare he give* my *best friend a hard time about that.* "You shut up about that, Nick," I growl. "You don't know anything about it."

Nick blinks at me a couple times, but when he gets over his shock, he gives me a hard smirk. "Your boy toy here is wasting his God-given talent."

"So what? You get off his case about it."

Nick matches my anger, leaning forward in his chair, both hands in fists on the table. His eyes lock on mine, and I stare him down right back. It's as if we've both forgotten Oliver is in the room. This fight has somehow become between Nick and me. "Someone has to get on his case about it," Nick growls.

"Director West is too soft on him. He needs to step up and become the man he's supposed to be."

"You weren't there that night!" I scream, angry tears misting my eyes. "You don't know what it was like for either of us!"

Nick is relentless. "I know it was worse for you, but you don't let that night rule your life."

"The *hell* I don't!" I slam to my feet, banging the table with both hands, and my chair goes flying out behind me. "Why the hell do you think I don't date, or even have any friends? I get sick to my stomach every time someone touches me! Every damn time someone gets too friendly, I relive that night. It's called Post Traumatic Stress Disorder, asshole, and it's real! And just because Oliver suffers from it differently than me, doesn't mean he's not *suffering.* If you want him to use his magic again, then get him help. Don't sit around making him feel like less of a man for a problem he probably doesn't even realize he has. He wasn't like me. He wasn't sent to years of therapy. He never told anyone what happened. Nobody knew what he went through. He needs compassion and support, not a kick in the ass, and if you can't leave him alone, then you can get the hell out of here. I'll find Shandra without you."

My chest is heaving, and my tears are streaming down my cheeks, but I don't care. I'm so angry. And maybe my anger isn't for Oliver. Well, not only for Oliver. Maybe I have anger issues after my sad story of a life. But just because I lost it doesn't make what I said untrue. I'm not going to back down.

Neither is Nick, apparently. Or maybe he's just reacting to my display of dominance. I don't know what kind of underworlder he is. Maybe he *can't* back down. He rises slowly to his feet and does that freaky eye thing where his pupils turn into slits and he emits power. When he gets like this, the room gets hotter, as if he's radiating heat. "You," he says, shaking with fury, "will not do anything else regarding this case unless I say so and am there to supervise you, or so help me I'll throw you in jail for hindering my investigation!"

And that is just enough to send Terrance over the edge. "ARE YOU *THREATENING* HER?" he roars.

His eyes are now all black, which has previously scared the piss out of everyone around him, no matter how badass they are. Not now, though. Apparently, Nick Gorgeous is the Agency's go-to guy, because he's even more badass than a raging troll. His gaze snaps from me to Terrance, and he stands up straight, seeming to grow taller and broader as he does. And something happens to his skin that I'm not sure how to describe. I'm not close enough to him to get a good look at it, but I'd swear it's shiny now, as if it turned to armor. *What the hell is that guy?*

"I'm doing my *job*," he says, his voice echoing with power. "After Oliver called about the black magic, Madison told me to babysit these two idiots"—he waves his hand at Oliver and me—"the unsolved human puzzle, and the Agency's golden boy because they know Nora won't stop meddling until she gets herself killed, and Oliver will go along for the ride because he's infatuated with her."

What? How rude.

"I don't mind letting Nora do her thing," Nick continues. "I want to find our missing underworlders, too, and she seems to be our best bet for that so far. But make no mistake, Terrance, I will protect her from herself if I have to, whether it pisses you off or not."

Terrance calms down, seeming pleased with Nick's explanation. I groan, and suddenly both Nick and Terrance are looking at me. I went from no one in the world caring about me to having two extremely overprotective big brother types in one night. I would tell Nick where he can shove his babysitting, except the man has a point. I'm just reckless and stubborn enough to get myself into serious trouble. And I honestly wouldn't mind having whatever the hell he is at my side tonight when I go serve myself up as bait in order to find Shandra. "Well," I grumble, because they're both staring at me as if waiting for me to say something. I give Nick a flat look. "At least you can recognize my skills for how useful they are and aren't trying to ground me."

Nick surprises me with a chuckle. "You are pretty badass, little human. You've proven to be more than resourceful. I've got no problems letting you put that arsenal of unique abilities to use. But if you insist on doing this, then I'm coming with you."

"Fair enough." I shrug. "Just respect Oliver, and we won't have any more problems."

"Fine." Nick matches my shrug. "I can do that. I guess I didn't look at it from that perspective before. I'll try not to be too big of an ass from now on."

I snort, and turn to wink at Oliver. Only he's not standing next to Nick anymore; he's come around the table and is right beside me. When I meet his eyes, I notice they're shining with unshed tears. Then, without warning, he throws his arms around me. The hug is so tight, and so desperate, that I let him hang on to me. "Thank you," he whispers in a shaky voice.

His thoughts flood me, only they're so jumbled I pick up emotions more than individual thoughts. The main theme is gratitude. I'm the first person who's ever defended him about his refusal to use magic. I'm the first person who's ever understood him. He's so grateful to have me in his life now. He loves that I call him Ollie and refer to him as my best friend. He's never had a best friend before.

He's always been misunderstood. He's been ostracized in the sorcerer community, and he's a disappointment and an embarrassment to his parents. He's so glad that I seem to genuinely care. He wishes I wanted more than friendship from him, but he understands my aversion to dating and is determined to ignore his feelings for me and just be the best friend I could ever ask for.

For once, hearing someone's thoughts doesn't upset me. I smile as I return his hug. "Of course I understand you," I whisper, not hiding the fact that I know what he's thinking. There's no point when he knows what I can do. "I'm just as screwed up as you are. And I do care. Maybe I can't date you, but I *do* care. It's you and me, Ollie. Against the whole damn world, if we have to."

"Aww, misfit love. How adorable."

Oliver rips himself away from me, his face flaming. I lift my middle finger to Nick. "Thought you said you'd stop being an ass."

He grins at me. "I said I'd try. You're making it too difficult."

I roll my eyes again. I feel like he makes me do that a lot. And yet...I kind of like the cheeky bastard. "Okay, are we done with the drama now? Ready to hear my plan?"

We all sit back down, and Nick waves a hand toward me. "Take it away, Spitfire."

"Well, *Gorgeous*..." Okay, I have to use the ridiculous name this once to butter him up. It works, too, because he grins and winks at me. It takes everything in me not to roll my eyes again. Or smile. "We're going to rush them."

He leans forward, his smile transforming into a confused frown. "Beg your pardon?"

I shrug. "It's Rush Week. They're going to a sorority mixer tonight at Alpha Gamma Delta, and they need one more guy and one more underworlder. So, since you insist on going with me, you're going to be my date tonight, and we're going to rush

—me a sorority and you...an evil cult with an affinity for dark magic and sacrifice."

Nick purses his lips as if he's doing everything he can to not laugh at my antics. When he can speak without grinning, he simply says, "Explain."

I take a deep breath, unnerved a little to have the attention of everyone in the room. They're ready to listen to my plan and take me seriously. As if I've ever been a leader or made a plan in my life. But I'm the one with the knowledge this time, and I vowed I'd do everything I can to get Shandra back.

"They need twelve," I say. "Muscle Head and Shandra were only eleven. They said the ceremony has to be done on the blood moon—which is Tuesday—but they're still a guy and an underworlder short. Xavier was supposed to be their twelfth, but I botched that plan when I fed him to Cecile."

Both Terrance and Nick snort at my wording, and Oliver grins, but come on. How else would you say it? I mean, succubi feed off of lust. I *literally* fed my neighbor to her.

"Anyway..." I roll my eyes. Again. I need to stop doing that so much. "They sounded desperate. They want Xavier, but he ended up in the hospital, and the cops were on him about what 'drugs' he OD'd on. The guys were pissed that he made such a stupid mistake and had all that baggage with cops watching him now, but they said they'd give him one last chance. They're supposed to meet him at the party tonight, and he's supposedly going to bring his vamp—I'm pretty sure they mean Parker."

This earns me another round of snorts. From all three men this time. "As if Parker would let himself get taken," Terrance says, his voice rumbling with laughter.

"I can get Parker to take care of Xavier. Then Nick and I show up under the guise of me rushing Alpha Gamma Delta, but we let it slip that I'm an underworlder and Nick's a human that knows the truth of the underworld. We'll give them something too good to pass up."

"Hang on." Nick laughs. "I'm the human in this situation, and you're the underworlder?"

"Hello. They're a fraternity. They need a dude. And look at yourself—tall, dark, and dangerous looking. You're exactly the kind of guy they want."

Nick smirks, preening at my description of him. "Aw, shucks, Nora, I knew you thought I was gorgeous, but damn."

"Whatever, like you don't know what you are."

"True, I'm irresistible, but you're still human. They'll probably be able to tell."

"Not necessarily," Oliver chimes in. "If they're human, they probably won't. And if they need confirmation, Nora's not without her own tricks."

"True!" I clap my hands, feeling the excitement of a plan coming together. "If their point is to steal the power of the underworlders they take, there's no way they'll be able to resist a mind-reading ability."

Nick and Terrance pass a look so long between them that one might think *they* had the mind-reading ability. When it's over, Terrance sighs and Nick weighs me down with a heavy stare. "This will be dangerous, Nora. You're talking about offering yourself up as bait to find their sanctuary."

I nod, and for once I'm completely serious with Nick. "I know. That's why you're going with me. Are you saying you can't protect me?"

Nick's eyes narrow. "I'm not infallible."

I hadn't expected him to admit it. I respect that he did, and so I give him a straight-up answer in return. "No one is. I know the risks, but there are eleven missing people out there that I can help rescue before they're killed. It's worth the risk, even if there's only a possibility of success."

"So brave," Terrance murmurs.

A long pause descends on us until Nick flashes a small smirk. "Or foolhardy." He sighs. "I guess it's a good thing I'm a little rash, too." He leans back in his chair and raises his arms above his head in a big stretch. "All right, Spitfire. You've got yourself a date. Let's go rush."

"I go, too," Terrance demands, crossing his huge arms over his barrel of a chest.

"Me too," Oliver agrees.

Bless their hearts. My new friends are the best. Unfortunately, neither of them can come. "Sorry, guys." I meet Terrance's glare with an equally stern gaze. "As much as I'd love to have you there, you'd scare them off in an instant. They know you, Terrance," I say when he starts to argue. "They stole your friend from under your nose. They'd recognize you and panic."

"And you..." I shoot Oliver an apologetic smile. "They might not be able to tell you're an underworlder, but they might, too. At the very least, if they all have a bit of dark magic, they might be able to feel yours. They're after powerful underworlders. You're one of the most powerful people in the city, and as much as I don't care that you don't use your magic, the fact that you don't makes you extremely vulnerable. I'm weak enough as it is. If you came with me, that would leave two people Nick would have to protect instead of just one."

Oliver grimaces. "You're right," he says. "You should be Gorgeous's only priority. I have to work anyway. But I'll be standing by and ready to send the whole Agency to you at a moment's notice."

I grin at him. "Awesome. That makes you Watchtower."

He can't help smiling. I knew the comic book reference would cheer him up.

"I'll wait in the car down the street," Terrance says stubbornly.

I can't argue with that, and I can't blame him for wanting to be there if we figure out where Shandra is. Honestly, I'll be glad for the backup. "All right. I can live with that. Every team has a guy in the van. You're the backup muscle and the getaway driver."

"Backup muscle?" Nick asks, that begrudging smile back in place. "Does that mean I'm the muscle?"

I flash him a killer smile. "Yep. And I'm the brains of this operation."

Nick snorts and shakes his head. "Whatever you say, 007. But you know, team lead or not, this *operation* is going to require you to wear a sexy dress."

Shit! He has me there.

CHAPTER FOURTEEN

I**'ve only got a few** hours to go shopping for a dress for the party tonight, so Nick takes Oliver home. As soon as they're gone, Terrance hands me a wad of cash. "What—Terrance! *No.*"

He shoves the money at me again. "For your dress. Get something nice."

"Terrance."

I give him my best no-nonsense stare, and all it does is cause him to retaliate with a much more serious I-mean-business scowl. I'm not ready to back down. "Oh," I say, throwing a bit of sarcasm into my voice, "and while we're having this conversation—"

"No." Terrance grunts.

"That car outside—"

"It's yours. I said no arguments."

"It's a *car*, Terrance. I can't accept that."

He grunts again and flops down on the couch, looking anywhere but at me. "I own the dealership. It's not a big deal."

I blink. And then I laugh. Of course he owns the dealership.

"Even still. I hate feeling like I owe people, and I'm not a mooch. I didn't earn that car, or the laptop. I can't accept any of it."

"Didn't earn it?" Terrance finally looks up at me. "You're risking your life to find my clan member. If you need a reason to accept my gifts, consider them payment for a dangerous job."

I suck in a deep breath through my nose, still feeling annoyed, but seeing his reason. "Well, when you put it that way," I mutter. I plop down on the opposite end of the couch, scowling at my lap, and grumble, "It still feels like too much."

Terrance sighs. "You are doing a service for my clan that we can never repay. We are the ones indebted to you. Especially me. If you bring Shandra home, I will be in your debt for life."

I'm shocked by the admission. A life debt is a huge deal. People don't just spout off something like that. If Terrance says it, then he means it. "Because she might be your mate?" I ask.

Terrance flinches, and all of the blood drains from his face. I duck my head, cringing. "Sorry. Your sister mentioned it in the vision I saw of her and Shandra at the bar. Shandra was so nervous. She didn't think you were going to be happy about your clan sending her."

Terrance's entire body deflates. After a long sigh, he shakes his head once. "I wasn't happy. I was shocked more than anything. I sort of freaked. That's why Shandra walked off by herself."

And now I see why he'd consider it a life debt. "It wasn't your fault, Terrance. It may have been your club, and she may have been upset because of you, but *you* didn't get her kidnapped. It's not your fault."

Terrance lifts his head, his lifeless eyes meeting mine. "She was my responsibility, potential mate or not, she and Nell both. Our clan is not in this city. Here, I am their head of clan. I was her protector, and I failed her."

I feel awful. I want to make him feel better, but I don't want to be inside his head right now, so I gently pat his shoulder once and then sit back. "You haven't failed her," I promise. "You're doing everything you can to get Shandra back. You haven't given up. You even went as far as to hire a crazy human psychic to find her." When he looks at me again, there's a spark of hope in his gaze. I shoot him a wink and then make him a promise. "I'm going to find her, T-man. I'm going to get her back for you, and when I do, you'll be a hero to your clan—a hero to Shandra and your sister both."

He sucks in a deep breath, swallows hard, and then clears his throat. In a husky voice, rough with emotion, he says, "Thank you, Nora."

"You're welcome, Terrance. And I suppose...thank you for the gifts. I admit I do love the car. It's very badass."

Terrance grins. "I thought it suited you."

"Very much so. Now if only I had any freaking clue where and how to buy a dress."

"I don't know a thing about that." Terrance lifts his arms above his head and stretches deep while he releases a mountain of a yawn. "But I do know someone who can help."

I glance his way, curious as to who he might recommend.

"You met Cecile at the club the other night."

I want to play it cool, but my eyes bulge of their own accord. "The succubus?"

Terrance laughs. "She's safe. Or...she will be with you, if I call her."

"That's reassuring." Yes, heavy sarcasm.

Terrance chuckles again. "You have my word, Trouble. She won't mess with you now that you're under my protection. She works at the club."

"She does?"

"Sort of hired eye candy."

I snort. "Yeah, she's good at that. It's probably a mutually beneficial arrangement, too."

"Very much so. Trust me, she doesn't want to be banned from my club. She was curious about you anyway. She said she didn't affect you. That doesn't happen a lot. She wanted to meet you again. She'll be good, and I'm sure she'll know exactly where you can find a dress."

I sigh. "I'm sure she will. Okay, go ahead and call her. But I only have until seven. I have to meet Parker and get him all caught up."

Terrance raises an eyebrow at that but doesn't say anything. He pulls out his cell phone and calls the succubus.

Truth be told, I'm nervous to see the seductress again, but I genuinely have no clue about dresses. I couldn't find a store that sells them, and even if I could, I'd have no idea how to pick one out. I need her help.

I'm still fretting when Terrance hangs up his phone. "She says two hours isn't enough time to go shopping, but she should have something in her closet. I'll give you her address. She's not far. She says she can help with your hair and makeup, too."

Terrance laughs when I cringe. "Oh, come on now, Trouble, you're a beautiful woman; don't be so afraid to show it off."

My grimace turns into a scowl. "Remember what I told you about self-preservation? I'm not afraid of my looks, I'm just not stupid about them." Terrance's confused frown doesn't surprise me. He doesn't understand yet, but he'll learn. "Nothing good will come from me in a dress all dolled up with hair and makeup done."

Terrance doesn't believe me. His grin is positively wicked when he says, "I can't imagine it, so I told Cecile to bring you to the club when she's finished with you."

I shake my head and do my best not to laugh. "Am I going to a party or the prom?"

T-man's eyes start to sparkle. "Cecile won't know the difference."

I sigh. This is going to be a long night.

CECILE LIVES in one of the few high-rise apartment buildings downtown in a penthouse suite. Let's just say it's so nice I feel like I lower the resale value when I step through the front door.

"Nora!" Cecile cheers, clapping her hands together when she sees me. "Welcome, you beautiful woman!"

I smirk. "So I've upgraded from vapid human, then?"

Cecile slices a hand through the air as if to wave off my sarcastic comment. "Bygones, darling, bygones. I can't tell you how excited I was when Terrance told me what you needed."

I'll bet. She has *makeover addict* written all over her. She's wearing black leggings and some kind of baggy shirt that reaches to her mid thigh and hangs off one shoulder. She looks tall, leggy, and willowy, like some kind of wispy, delicate faerie, and yet I know she's got a set of voluptuous curves hidden somewhere. I never knew clothes could change a person's looks so much. Still, either look works for her. The woman is flat-out gorgeous.

"You're such a natural beauty, you know. I didn't realize it the first time I met you, but you are. I'm excited to give you a proper makeover."

My stomach flips, and not in a good way. "Let's not get too crazy now. I just need to look acceptable for a sorority party over at Wayne State. This isn't a wedding or anything."

"So we need fun, flirty, sexy. Got it." She looks me over from head to toe in an appraising manner, chewing her bottom lip as she thinks. "I think I know what we want to do."

She cocks her finger in a come-hither manner and heads across her apartment to her bedroom. Her room is everything I'd imagine a queen of the night's bedchamber to be. And I use *bedchamber*, because that's what it is. *Room* just doesn't cut it. The four-poster canopy bed with draping curtains is the focal point, but there's a lot more going on in here. If I wondered before, stepping into this room, I now know Cecile likes to bring her work home with her. I shiver as she leads me into a walk-in closet.

The closet is almost as big as the bedroom and looks like something you'd see on TV in a rich person's house. There's a padded bench in the middle—drawers, shelves, and racks galore—and several kinds of lighting options. Cecile goes for a brighter light setting and directs me to sit on the bench seat.

While she sorts through a rack of dresses, I fumble for something—anything—to say. I can't think of a thing. I've never been good at being a girl. Cecile glances over her shoulder with a smirk, as if she knows what I'm thinking. She pulls down a green, a blue, and a pink dress from the rack and tosses them beside me. "Okay, honey, level with me," she says as she continues to hum and haw through dress after dress. "I know you're downplaying the looks on purpose. You do everything you can to hide from the world. Why, when you are so gorgeous with that shiny straight hair and that hourglass figure?"

She brings over a ruby red dress and snaps her fingers as if she wants me to stand.

"I just don't like attention," I say, rising to my feet. "I get too much of it."

She sighs wistfully as she holds the dress up to me, then spins me around and holds it up to my back. "Is there such a thing as too much attention?"

"When you aren't strong enough to defend yourself?" I ask, voice hard. "Yeah."

She turns me back around, dress forgotten, and stares deep into my eyes as if trying to peel back every layer I have and figure me out all the way to my soul. I decide to save her the trouble. "There's something...off about me. I'm cursed. I draw men to me. The stronger their attraction, the more they tend to lose their sense of reason. And they generally don't take no for an answer. I've had admirers, stalkers, and abusers my entire life. I don't know what it is, but I know I'm not imagining it."

Cecile takes a step back and smiles softly as she looks me over again from top to bottom. She shakes her head. "No, you aren't imagining it," she says quietly. "I, myself, am quite taken with you. Not in a sexual way, but I find myself curious, and pleasantly drawn to you. It's very similar to the allure we succubi and the incubi have on our prey, though we choose when to send out that allure, so to speak."

My eyes pop wide open. "You can control it?"

"Of course, dear." She grins and lifts the green dress. "I think this one."

She points to a privacy screen, and I know that's my cue to try the dress on. She explains a little about her kind as I move behind the screen and begin to undress. "We lust demons feed off of sexual energy. In order to do that, we must have control of our pheromones so that we can naturally attract our prey. The more pheromones we push into the atmosphere around us, the more anyone in the vicinity will react to us. Like you spoke of, the more natural attraction one might have to myself or others of my kind, the easier they'll succumb to our charms. However, we do always give off a little more pheromones than any non-lust demon, so we do usually have a little of that natural allure that you speak of. I must admit, though, Nora, darling, you have almost zero reaction to it. You are the least lustful person I've ever met."

I pull the dress up over my hips. It has spaghetti straps and is low cut, tight through the waist but loosening into a small flair at the hips, reaching mid thighs. It's actually a cute dress that I might like if I didn't know it would make everyone in the room stop and stare at me.

"It's actually quite refreshing," she continues. "I do believe that's what originally piqued my interest about you." She chuckles at the memory. "I am not often turned down by anyone once I've set my sights on them—male or female."

"Well, don't be offended. After what I've been through, I have a hard time with anything sexual."

"Hmm... I suppose you have a point. I'm sorry your sexual experiences have all been so negative. It really can be a wonderful act."

I'm sure it's supposed to be, but I don't think I'll ever be ready to experience sex the way most do. I'm pretty sure I'm broken. I zip the dress up on the side and am surprised at how well it fits. The green looks great with my dark hair and fair skin tone. Cecile knows her stuff, I'll give her that.

I walk out from behind the privacy screen slowly, feeling self-conscious since I'm never so exposed. Cecile gasps softly and smiles. "You are positively stunning." After a moment's perusal, though, her face falls into a concerned frown. "I see what you mean about attracting attention. You will have someone with you at this party, right? Someone who can protect you?"

I nod. "Nick Gorgeous will be with me. We're working undercover together tonight, trying to find the missing underworlders."

"Mmm." Cecile has her eyes closed, and the moan she's

making is causing me to blush. "Now that man is something else."

"Do you know what he is?" I ask.

Cecile opens her eyes and focuses her gaze on me. There's a twinkle in her eyes that makes her look more playful than I've ever seen her. "He hasn't told you what he is?"

"No. And I can't figure out if it's polite to ask underworlders what species they are or not, but I'm thinking it's probably rude."

Cecile chuckles and heads to a wall of shoes. "No heels," I say quickly. "I can't walk in them. Something flat. *Please.*"

She picks up a pair of flat, strappy green sandals and winks at me as she hands them over. "It *is* considered rude to ask an underworlder's species if you can't naturally tell. And if Gorgeous hasn't shared that information with you, then it's not my place to tell you. But rest assured, little darling, he is a magnificent creature, and you are safe with him." Her face is overcome with lust again, and she adds, "He's magnificent in every way, Nora. If you ever get the opportunity, I do hope you find the courage to give him a go. He'll change your mind about sex. I promise."

I choke on a laugh. "You and Nick?"

Her grin is 100 percent seductress. "Every decade or so. I don't even feed from him. I simply take him for pleasure. His kind are irresistible to mine."

"And to Ren?" I ask, remembering the charming incubi I met at the Agency who seemed hopelessly in love with Nick.

Cecile laughs a light, tinkling laugh. "Yes, and to Ren's kind, too, the poor man. Gorgeous seems abnormally immune to Ren."

"He was certainly resisting with everything he had the other night. I was more affected, and I'm almost never affected by guys."

I choose to push away the thought of Parker that suddenly jumps into my mind.

"You were affected by Ren?" Cecile asks, pushing me back out into her room where she sits me at a vanity.

"Yeah. But I also couldn't breathe or move. I think he had his setting on full blast trying to get Nick to feel it."

Cecile laughs again. "I'm sure. I do love watching those two in the same room. It's entertaining, is it not?"

"Maybe for you. For me, it was just painful. I've never felt lust like that before. I could literally taste it. But again, the whole not breathing thing was unpleasant."

"Oh, sweet Nora. That you didn't rip your clothes off and climb up Ren's body is a testament to your resistance. You, darling, are a conundrum."

She plugs in a curling iron and begins brushing my hair out. For a moment, I close my eyes and enjoy the feel of her pampering me. I had one or two decent foster mothers, but for the majority of my life, I've never had someone to dote on me like this. I am starved for affection and touch that doesn't repulse me, and I absolutely love this.

As if she can sense me relaxing, Cecile falls quiet and works on my hair in silence. She curls it into big, long ringlets and puts enough product in it to make it really shine. My hair has never looked so gorgeous in all my life. Honestly, I didn't know it was capable of looking so pretty.

While she starts pulling out makeup and skin products, I reflect back on our conversation. I can't stop thinking about how she said she could control her allure. I can't imagine that. Being able to shut it off? Or at least turn it down to low? "Do you think, maybe, I'm like you?" I ask, finally breaking the silence.

Cecile smiles at me as she begins to brush a light foundation powder over my face. "What do you mean?"

"Everybody keeps saying I probably have a little underworlder blood in me. Do you think maybe it comes from a succubus? Like, way down the line or something? Maybe that's where my curse comes from. Maybe I could learn how to turn it off, or at least control it like you do."

Cecile's smile turns sad. "As much as I would enjoy that—my kind are so very rare—I can't smell a single hint of demon energy on you. Not to mention, I can smell and taste pheromones. If your allure was from that the way mine is, I would know. I'm afraid you must be something else. Something extraordinary, darling. Close your eyes for me."

There goes that theory. I'm glad I have to close my eyes so she can't see the disappointment in them. Not that I would want to be a succubus or anything, but answers would be nice. And a mentor who could teach me to control my curse would be amazing. Instead, my hopes are dashed. But it does make me determined to try and figure out what I am. With my powers, everyone is probably right; I have to be some kind of underworlder. If I could just figure out what kind, maybe I could get some answers.

"Beautiful," Cecile murmurs. "Okay, open your mouth and relax your lips. It's time for some light strawberry-flavored gloss."

I let her gloss my lips, and then open my eyes. I hardly recognize the person staring back at me. "Wow, Cecile."

She smiles sweetly. "I had a beautiful canvas to work with."

CHAPTER
FIFTEEN

T**errance changes his mind** about having me come to the club the second I get to Underworld. He's working the floor when Cecile drags me into the main dance hall of the club. He sees me about the same time as everyone else in the room. It doesn't help that I'm standing next to the gorgeous succubus. Together, we stop all movement. Everyone in the room stills to watch Cecile and I head to the bar.

Because it's Friday night, the club is three times as crowded as it was on my first visit. Cecile waves at Terrance across the room, and then drags me toward the bar. Two guys immediately stand up, offering us their stools. "Why, thank you, Pellitoris," Cecile purrs, kissing the cheek of the man on the right that just gave her his seat.

"Anything for you, Cecile," Pellitoris says. His voice is every bit as smooth as hers had been. His eyes drift to me along with the guy who gave me his seat. "Who is your exquisite friend?"

Cecile breathes in deeply, her pupils swelling as she skims some of the lust coming from the two men. "Mmm," she says. "Exquisite indeed. This lovely darling is Nora."

Pellitoris takes my hand before I can stop him and brings it to his lips. I don't hear whatever greeting he gives me; I hear his thoughts. She's the most beautiful creature I've ever seen. I need to get her on the dance floor so I can feel her body against mine and become the envy of every man in this club. Then perhaps I can bring her back to my kingdom. A little faerie food and wine, and she could be my human pet forever.

I pull my hand away while forcing him a tight smile. Yeah, I'm not going to be some summer fae's plaything for eternity, thanks, but I keep my mouth shut. I know not to insult a sidhe. They're a very prideful race and downright nasty when you slight them. "Nice to meet you."

"And you, love. Perhaps you would do me the honor of a dance?"

Shit. How to say no without insulting him?

"Sorry, Pellitoris," Terrance grumbles, having finally made his way to us. "This human is not available."

Pellitoris frowns at Terrance and looks to me for confirmation. I shrug apologetically. "I'm waiting for my date right now. He'll be here any moment."

Pellitoris considers this and then grins at me. The sight gives me the bad kind of shivers. "And who is this man that didn't have the decency to pick you up?"

"Parker Reed," Terrance says, as if the name should scare the faerie away. "And he would have picked her up, except she's staying at *my* place, and my wards are harmful to vampires."

I glance at Terrance, wondering if that's true. I'll have to ask later, but I know better than to question him now. His face has gone dark enough that Pellitoris does a double take and then studies me again. "You're staying with *Terrance?*"

I nod slowly. So does Terrance. And he's taking on his badass-troll-bouncer stance. Pellitoris looks Terrance over from head to toe and then sighs. "Very well. I shall find another dance partner. It was still a pleasure to meet you, m'lady."

"Pellitoris, love." Cecile holds out a hand to the faerie. "Perhaps a dance with me instead?"

The sidhe's face lights up, and he escorts Cecile to the dance floor. She shoots Terrance a subtle wink as she walks away. She offered to dance with the faerie to smooth over the situation, and I wonder if that's not a big part of her job—playing peacekeeper for the surly troll. It would make sense.

"Nora, darling." I glance at Cecile in time to see her flash me a brilliant smile. "Tonight was so nice. Do call me again some time. I hope we shall be great friends."

Oddly enough, I like the idea of being her friend, so I nod. "I will."

She walks away, and Terrance takes her place on the barstool next to me. He faces outward, scowling at everyone who looks our way. "Can't leave you alone for a second in this place," he grumbles. He eyes my outfit, and his frown deepens. "Damn succubus did too good a job. Is Parker on his way yet?"

I nod. "Texted him on the way. He should be here any minute. We'll go somewhere else."

Terrance growls at a man that sits on the stool on the other side of me. The man scampers away immediately. The poor guy must have made the mistake of checking me out. "Are you sure I can't come tonight?" Terrance asks gruffly.

I shake my head. "As much as I'd love to have you backing me up, you really can't. You'll scare away our only lead, and we might not find Shandra in time. But don't worry. I'll have Nick with me every second."

Terrance grunts. I take that to mean he's satisfied with my answer. After a moment of silence, Terrance sighs. "You want something to drink while you wait?"

The offer makes me smile. "Sure. A Coke would be nice."

Terrance disappears to make that happen without a word. It

only takes him a minute to walk around the other side of the bar and shove a glass of Coke at me. "Thanks, T-man."

"I was right, you know," he says as I down half of the Coke. I didn't realize how parched I was. Must be the stress of being so dressed up. "You *are* trouble."

"You're the one who wanted me to come here first."

Terrance grunts again and folds his arms across his chest. I get the T-man scowl. "My wards keep out anyone who isn't expressly invited. I didn't want Parker invited to my place because vamps are all connected by a mental link to their sire. Invite Parker, and the magic wouldn't be able to tell the difference between him and any member of his clan."

So then Henry or any of his cronies could theoretically sneak in. I shiver again. "Good call, then, T. Thanks."

His face softens. "I'll keep you safe, Nora."

My throat closes up at the promise. It's still overwhelming to have someone I trust looking out for me.

"I'll always protect you, too," a smooth, soft voice says from behind me.

The hairs on my neck stand up, and I have to take a deep breath and smooth out my face before I turn to face Parker. My heart skips a beat when I see him. I can't help it. He's dressed in designer jeans that fit him like jeans should fit a man, and a nice button-down shirt the same color blue as his deep blue eyes. The sleeves are rolled up on his strong forearms. And he's looking at me as if I've stolen all the air from his lungs.

"Hey," I say. I cringe when the word comes out raspy.

He doesn't speak right away. He's still taking in the sight of me. "Nora," he finally whispers, slowly shaking his head. "You look..."

Before he can find the right word, Terrance clears his throat. Parker blinks a couple times and flinches as he breaks from whatever spell he was under. Knowing that I was the cause of his trance, heat rushes to my cheeks. He clears his throat. "Thank you for agreeing to meet with me."

"It's just business." At least, that's what I keep telling myself.

Parker's lips twitch, as if he can see right through my no-nonsense attitude. Considering the man can sense my attraction to him, he probably does. That only makes me more determined to keep things professional. "We have a lot to discuss, so let's get a move on."

His lips twitch again. "Anywhere in particular?"

"Nowhere underworld affiliated," Terrance orders. He's gone back to scowling at all the hovering men.

"How about Greektown?" I offer. "That's not run by the underworld, is it?"

Parker laughs. "Nope. Just the Greek."

"Great. I'm starving, and I love me some falafel."

"Greektown it is." Parker's eyes sparkle with amusement. It only makes him look hotter.

Parker grins as if he knows why I'm suddenly scowling, and moves to place his hand on the small of my back.

"No touching!" Terrance snaps as I sidestep Parker's hand. "And keep a damn eye on her."

Parker drops his hand and gives Terrance a grave look. "I'll keep her safe, Terrance. You have my word."

"You'd better."

"I will."

The two share a look that I want to roll my eyes at. I'm not some fragile doll. But I'm not ungrateful to have people looking out for me while I'm wearing a dress, so I resist the urge.

Parker, keeping to the no-touching rule, waves his hand, signaling for me to lead the way. We head out the front door, and I have no doubt the Mercedes Coupe waiting at the valet is his. He hurries forward and opens the passenger door for me, and now it really feels like I'm on a date. For the first time in my life, I'm conflicted by that feeling.

I shouldn't want to date Parker. In my head, I know he's a vampire. He's one of the same disgusting, murderous things that killed my mother. He drinks *blood*. But the more I get to know him, the harder it is to see the vampire, and all that's left is the man.

I've never been interested in guys before. Normally when one gets too close, all I feel is fear. When Parker slides into the car and his heady cologne fills the air, fear is not the feeling that overtakes me. I don't understand why he has this effect on me, and I don't like it. It makes me nervous.

"You okay?" Parker asks as he pulls away from the club.

"Fine." I realize I'm completely stiff and that my answer came out clipped, but I can't seem to relax.

I don't say anything else until we reach the restaurant Parker insists is the best in Greektown. It's too nice for my taste and has a romantic atmosphere, but since it smells heavenly, I don't argue.

We're escorted to a small, candlelit table for two. Parker pulls out my chair for me, and now I know I'm on a date. How the hell did he trick me? What have I gotten myself into?

I startle when I hear my name called. Parker and the guy who escorted us to our table are both looking at me. "Wine?" Parker asks again.

"I don't drink."

I cringe inwardly for sounding so bitchy. But I'm on a date with a vampire, and I'm so nervous I'm about to start shaking.

Parker mutters something to the host, who scampers away, and then Parker settles his eyes on me. His gaze roves over me again, as if he can't help himself.

"Nora—"

"What's good here?" I ask, scooping up my menu and

ducking behind it to hide from his penetrating stare. I can still feel him watching me.

"Everything," he answers. "Especially the falafel. That is what you wanted, isn't it? They have an especially excellent dish here."

I lower my menu and frown at him. "So you eat food, then?"

His eyes spark with amusement again. "Yes. I do. It won't sustain me, but I enjoy it, and will be ordering dinner with you."

Well, that's a relief. A small one.

As if his comment conjured him up, a waiter appears beside our table, dropping off water glasses with wedges of lemon. I order the falafel, and Parker opts for some kind of Greek lamb chops that actually sound awesome. When the waiter is gone, I grab my water and chug half of it down.

"There's no need to be nervous, Nora."

"Right," I grumble under my breath from behind my water glass. "I'm only on a date with a vampire."

I forgot vampires have really good hearing. Parker hears my comment, and his face lights up with pure pleasure. Damn. Now he knows it's a date. What the hell is wrong with me?

"I'm really glad you agreed to see me tonight, Nora." He holds up a hand when I open my mouth to argue. "I know it's only because we need to find the missing underworlders, but I'm still grateful. Please, allow me to apologize for my part in your experience with my clan." I scoff but don't interrupt him, because his face looks so sincerely regretful. "If I'd had any idea of your gifts, or that you most likely have underworlder blood in you, I never would have brought you to Henry."

No. You'd have tried to keep me for yourself.

"Whatever. It's over now, so let's just forget about it, okay? I know you didn't mean for all that to happen. I'm still mad, but I don't blame you. I blame Henry."

"Henry is not all vampires," Parker says softly.

Parker meets my stare, and I can't look away. I'm so grateful for the table between us. If he touched me right now, I don't think I'd have the willpower to stop him. "It doesn't matter," I whisper. "Vampire or not. I don't do dating or relationships or anything physical."

"You're attracted to me."

He's right, but that's not enough. "I'm afraid of you," I admit. "I'm afraid of all men. I've been hurt by nearly every single one I've ever met."

Parker's eyes fill with sadness. "I would never hurt you, Nora."

I gulp. I don't want to trust him, but my heart is starting to believe even if my head doesn't. "It doesn't matter," I say again. It's barely a whisper.

"How can I prove myself to you? Tell me how I can gain your forgiveness and your trust."

I shake my head. It wouldn't matter if I forgave him, and I already do trust him, or I wouldn't be here with him now. But I can't get into a relationship. It wouldn't end well. He's too drawn to me. If I gave him an opportunity, he wouldn't be able to stop himself. *No.* Until I figure out what I am and how to control this curse of mine, I can't date anyone. My body is just going to have to cool down.

"I'm not looking to date, Parker. But I could use your help tonight."

"Anything."

Our food arrives, and as we eat, I tell Parker about my day, about going to the university and discovering the fake fraternity full of dark magic users. I tell him about my vision in the car and about the plan I've concocted with Nick for the party tonight. Parker doesn't like this idea, but he doesn't get a say. "So what would you like me to do?" he asks, not quite able to mask his annoyance that I refuse to stay away tonight.

"I need you to keep Xavier away. I'm sure he'll call you."

"He already has. I haven't returned his call, but he invited me to come to a party with him tonight."

I grin, feeling the excitement from earlier when I was plotting this undercover operation with Nick. "That would be the one we're going to."

"So why don't I just come? At least that way I could help Gorgeous keep an eye on you."

I shake my head and scoop up the last bite of my falafel. Parker's right: This is the best falafel I've ever had. "You can't. These guys know Xavier. They like him and trust him already. He's the one they want. If he shows up tonight, they won't look twice at Nick and me."

"That's not a bad thing," Parker says dryly. He glances at my empty plate and adds, "Shall we order some baklava for dessert?"

I should say no; dessert feels like it brings us back into date territory after I've finally got us in business mode. But come on. Turn down free baklava? I don't think so. "Hell yeah. I love baklava."

Parker laughs and flags down our server. After the guy is gone, I resume our argument because Parker is looking at me all lovingly again. "You can't bring Xavier," I say.

"But if I'm there with Xavier, then they can just take me instead."

"Yeah, and then you'd end up missing, just like all the others. They're using dark magic roofies, remember? You'd wake up trapped in a cage somewhere, and we wouldn't be able to find any of you. The point of all this is not for me to be bait, but for Nick to rush. We need them to accept Nick so that they tell him where the ritual is. If you go with Xavier, we still don't learn anything."

Parker sighs. He knows I'm right.

"Please just keep him away from the party. Take him out somewhere else, compel him if you have to."

Parker raises an eyebrow at me. "You'd have me compel him? I thought you hated us doing that."

"To innocent people, yeah, but to dangerous, psycho creeps? I'm not going to lose sleep over it."

Parker chuckles quietly and shakes his head once. He pins me with a considering look, and I see the precise moment he agrees to my plan. "Okay," he says. "I'll keep Xavier away for you tonight. Under one condition."

"And that is?"

He leans forward in his chair. "You allow me a kiss goodnight before I have to hand you over to Gorgeous."

My mouth goes dry, and all the air is sucked from my lungs. I hesitate just a moment too long, and then the server is there with our dessert. He sets the plate in the middle of the table between us and lays down two dessert spoons. As soon as he's gone, I grab my spoon and dig right in. "Oh, wow. This is good."

"Nora..."

I refuse to look at him. "You have to try this. Seriously."

"Nora."

Sighing internally, I clear my mouth and force my gaze up. "No."

His damn lips twitch again.

"No. Not happening." This time, I sound like I mean it.

"On the cheek, then," he counters. "I want to prove to you that not every experience with a man has to be a bad one."

I swallow. Hard. Even though there's no more food in my mouth. Then I take another bite of the baklava. "You'd better get in on this before I eat it all."

"Nora..."

He's not going to let it go. Closing my eyes, I set my spoon down. "Fine," I whisper.

When Parker sucks in a breath through his nose, I finally look at him. I shouldn't have. His eyes are swirling with desire, and the intensity of it makes my stomach flutter. I'm excited, but I'm also terrified. "On the *cheek*," I demand. "And that is it. Nothing else. You try anything funny, and I'll sic my troll on you."

Parker smiles as if he's just won, and my stomach cramps with nerves.

"I'm going to win you over, eventually," he says as he finally picks up his spoon and dishes himself a bite of our shared dessert. "I'm a very patient man."

CHAPTER SIXTEEN

Nick picks me up from the restaurant. Parker and I wait at our table until he texts, then Parker pays the check and walks me out the door. Nick is leaning against his motorcycle, waiting for me when we come outside. When he sees me, he lets out a long whistle. "Well, damn. Now I feel underdressed."

He's wearing jeans and a Metallica T-shirt under his leather jacket. He's left the cowboy hat at home today and has traded his cowboy boots for a pair of black motorcycle boots. I smirk. "Actually, I think you'll fit right in."

This makes him grin. He takes off his jacket and holds it out to me with a waggle of his eyebrows. I hate to encourage his antics, but I laugh despite myself. As I take my first step in his direction, Parker clears his throat behind me. Oh yeah. I owe him a kiss.

I take a moment to steady myself before facing the music. I can feel him close the distance behind me. "My hands are clasped behind my back, Nora. You have nothing to fear."

Except maybe how much I like it. He's so close his breath tickles the back of my neck. A shiver rocks my entire body.

"You want this. Don't you?"

I'm honestly not sure. Part of me does, and part of me thinks if I do this, there's no turning back. This isn't safe, no matter what Parker claims.

"Turn around, beautiful."

I can't breathe. My anxiety is locking up my entire body. I'm shaking. It's just a kiss on the cheek. It's not even the lips. But it's what it means that scares me. It's a move to get closer. It's a stamp on the end of a night. It's a goodnight kiss.

"Nora, sweetheart," Parker murmurs, "if you really can't do it, it's okay. I'll still keep Xavier away from the party."

I let out a giant breath of relief. My entire body deflates, leaving me feeling like rubber. I hadn't realized I was so tense. I can't even accept a kiss on the cheek from a guy I'm attracted to. "I'm sorry," I croak.

I feel like an idiot. There really is something wrong with me. My shoulders sag at the thought. I'll never be normal. I'll never have love or a regular relationship.

"It's all right, sweetheart. I'm sorry I pushed it. I didn't realize how serious it was."

"It's stupid."

"It's understandable."

I still can't even turn around and look at him. I'm on the verge of tears, and I just want to get out of here. Nick is waiting patiently at the curb, watching the two of us with a curious expression. No doubt he can hear every word we're saying. "Thank you for dinner," I say, not knowing how else to get out of this conversation.

"It was my pleasure," Parker says. His voice has returned to normal, as if nothing awkward happened at all, as if I'm not a hopeless wreck. "Be careful tonight, Nora."

"You too."

I head toward Nick without looking back. When I get to the

bike, Nick slips his jacket on my arms without saying anything. I appreciate him not asking me what all that was about. I climb on behind him, and as he revs the engine, he says, "You want to ride for a bit first? We've got a little time if we want to be fashionably late."

He is a wonderful man. A motorcycle ride to give me time to compose myself and get my head back in the game is exactly what I need. "Yes, please."

We take off, and I immediately lose myself to the thrill of being on the bike. I feel better within minutes, but we drive for twenty before we arrive at the sorority house. It seems to be a casual party, not a wild rager like you see on TV. I'm glad for the laid back atmosphere. It's perfect for mingling, which is exactly what Nick and I need to do.

As I hand Nick his jacket back, I give him one last pep talk. "Okay, once we're in there, you have to act annoyed with me behind my back."

Nick shoots me a questioning look as he straightens his leather jacket. "Why?"

"Because this is a *sacrificial* ritual. They have to believe you're only using me for my power and that you'd be willing to kill me, or they won't go for it."

Nick lets his eyes drop to my feet and slowly pulls them back up, smirking. "I can't want you for your legs?"

I roll my eyes. "Of course that, too, or we won't look sincere as a couple. Come on, we've got to sell this. It's our only chance."

"Okay, okay, I promise I'll be the douchiest boyfriend ever."

"Thank you."

Nick laughs, shaking his head. "You ready, 007?"

I look at the house again and take a deep breath. "Yup. Let's do this. Let's go rush."

One of the Alpha Gamma Delta girls is standing at the door,

greeting guests. Her eyes light up as Nick and I arrive, but the look is for me and not Nick. I have to hold back a laugh at his soft snort. I guess he doesn't get passed up by women often. "Hello!" the girl greets, taking my hand and shaking it with both of hers. She lets go quickly, so I only get the briefest thought from her. *She's so gorgeous. She looks fun. I hope she wants to rush.* "I'm Stacia. Welcome to Alpha Gamma Delta. Are you thinking of rushing?"

"Considering it," I lie as I pull my hand back. "I'm mostly curious about sorority life. I want to figure out if it's for me before I decide to rush anywhere. Someone on campus told me about your mixer tonight. I hope you don't mind that we came."

"Oh, of course not! That's what this party is for. To welcome any who are interested," Stacia says. She's got a nice attitude about her—very happy and friendly. I kind of like her. "Drinks are in the kitchen," Stacia goes on, "and anyone wearing the Alpha Gamma Delta T-shirts are here to answer any questions you have or show you around. Please, come in and enjoy yourselves."

I reach deep down inside me and pull up my best happy-go-lucky bubbly Nora. It's not easy, and I know even though I like Stacia's outgoingness, I'm 100 percent *not* sorority material. "Thanks! It's nice to meet you. I'm Nora, and this is my boyfriend, Nick. We'll be sure to talk to a few different people while we're here. Thanks for having us. It looks like a great party."

Nick slides me a glance once we're finally in the door. I match his wry look. "Don't even say a word."

"I wasn't going to," Nick says. His laugh makes me think he's lying. "So, should we hit up the kitchen for a drink and then do a lap? You can point people out to me, since you're the only one who knows what any of them look like."

"Sounds good, but just water for me. I don't drink."

Nick grins. "Well then, I guess I'll have to drink for the both of us. Gotta blend in, right?"

"Don't get slobbering drunk. We're working tonight, remember?"

Nick shrugs. "My metabolism burns off alcohol too quickly for me to get drunk. I'll be fine."

I want to ask so badly what kind of underworlder he is, but he doesn't offer, and Cecile confirmed my suspicion that it's rude to ask, so I hold my tongue and let him lead me to the kitchen.

Once I have a bottled water and Nick has the customary red Solo cup in hand, we wander through the house. It's huge and nice, though it's not fancy like I would think a house this big would be. It's very normal feeling, homey. Another point for the sorority. Who knew I'd like it?

"Bingo." Seeing a familiar face, I nod my head in the right direction and murmur behind my water bottle. "Blondie with the muscles, at two o'clock. That's the guy who took Shandra. The even bigger guy next to him with the sandy hair is the owner of the one and only banana boat hooptie."

As Nick casually looks them over from behind his plastic cup, I add, "Look for a shorter redheaded guy. That's Elijah. He seems to be the human in charge."

"Excuse me," says a voice behind us, clearly trying to get our attention. We both turn to find none other than Elijah standing right behind us. "Correct me if I'm wrong, but did I just hear you say you're looking for a *human* in charge of a fraternity?"

I'm busted. But how to play it off? He obviously heard me, and he's looking at me with dangerous suspicion. Hopefully he didn't hear me mention Shandra by name. I'll have to be more careful. For now, I may as well own it.

I pull out Bubbly Nora again and give the guy a huge smile while bouncing up and down a little. "Oh! You're him, aren't you? Are you Elijah?" I grip Nick's arm, grateful for his long-sleeved leather jacket. "Oh, Nicky, I told you we'd find him!"

Nick grimaces at me. It could be because we got caught, or it could be the girly whine I throw into my words, or more likely, it could be that I called him Nicky. Either way, the grimace is perfect, because Elijah looks between us and his eyes narrow even further. "Yes, I'm Elijah. Is there something I can do for you?"

There's more disdain in his voice than wariness. Condescending asshole. I want to tell him where he can shove his self-importance, but I have to keep up the act of the annoying underworlder. "Actually, there is." I giggle. It almost kills me.

In a bold move, I take Elijah's arm and drag him into the living room to snag a seat on an empty couch. "You see, my boyfriend Nicky wants to rush your frat, but we looked everywhere for information on you guys and couldn't find anything."

Elijah sits down with me but pulls his arm out of my grip, making me lose his thoughts. All I got from him on our short walk across the room was that he's really irritated for several reasons. First, he thinks it's a pity I'm so hot, because I'm super annoying. He doesn't like that I know about underworlders—and I must, because I mentioned humans—and wants to know how I know about him and his brotherhood.

"Unfortunately," he says, frowning at me with all the arrogance of Mr. Darcy, "joining our brotherhood is a private thing. It's by personal invitation only, and all of our slots are full for the year."

"Oh, bummer." I pout for all I'm worth. "That's a shame." I duck in close to his ear and lower my voice. "Nicky was so excited when he learned there was an underworld fraternity."

Elijah can't help himself; he's as drawn to me as any man. His hand falls to my thigh, half on my dress and half on my bare skin. I hate his touch, but I swallow back my revulsion and let him leave his hand there. "And how is it that you came to know about us?" he asks, sugar in his voice now instead of irritation.

His thoughts haven't changed much; he still wants to know how I know who he is, but he's a lot less annoyed with me. Now, instead, he keeps thinking about how beautiful I am, and he's wondering how serious Nick and I are. We don't seem to be that serious, because Nick hasn't stopped me from talking to Elijah and sitting so closely to him, and Nick's eyes keep drifting to other girls.

"Oh!" I say, laying my hand on top of his. "Well, that's a funny story. I met your friend Xavier at Underworld the other night. He was with a friend of mine. He was cool, but he kept hitting on me. He kept trying to get me to come home with him even though I told him I had a boyfriend. I sort of had to glamour him a little to get him to back off." I make an *oops* face and giggle conspiratorially.

Elijah perks up at this. "Glamour? You're fae?"

I bite my lip and try to look nervous since underworlders aren't supposed to talk about the underworld. Elijah begins rubbing small circles on my bare thigh with his thumb. "You can trust me, Nora. I myself am a sorcerer. I'll keep your secrets."

I pretend to consider it while I listen to his thoughts. He's excited at the possibility that he's found another underworlder, but he's not sure he believes me. I seem human to him.

"Okay," I say, biting my lip again. It draws his gaze to my mouth. "I'll tell you, but you have to keep it secret. It could be dangerous if the wrong person found out about me."

He grins and grips my thigh in a gesture meant to be supportive and comforting, but his thoughts say, *Oh, honey, I* am *the wrong person, you just don't know it.*

And then I get images of past rituals. I see him sacrifice a water sprite—a young woman, looking so sickly and helpless, drugged by a dark magic roofie—and he takes her life force by drinking her blood. I want to be sick. I want to kill this jerk.

Nick must see the change in me, because suddenly he's right there, grabbing Elijah's hand and taking it off my thigh. I don't want to know how hard he's crunching it, but Elijah's face flushes red and he winces, flexing his hand when Nick finally lets him go. Nick leans in close to him as he hauls me to my feet and says, "Get your own. This one is mine."

It's the perfect line, because it challenges Elijah, who is obviously prideful; it clarifies that I am indeed an underworlder; and most importantly, it tells Elijah that Nick only wants me because I'm an underworlder. For these reasons, I don't kick Nick in the balls for treating me like a possession.

Nick pulls me away from Elijah, but not far enough that he can't still hear us. "Baby," he admonishes me quietly, "what are you doing? You can't tell people what you are. The sidhe are so powerful, especially the Summer Court. You're fae royalty, baby. People would kill you to get your power."

Nice. Now I don't have to come up with a type of fae on my own. Nick's just given me the perfect cover story. I love that he's right in sync with me on this mission. He's the perfect partner. "But Nicky," I whine. "He's the leader of that group you want to join. We want him to trust us. I thought if he knew I'm an underworlder, maybe he'd let you in."

"But we don't know him yet. We're just checking them out, remember? We don't know if we can trust them."

"Don't forget I'm powerful, Nicky," I say in full-on girly pout mode now. "I can take care of myself."

Nick smiles at me and caresses my cheek. He lets his fingertips linger near the corner of my mouth. I'd be shocked by the move if it weren't for the thoughts he's sending me. It's startling to hear him talking directly to me with his mind. He's the first person who's ever done that. *You're a hell of an actress, Spit-*

fire. Too good. I didn't like the way he was looking at you. Let's just lie low for a bit. Let them chase us now.

I nod to let him know his message was received, and he lowers his fingers. "Come on," he says. "Let's go mingle with sorority girls."

I snort, but we go find a couple of girls in Alpha Gamma Delta T-shirts and start learning about sorority life.

Nick and I kill about an hour chatting with sorority girls and having drinks. Nick even talks me into a dance. The entire time, members of Elijah's brotherhood keep a close eye on us and start seemingly random friendly conversations with us. We can always tell when it's one of them, and I'm pretty sure we've met all eleven of them now. They're vetting Nick pretty hard, so I think they've decided they believe I'm sidhe, and now they're just trying to find out if Nick would be willing to play along with their sick game.

They've managed to separate us, but we're still in each other's sight. Hooptie guy and a couple of his brothers have Nick cornered in the kitchen, where he went with them to get more drinks. The second I was left alone, Elijah reappeared, and now we're sitting on the same couch as before. He's got his arm around the back of the couch behind me and is leaning in very close.

He might be trying to seduce me, but his intentions are a lot more nefarious, because from the moment he came over to me, my intuition kicked in, sending tingles up my spine. Elijah means me harm. The feeling that I'm in danger isn't too bad, so he must not mean to do anything to me tonight. My guess is that he's decided to let Nick into his brotherhood, and he plans to have Nick sacrifice me on Tuesday during the blood moon. Every instinct I have is screaming at me to get the hell out of here, but I force myself to keep playing my part. We're so close. We're going to get Shandra and the others back.

"So you said you met Xavier at Underworld?" Elijah says. "Is he the one who told you about us?"

Xavier is a great out, considering he isn't here and won't be showing up to contradict me. I bob my head in a nod. "He wasn't just spilling your secrets, of course. He met Nicky. See, there aren't usually any humans in Underworld. Most humans don't even know the underworld exists, so Nicky can't ever talk about the things he's learned with anyone. When I saw Xavier there, I got a little excited and told him Nicky was human, too. They hit it off right away.

"That's when he told Nicky about your brotherhood. He said he thought there might be one spot left, and he'd rather Nicky join than some guy named Noah. He said he'd ask you about it, but then he ended up in the hospital. When he called to tell us about this party tonight, he said he didn't get the chance to talk to you about Nicky yet, but that we should come and meet you guys anyway."

Elijah sighs. "Not that I don't like both you and your boyfriend, but Xavier still should have been more secretive about us. That's one of the rules when joining; you don't tell people about us."

"Oh, I know all about that. Rule number one in the underworld is don't tell humans about the underworld."

Elijah gives me a wry smile. "Then how is it that your boyfriend knows all about it?"

I look away and try to blush. Who knows if it worked? But the feigned shyness does have the desired effect. Elijah moves his arm from the back of the couch to officially around me, letting his hand fall on my shoulder. His thoughts are a little jumbled. He's attracted to me, and interested in my power, but he's still suspicious. The fact that I feel human to him is keeping him wary. He doesn't like how much I know about him. He doesn't think Xavier would have blabbed about the brotherhood. He was a solid recruit. He's also a little wary of Nick still. Nick is too perfect of a candidate. Elijah is concerned about the coincidence that he found us right when he was so desperate for one last member of his circle. He doesn't like coincidences. He's not quite ready to trust us yet.

"What are you doing dating a human anyway?" he asks in a soft voice. "Aren't you supposed to keep to your own kind?"

"I'm sidhe," I say in the demurest voice I'm capable of. "I'm part of the Summer Court. But I don't like to stay there much. The sidhe are so emotionless and aloof. It gets boring." And...I look up at him through my eyelashes. "Humans are a lot more fun. I don't normally tell them my secrets, but Nicky is special. He's so persuasive. I've really fallen hard for him." I glance around us as if to make sure no one is listening, then whisper, "He wants me to petition the Summer King to turn him fae. He says he loves me and wants to be with me forever. It doesn't happen often, but it *does* happen when the humans are intriguing enough. I think Nicky has a chance. He'd make such a handsome faerie, don't you think? He's so strong and good-looking already, I can't imagine him with the power of my people inside him as well."

There. Let Elijah chew on that. He drops his arm from around me so that he can lean back. He looks me over with a very considering stare. When I frown at him, he forces a smile. "You're a very interesting woman, Nora. And, if you don't mind my saying so, the most beautiful one I've ever met."

I giggle and swat his arm lightly. "Thank you for the compliment, but don't let Nicky hear you say that. He wasn't happy earlier. He thought you might be trying to steal me from him."

Elijah leans in, and his eyes flash with intensity. "And what if I am?"

I allow my eyes to grow big, then I giggle again and shake

my head once. “Then I’d say you have your work cut out for you. I’m devoted to Nicky. He’s so strong.”

He wets his lips and drops his gaze to my mouth. “What if I could prove that I’m stronger?”

I’m not sure how to answer. I’m not touching him anymore and am surprised by this line of questioning. I thought he didn’t trust me, and now he’s trying to steal me from my boyfriend? Does that mean he wants me, but not Nick? Or is he trying to prove the two of us are untrustworthy somehow?

I glance across the room at Nick, stalling while I try to piece together the best response, and am startled to see who’s joined him. Parker promised me he’d keep Xavier from the party. But then...I don’t see Xavier. Parker is here alone.

It’s the perfect out. I gasp and call loudly, “Parker!”

CHAPTER
SEVENTEEN

When **Parker turns in** my direction, I beam a smile at him, stand up, and meet him halfway across the room. Elijah follows me, keeping a set of hawk eyes focused on Parker. I don't think the two have met before, but somehow Xavier figured out who Parker is, and he told Elijah that Parker is a 400-year-old vampire.

"What are you doing here?" I ask, surprising Parker with a hug. I lean my face in next to his and whisper in his ear as soft as I'm able. "Just play along."

Parker doesn't miss a beat. "It's lovely to see you again, Nora. Xavier called and invited me tonight. It's not Underworld, but it's something to do. What are *you* doing here?"

"Xavier called me earlier and told me about it." I look all around, even though I know my creepy neighbor is not here. Parker might be here, but he wouldn't have gone back on his word to keep him away. "Where is he, anyway? Didn't he come with you?"

Parker shakes his head and looks me straight in the eyes. "I went to go pick him up because he wasn't answering his phone, and I guess he had some kind of mental breakdown after his trip to the hospital."

"Mental breakdown?" I gasp.

Elijah is concerned about this, too. No doubt he's afraid Xavier is running around telling people he's joining a brotherhood that sacrifices monsters in order to gain their power.

Parker shakes his head and gives me a small smirk. "It was the strangest thing. I guess he's been committing some very serious crimes against women for some time now, and this evening he randomly decided to come clean to the police about it. He turned himself in and asked them to lock him up and get him some psychiatric help."

My jaw dropped all the way to the floor. "What?" I squeaked. "That's *crazy!*"

"Yeah," Parker agrees, hitting me with an intense gaze. "I can't imagine what *compelled* him to do such a thing."

Oh! Oh, my! *Parker compelled Xavier to turn himself in?* The look he's giving me makes me certain he did it for me. Now I'm sorry I didn't kiss the man after dinner. I definitely want to do it now. I want to fling my arms around him, hug him tight, and thank him a million times over. I can't do this in front of Elijah, of course, but my eyes do gloss over with a layer of moisture. Parker sees me struggling with my emotions, and his face softens a little. Neither of us gets to say anything, because Elijah curses. "Xavier went to *jail?*" he asks Parker.

Parker nods, narrowing his eyes at the guy who is a total stranger to him. "Yeah. I watched him get hauled off in the back of the police car. And considering all the pictures and videos he handed over to the police of him doing unspeakable things to unwilling girls, I don't think he's coming home anytime soon."

Elijah huffs out a frustrated breath and rubs his hand over his face before raking it through his hair. He's too fidgety all of a sudden. He looks at me, then glances at Nick still laughing with his friends. After a moment, he sighs and forces a smile at me. "If you'll excuse me, Nora, I need to go talk to my brothers for a minute."

"Of course!" Go tell your brothers you have to let Nick into your whacked out circle.

Once Elijah is gone, I immediately throw myself at Parker. Rare tears leak from the corners of my eyes. "Thank you," I whisper, my voice raw with emotion. "I can't believe you did that."

His arms come around me, and for a moment he holds me tight. I can hear his thoughts, I know how much he's been longing for this, how much he likes it, and how much hope it's giving him, but I can't make myself let go. "I'm a good man, Nora. I couldn't let that creep keep hurting women the way he tried to hurt you."

"I've wished I had a way to turn him in for so long," I whisper, shaking my head while it's still buried in the crook of Parker's neck. "You don't understand how much this means to me. Seriously, thank you, Parker."

"You're welcome." Parker squeezes me even tighter and then lets me go, stepping back. "So...are you starting to believe me that we're not all bad?"

I'm not sure if he means men or vampires, but either way, after what he's just done when he didn't have to and wasn't asked to, I have to nod my head. "I guess some of you might be decent."

Parker smiles, but it's sad. "I'll have you know that I never chose this life." So it's vampires we're talking about, then. "I make the best of it now, but I never asked for it. It's not what I wanted. You, on the other hand..." His face changes to that same intense look he's given me a number of times, and he steps close, *really* close. I'm surprised that I don't back away from him. "I want you, Nora." He swallows and lifts his hand to my face. He drops it before touching me, though. "But I can't," he whispers. "Henry would kill me."

I gulp. "Do you mean that literally?"

"Possibly." He grimaces. "Nora, Henry has completely fallen for you. I've never seen him so besotted with anyone. As much as I want you for myself, and I understand why you chose to leave, I feel obligated to tell you that he's heartbroken by your rejection."

I feel no sympathy for the bastard. "He'll get over it the longer he stays away from me. At least, that's how it usually works."

"What?"

Parker's brows shoot up so high in surprise that I blush. I should have explained this to him sooner. "People are...drawn to me." When he gives me a look, I cringe. "Yes, humans and underworlders alike. You too, probably." He opens his mouth to ask questions, but I shake my head and cut him off. "I can't explain it. It's like all my other powers. I don't know where it came from or how it works, and I have no control over it. I just know it happens. It's why I've had so many problems with men my entire life. I was with Cecile earlier, and she said I'm definitely not a succubus, but I must have *something* in me that gives me this allure." I meet his eyes and give him a pleading look. "But until I learn how to stop it, I can't trust anyone with my heart. I can't trust that their feelings are sincere."

"Nora, I swear I—"

I hold up a hand. "You can't know that for sure. And besides, even if you could, or even if you don't care, I can't trust you not to get too...enthusiastic. People become obsessed, Parker. They can't help themselves. They get to a point where they *can't* take no for an answer. If I encourage you...you'll end up just the same way."

"I would never—"

"You can't promise that."

He shuts his mouth, brows pulled low over his eyes, as if he's trying to figure out how to argue. Before he finds that nonexistent solution, Elijah comes back, with all of his buddies and Nick trailing behind him. Nick moves to my side and slides an arm around my waist. It's a claiming gesture. I have to remind myself we're in character, because Parker had temporarily pulled me back to my real self.

"Hey, babe, I have some good news." I frown at him quizzically, and he nods to Elijah and his buddies. "I'm in."

"What?" I turn my frown on Elijah. "But I thought you said all the spots were full."

Elijah grimaces. "Xavier was supposed to be our final spot. Obviously he's not going to work out, so my brothers and I have decided Nick will make a good final addition."

"Yay!" I clap my hands together, ignoring Parker's secret smirk at Bubbly Nora. "Oh, Nicky," I whine, "I'm so happy for you! I *knew* you could get in!"

Nick grins. "Thanks, baby. It's all thanks to you, of course."

Elijah clears his throat to gain my attention. "As we've explained to Nick, to become a member, every man must have an underworlder officially sponsor him."

I almost snort. *Sponsor him. Sure. You mean forfeit our life force.* Still, I nod like a crazy bobble head. "Oh, sure! Of course I'll sponsor him!" I turn my pouty smile on Nick. "Whatever you need from me, baby. You know that."

Nick looks at me, face solemn. "Actually, there is one thing I need from you right now." He grabs my hand as if he's about to ask me a big favor and sends me a thought. *He wants some of your blood. You don't have to do this.*

Nick looks to Elijah to let him explain. Elijah gives me a very smarmy smile. "Our brotherhood is about trust, loyalty, and becoming one to reach a higher existence. That means we share things. We pool our talents and resources."

"This includes our underworld sponsors," Hooptie Guy adds.

Elijah nods. "In order to prove his loyalty and earn the final spot in our house, Nick must allow you to share some of your blood with us, and you must agree to it as well."

I know Nick told me they wanted some blood, but I can't help feeling surprised. They're not vampires. What do they all want with my blood? Nick reads the question in my eyes. Even the smallest swallow of underworlder blood gives a human temporary powers. It will also prove to them that you are, in fact, an underworlder. He sees my sudden panic, and he adds, Don't worry. I'm fairly certain that you have underworlder blood in you. It should work. And if it doesn't, tell them you've been cursed by your people and had your power repressed. Tell them you're cast out of faerie and that's the real reason you hang out with humans. If they don't accept us, I think Parker will stand in for you. But you don't have to do this. You can tell them the lie now and say it won't work. I'll pretend not to know and ask Parker to be my sponsor instead.

"Seriously?" I say, because it's been too long since Elijah spoke and I'm beginning to look suspicious. "You are aware that sharing blood is considered one of the most sacred, intimate acts in the underworld, right?"

Nick and Parker both shoot me secret smiles, proud of my quick lie. They underestimate me. Thinking on my feet is a skill I had to develop years ago to keep myself safe. I'm kind of a pro at it now.

Elijah takes my hand and speaks in a low, soft voice. "I know, Nora, and I am sorry to be so bold as to ask it, but don't you see? To earn our trust, there must be a sacrifice made." *Yeah, a sacrifice that includes my life...* "You do want Nick to become one of us, don't you?"

If I act too eager, they'll be suspicious. Elijah is still holding my hand, and so I know that he needs this. He needs to taste my blood to know that I am who I say I am and that he can trust Nick. He likes Nick, but he's still not quite certain he can trust us. I can see that having Parker give his blood won't work. Elijah is already being drawn to me. My blood is the only thing that will convince him to let Nick in.

"All right," I say. "I'll give you blood. But just you for now." I glance at his brothers. There is no way I'm letting all of them drink from me. When Elijah frowns and shakes his head, I shake mine as well. "I'm sorry, but trust has to be earned both ways. I've spent time with you tonight. I'm comfortable with you only. I'll give you my blood, and if that's enough to get Nicky in, then I'll be willing to share myself fully as Nicky's sponsor."

Just as I'd hoped, my singling Elijah out plucks at his pride and puffs up his ego. He's flattered and excited that he'll have something that none of his brothers have. For all his talk about sharing everything and becoming one, he relishes being their leader. "Okay," he agrees. "That's fair enough. Just me tonight. You can share with the others after Nick is officially initiated."

"Okay," I say. "I can agree to that. Thank you for taking my feelings into consideration."

"Of course. You are Nick's girlfriend, after all, not just his sponsor. We wouldn't want to make either of you uncomfortable," he purrs. "Shall we go someplace a little more private?"

"There's no one out front anymore," Nick says, looking out the curtain. "It's chilly, so everyone has come inside. We'll have privacy out there."

And we can make a swift getaway, if we need to. Smart thinking, Nick.

Elijah gestures with a hand for me to lead the way. Nick slips his arm back around my waist and escorts me outside. I love how he always makes sure not to touch my skin unless he wants me to hear him. Mind reading wouldn't be so bad if everyone were as conscious of my ability as he is.

Unfortunately, not everyone pays as much attention as Nick. As we head down the front steps and to the corner of the yard near a large tree, where we'll have cover from the house and the street, Parker grabs my hand. I'm flooded with his angry, afraid, and jealous thoughts as he says, "Nora, you don't have to do this. Those jerks shouldn't be asking you for this."

It's hard to feel his concern for me when his thoughts of thirst, lust, and his desire to share blood with me, to form a bond, are shouting at me. I rip my hand out of his and wince when he jerks back, offended. "Sorry. I can hear your thoughts when you touch me like that."

Parker grimaces. He knows exactly what I think is unpleasant at the moment. "I'm sorry. They're just thoughts. I would never act on them."

"I know, but I don't need to hear them."

"Sorry. But still. You shouldn't do this. If they just need underworlder blood, I'll give them mine. I'll be Gorgeous's sponsor."

I'm not surprised by the offer, but I do know it won't work. Having heard Elijah's thoughts inside, I know he's already starting to fixate on me. Drinking my blood is only going to make his obsession worse, but it's the only way to get us to the sanctuary and the missing underworlders.

All of Elijah's brothers have followed us outside, and all of them hear Parker's angry comment. Eleven angry faces stare at me, waiting to hear my answer. I give Parker a reassuring smile. "It's fine, Parker. It's only Elijah right now, and if these men are really going to be his brothers, then I don't mind. Are you going to be okay once I bleed?"

Parker sucks in a sharp breath through his nose and his eyes flash with desire, but he nods. He glances around and then lowers his voice. "I'm a very old vampire, Nora; my control is impeccable. Still, because it's you, I fed before coming here tonight just to be safe. I will be fine."

Parker glances at the group of humans staring at us. I can tell he hates that we've just confirmed their suspicions about his underworlder status. I feel a little bad about that, but I also needed the answer to his question. I don't think I'd have been able to cut myself in his presence if I thought he was going to vamp out on me.

"Is her blood really that much more enticing to you?" Elijah asks.

The glare he gets from Parker is 100 percent vampire. His eyes turn red, and his fangs descend. It makes Elijah and his friends all back up.

"You will keep his secret," I say calmly to the group of curious onlookers, "or we will kill you. All of you."

Whoa. I don't know where that threat came from, but I kind of mean it. Not that I'm a murderer, but I suddenly feel this desperate need to protect Parker. I guess that makes him one of my friends now, too, because I would only ever be that loyal and protective of someone I care about.

Elijah must believe I'm serious, too, because he steps over to me with a hand up in surrender and speaks to me like he's trying to calm a raging child. "It's all right, Nora. We would never do something to harm your friend. We do not do things to hurt our brothers or their sponsors." His smile turns rueful. "Besides, we know better than to cross a vampire." He nods when Parker growls softly once more. "Your identity is safe with us. You have my word."

After a moment of tense silence, Elijah turns to me with a smile. "It's time."

When I nod, he takes my hand in his and pulls a butterfly

knife from his pocket. His thoughts are a jumbled mess of excitement. He's addicted to underworlder blood, and he's so eager to try mine. He thinks there's something different about me, something powerful that I'm still keeping a secret. He thinks that's why he's so drawn to me and why Parker finds my blood more enticing.

"Well, get on with it," I rasp, shaking my arm at him.

He looks up at me with heated eyes and refuses to break my gaze as he makes a small but deep cut on my inner forearm over a vein. I wince but am rather proud of myself when I don't cry out because it hurts like a bitch, and pain brings out the sailor in me.

Keeping his eyes locked on mine in what I think is meant to be a sexy look—epic fail there—Elijah brings my bleeding arm to his mouth. At first, he just licks the beads of blood that have bubbled on the surface, but then he gasps and clamps his mouth down on the cut. He pulls a hard suck, and his eyes roll back in his head. He moans in a way that makes me feel dirty—though, that could just be his thoughts making me feel that way.

He's never had blood like mine before. He was right, and it's everything he expected. He doesn't know what's different about me, but mine is the sweetest, most vitalizing blood he's ever had. He can feel the power I'm giving him, and it's exciting him sexually.

Suddenly, the tingling sensation—that intuition that someone plans to harm me—disappears. Elijah no longer plans to allow me to be sacrificed. He has other uses for me now. He wants me to be his girlfriend, or, at least, some kind of sex and blood slave.

He was drawn to me before, but now, after sharing this intimate moment and tasting me, he's completely gone for me. It's more than bloodlust. He wants to claim my body as much as my blood. He's never wanted anything more. He plans to feel Nick out about ending his relationship with me before Tuesday, and he'll do whatever needs to be done if Nick's unwilling. He thinks Nick will go for it, though, because he didn't seem to really care about me, he only wanted my power, and Elijah can offer him a *lot* of power. It should be an easy negotiation. Nowhere in his thoughts does he consider *my* feelings toward himself or Nick. Asshole.

Elijah's thoughts disappear as he's ripped away from me. "Okay, that's enough," Nick says.

He takes his shirt off and wraps it around my bleeding arm before putting his leather jacket over my shoulders. I must be really out of it, because I'm shaking and I want to go home and I don't even care about the fact that Nick is shirtless and totally lives up to his name. Hell, he'd live up to Adonis's name.

"You okay?" he asks. I nod, but the simple action makes me sway, and Nick is forced to catch me. He glares at Elijah.

"You took too much," Parker growls.

He's keeping a lot of distance from me at the moment, and his eyes are burning red again. I must be the Bella to his Edward. That's comforting. Not.

"Sorry." Elijah looks completely drunk. His brothers are holding him up, and he's grinning at me with a wide, goofy smile. "You are incredible, Nora. So strong."

Really? That's strange, considering I'm human. Whatever little underworlder blood I have in me must be *really* kickass. But it's a mystery for another day, because I can hardly keep my eyes open.

"We," Elijah says, pressing a hand to his chest and then waving at his brothers, "the Brotherhood of the Highest Order, would be honored to invite Nick into our circle and have you as his sponsor."

"Super." I can't dial back the sarcasm. My head hurts too much.

Elijah's smile softens. "Go home and get some sleep. You'll feel better soon, and then we'll talk." His eyes shift to Nick. "We'll text you on Tuesday with the location for your initiation. Bring Nora. Once you've completed your initiation, you will be one of us. We'll move you into the house, and you can start to learn our secrets. Power you can only dream of right now will be yours in reality."

"Sounds good," Nick says, shaking Elijah's hand. "Parker, want to help me get her home?"

Parker looks at me, face pinched in pain and shame. "I'd better not."

Nick narrows his eyes at Parker as if he's now thinking the same thing I was a moment ago. What's so special about my blood? It should be normal human blood with maybe a drop of underworlder power in it. It shouldn't be so different that it's testing the control of a vampire as old as Parker, and who recently fed.

Nick turns me to face him and zips up his jacket while searching my eyes. "We need to get you home and in bed. Think you can hold on to me long enough for me to get you there on the bike?"

I'm honestly not sure, but my car is still parked at the club, and I'm not letting anyone besides Nick take me home. "I'm good."

"Okay. Let's get you home."

CHAPTER EIGHTEEN

By the time I wake up, having that psycho Elijah drink my blood feels like nothing but a bad dream. I vaguely remember Nick taking me for a burger before getting me home and putting me in bed, though, for the life of me, I can't remember what we talked about. It had something to do with me needing iron and waiting until Tuesday and having the Agency back us up, but I can't remember specifics.

I also don't feel like waiting.

I get up and shower, then wander into the kitchen. There's a note on the table near my keys, laptop, and phone. "Déjà vu," I mutter as I pick up the paper. The note is written in the same slanted all caps.

WENT INTO THE CLUB EARLY. HAD YOUR CAR BROUGHT HOME. GORGEOUS TOLD ME WHAT HAPPENED. TEXT ME WHEN YOU WAKE UP, AND LET ME KNOW YOU'RE OKAY.

I snort softly to myself. It's like having a dad—one that actually cares. I find it ironic that I didn't gain a real parental figure until years after I aged out of the foster system and went off on my own.

Checking the time on my phone, I'm surprised to find it's

after five p.m. I slept away the entire day. I've also got to still be iron deficient, because I've got a mad craving for a big, juicy bacon cheeseburger.

I rummage through the fridge for a minute, and after not finding what I'm looking for, I decide to venture out to the place I think Nick took me to last night. The one thing I really remembered is that the food had been awesome.

The drive isn't long, and the place isn't crowded. Best combination ever, as I'm still feeling weak. I claim a booth to myself and pull out my laptop. May as well look for a job while I wait for my burger. If we find Shandra and the others tomorrow, then I'm only stuck in Detroit as long as it takes for me to figure out where to go.

I find a job opening at a motorcycle shop in a town called Monroe. It's about an hour south of here on the coast of Lake Erie. Population says 20,000. I click on the job listing. I've always liked the idea of small town living. I've heard most underworlders prefer big cities—more people means it's easier to blend in. There may be a pack of werewolves out there—they prefer small towns with trees around to run in—but they are notorious for sticking to their packs. They wouldn't care about little old me.

I'm about to dial the phone number when my burger comes. The smell hits my nose, and the job is forgotten. The burger is even more delicious than I remembered. It's the best thing I've eaten in a long time. I scarf it down like I haven't eaten in a week, and consider ordering a second one, but decide to go with a chocolate butterscotch brownie with a Detroit signature—ginger ale ice cream. It's so good I'm literally moaning with pleasure when a shadow falls over my booth.

"I was going to say a woman like you shouldn't have to dine alone, but it sounds like you're enjoying yourself," Elijah teases, lust in his eyes. He smirks when I gasp, startled to see him. "Hello, Nora."

My shock of seeing him here overrides any embarrassment I might have felt. "Elijah!" My eyes flick to the man next to him. "Mark. What are you guys doing here?"

Mark would be Mr. Muscles, the infamous hooptie driver, who also seems to be Elijah's right-hand man. I don't like him. He's got a quality about him like Xavier has—the vibe of a twisted pervert. I grind my teeth at seeing them, looming over my booth while I'm all by myself, but I force a smile. "This is a pleasant surprise. I'm sorry Nicky's not here. He'll be sad that he missed you."

Elijah waves me off. "Never mind Nick. We'll see him soon enough. I came to see you." He slides into the booth on my side, and then adds, "You don't mind if we join you, do you?"

And how, exactly, am I supposed to say I do mind when he's already sitting down and blocking me in, no less?

I quickly exit out of my job search and shut my laptop as I scoot all the way to the wall. I want to put as much space between us as possible. "How did you guys know I was here?" I ask as Mark sits down across from Elijah and me.

Elijah's eyes flash with heat. He reaches out to touch my arm, and I flinch back before he can. He drops his hand, frowning, but quickly smiles again. "I have your blood inside me," he says in a low voice, thick with desire. "I used it to track you magically."

My eyes grow big. I let him think it's because I'm impressed. But really it's because I realize there's no escaping him. My psychic intuition isn't kicking in—apparently Elijah doesn't mean me any physical harm—but every instinct I have is screaming at me to get out of here, to call Terrance or Nick and have them come save me. I have my phone in my jeans pocket. I could discreetly call someone, but for some reason I don't.

Something inside me is telling me I should let this play out and see what they want. It could lead to finding the missing underworlders. "Why would you want to find me?" I ask, eyes wide, playing the innocent, unsuspecting underworlder.

"Nora..." His voice turns husky, and he scoots a fraction closer. "I haven't been able to stop thinking about you since the second we met. I know you're with Nick, but I was watching him last night, and, baby, he doesn't care about you the way you think. He's just using you for your power."

I put on my best pout and shake my head, because that's what the script calls for. "No...that can't be...I'm sure you're wrong. Nicky says he loves me."

Elijah gives me a patient, sympathetic smile. "If that were true, would he have been flirting with all the other girls at the party last night? I know you saw him."

Hmm. If Elijah saw me watching Nick, he must have been keeping a closer eye on me than I thought. I shake my head again—going for denial. "No...he's just a really nice guy. He's super sweet to everyone. Maybe he flirts a little, but—"

"He gave his number to three different girls while you were with Elijah," Mark interrupts. "When they asked about you, he said what you don't know won't hurt you."

I'm not sure if that's true, but since we wanted them to think Nick's only using me for my power, it wouldn't surprise me. I make my eyes big again, though I doubt I can conjure up any convincing tears—I'm not a weepy person—so I go for anger instead. "He did *what?*"

Elijah finally reaches for my hand. "Baby, don't get angry," he murmurs. "You guys are just wrong for each other, that's all. He doesn't appreciate you. Not like I will."

I'm surprised when his thoughts are an echo of his words. He really does believe Nick isn't good enough for me, and that he could do better. He really does want me to be his girlfriend.

And once we're bonded, I'll never be able to leave him. I'll be devoted to him.

Wait, what? Bonded? I don't know what that's about, but it doesn't sound good. I know he's a sorcerer, but from the way he sucked my blood last night, I'd bet he has some vampire powers, too. I'm guessing he's got traits from every underworlder he's ever sacrificed. Could he perform a vampire sire bond on me? Or a werewolf mate bond?

"I don't know..." I bite my lip, turn my chin to my lap, and look up at him through my lashes as I squeeze his hand. "You're very handsome, and sweet, and powerful and all, but you're about to be Nick's fraternity brother, and I'm about to be his sponsor. Wouldn't us getting together cause a lot of problems?"

"Not if we initiate Xavier instead of Nick," Elijah says. "We could post his bail."

That's not good. "You're not going to initiate Nick?"

Mark pipes up. "We've already voted on it. Nick's out, and Xavier's in. He's going to get Parker to sponsor him. Xavier and a few of the other guys will talk to Parker after sunset." When I frown at him, he shrugs. "The brotherhood is about loyalty more than anything. We don't want a guy who cheats on his girl. If he can't be loyal to the woman he claims to love, we can't expect him to be loyal to the brotherhood."

Oh, shit. Nick was our key to finding the sanctuary. And they're going after Parker tonight. He'll be kidnapped, Nick will never get the text with the sanctuary location, and we'll never find Shandra before tomorrow night. How the hell did our perfect plan fall apart so fast?

Now I have to play along. I have to let Elijah convince me to be his girlfriend. It's the only way. Or maybe not. Would he show his underworlder girlfriend to the sanctuary where he's sacrificing underworlders? Doubtful. Instead, he's probably going to use his dark magic on me to form some kind of bond where I'll turn into his whacked-out love slave/blood whore. *I am so screwed.*

I can't panic. I know that much. And I can't just go along with his plans. That would be too obvious and wouldn't get me to the sanctuary. Maybe if I refuse him. If I put up a fight and he has to kidnap me.

Shit. I so don't want to get kidnapped and magic-roofied.

I should just get out of here.

Before I can make up my mind, my server comes with my check. "I'll take care of that," Elijah says, beaming me a smile that makes my skin crawl. He thinks he's already won, that I'm already his. He must really plan to magically drug me.

"Oh, um, thank you, Elijah, but you don't have to do that."

"Nonsense. Let me buy my new girl dinner."

While he hands the server his card, I gulp. I really need to get the hell out of here. "I don't know, Elijah."

"Baby, it'll be fine. You'll see. I promise you don't want to be with that cheating jerk. I'll take care of you. I'll be truly devoted in a way Nick never was to you. And I'm powerful, baby. You have no idea how powerful I am."

"Yeah, but—"

"Why don't you come back to the house with me?" Elijah suggests when he sees how nervous I am. He takes my hand again and gives it a squeeze. "We can just talk and get to know each other a little. You can talk to the rest of the guys, too. I'm sure they'll all tell you what they saw with Nick last night. I know you don't want to hear it, but I hate the thought of you being with someone who isn't faithful to you."

I want to leave. I know better than to go with him, and to jump into something like this all by myself. I feel bad about Shandra and all, but getting myself kidnapped isn't going to help her. It's time to escape and regroup.

"Gee, Elijah, that's really sweet and all, but I can't just start being with you when I love Nicky. I need to see it with my own eyes or hear it directly from him before I believe it, you know? I don't know you guys very well. I can't just take your word for it. Not that I don't believe you, but I owe it to Nicky to at least talk to him first."

Elijah sighs as the server returns with his credit card. He looks at me again, long and hard, after he signs the slip. "He doesn't deserve you, Nora."

I shrug, not knowing what to say to that.

Elijah taps his fingers on the table as he devises a plan. I want to hear his thoughts, but not enough to touch him. I wouldn't be able to explain my sudden need to hold his hand anyway.

I know the second he changes his plans, because that tingling feeling creeps up my neck and the dread settles in my stomach. It's not extreme, so he doesn't plan to kill me, but he's definitely planning to bring some kind of physical harm to me. I'm definitely getting drugged and kidnapped.

"All right, baby," he says, taking my hand again and rubbing his thumb over the back of it. I let him so I can get a read on his thoughts. "I can see you need some time. Go talk to Nick. If he isn't honest with you, then bring him to me. I can cast a spell that will keep him from lying. I can get the truth from him for you. But promise me that you'll come to me when you learn what kind of guy he is. Promise me you'll give me a shot."

I'm not even listening to what he's saying, because I'm watching his plan unfold in his thoughts. He needs me alone before he can use his magic dust. He can't risk witnesses. He plans to follow me to my car when I leave, and then he'll drive me in my own car, since he caught a ride with Mark and he doesn't want anyone to suspect I am missing or that something's wrong.

He plans to knock me out and take me to the sanctuary,

where he can hold me until he can perform the bonding. There's a chance he might not be strong enough if the bond is against my will, but it will be nothing at all after the ceremony tomorrow night. Elijah wants me badly enough he's willing to keep me locked up for a couple days, if he needs to. Once the bond is formed, he thinks it won't matter. He thinks I'll love him and be devoted, despite the kidnapping.

Though this is what I want, I'm still freaked out, and I definitely don't want to go it alone. I need backup. I know they plan to jump me at my car, so I need to make some calls before I leave. "Okay, I promise I'll call you after I talk to Nicky. But I'm supposed to meet up with some friends soon, so I should really get going."

Elijah kisses the back of my hand before he lets go, then both he and Mark stand up to let me out of the booth. "I'll walk you out," Elijah says to me, with a knowing smile he can't quite hide. "This is Detroit, after all, and a pretty thing like you shouldn't go anywhere alone after sunset."

Since I know it's coming no matter what, I don't try to fight him. He might get suspicious of me if I refuse the seemingly innocent offer. "That's sweet of you," I say, gathering up my laptop into its case. "Give me just a minute to use the restroom first, and then I'll be ready."

"Of course."

He and Mark escort me through the restaurant to the bathrooms and then move to stand beside the door. Elijah holds his hand out to me. "Let me hold that computer for you while you go."

"Sure."

I hand over the laptop case, grateful that my phone is in my pocket and not in the case where Elijah probably thinks it is. I pass off the laptop, hoping I get it back eventually, because I'll feel terrible if I lose Terrance's gift. Then I slip inside the ladies' room into one of the toilet stalls.

My first instinct is to call Nick, but when I try, it's like my finger won't follow directions. I can't hit the button. I don't understand what's going on. I try to call Terrance next, and the same thing happens. It's the same with Oliver and Parker, too. I can't call any of them for help, and the more I try, the more I feel a weight press down in my brain.

It's the heaviness in my head that makes me figure it out. I felt this same feeling the day Henry compelled me to find Nadine. "Shit!" I hiss.

I'm still compelled to do everything I can to find her. Elijah plans to take me to his sanctuary, where Nadine is being held. I know if I go with him, I will find her. The compulsion doesn't seem to realize that if I get kidnapped, it won't matter that I find her; I'll be stuck with her. But it does realize that if I call someone for help, they'll come and get me, and I won't make it to the sanctuary.

Damn it, Henry! The bastard is still causing me a shitstorm of problems. "*Think*, Nora," I whisper to myself. "You need backup. You need them to come get you at the sanctuary, not keep you from getting there."

That's it! If I can't call for help, I can at least leave them a clue, right?

I click on my messenger and look up Oliver's name. He's currently offline, which is perfect. I try to type a message and sigh in relief when the compulsion allows me to do it. If he doesn't get this message right away, he won't come and try to stop me. But I know Oliver doesn't go long without logging in. If he finds it in half an hour, that should be more than enough time for me to find the sanctuary. Then he can call Nick and send in the cavalry.

> PsychoPsychic: Elijah and Hooptie Boy showed up and are kidnapping me. They're taking me to their sanctuary. Track my phone like you did at the college the other day, and come get me. Call Nick and Terrance and tell them to bring lots of backup. I think it's going to get ugly. Don't call me. If they know I have my phone, they'll probably take it.

After sending the message, I silence my phone and hide it down the front of my underwear. Gross, but hopefully effective. There's a chance they'll pat me down after they kidnap me, so the bra may not be safe. Pockets are out, and probably my socks, too. But I doubt Elijah's going to stick his hands in my pants. At least, not before our sick little bonding ritual.

I quickly wash my hands and then head back out of the restroom. Elijah and Mark immediately meet me. Mark blows what looks like cigarette smoke in my face, but it smells tangy and tingles like magic. "What the hell?" I ask, but can't get anything else out before I start to get woozy.

"It's okay, baby. I'll take care of you." Elijah pulls my arm over his shoulder and starts walking me out the front door like I'm his girlfriend who's had one too many drinks.

Outside, he reaches into my pockets, looking for my car key. Score one for me for moving my phone! He lifts my key from my pocket and pushes the button on the fob. He grins at me when my car's headlights flash. "Nice ride."

I want to tell him where he can shove that ride, but I'm afraid he'll take that the wrong way, and he'll end up finding my phone after all.

He gets me to the passenger seat of my car just as everything goes black.

CHAPTER NINETEEN

I **wake up in a cage**, with a raging headache and an upset stomach. The only thing I have the energy to do is roll over and grab the bucket someone was thoughtful enough to leave beside the mattress I'm lying on. I pull it to my face just in time to yack up my entire burger, fries, and brownie sundae. It's not the same experience coming back up as it was going down.

I puke and puke and puke until there is absolutely nothing left in my stomach, and then I roll back onto my mattress with another groan—a much weaker one. I'm sweating and shaking as if I'm coming off the worst withdrawals ever.

"Damn, girl," a weak voice rasps from the cage next to mine. "And I thought I felt like shit."

The lighting in here is dim and my vision's a little blurry, but it's enough to make out that I'm in a large warehouse and a bunch of iron cages are lined along the back wall like a row of jail cells. The girl in the cage next to me is not one I recognize. "Are you Nadine?" I ask, because the smaller woman is not the troll from my vision.

"That vampire bitch? Hell no. I'm Maya. Part of the Huron River werewolf pack out in Flat Rock."

Oops. I give my werewolf neighbor a cringe. "Oh. Sorry. I'm Nora, by the way."

I go to shake her hand through the bars but she holds up her arms, and I realize she's chained at the wrists and ankles to the back wall of her cage.

"The werewolf is calling *me* a bitch?" a silky voice calls from somewhere down the line of cages. "Hello, pot meet kettle. How do you know my name, human?"

She said *human* as if it were a dirty word. "Your bastard clan master compelled me to find you."

Nadine snorts. "Some rescue. Nice job."

"Again, you can blame Henry. His compulsion wouldn't let me call for help when Elijah tried to kidnap me."

Nadine doesn't respond to this, and things go quiet. I turn to Maya again. "Do you know if Shandra's here?"

Maya cocks her head to the side. "The troll? Yeah. She's here."

The werewolf rolls her head to the side to nod at the cage on the other side of her. I squint past her but can only make out a large lump on the floor. "Is she okay?" I ask.

The woman shrugs. "Probably. They're monitoring her, but they've kept her unconscious the entire time. I think they're afraid of her being awake. Not sure her bars can hold her."

Yeah, that's doubtful. I don't think there's much that could stop a raging troll. But then, I'd have thought that about a werewolf and a vampire, too. "How are they keeping you and Nadine in here? Are the cages magic?"

Maya shakes her head and rattles the chains cuffing her wrists. She winces as if the action burns her. That's when I notice the chains are made of silver. "I think the cages are normal," she says, "but I can't do anything with these damn silver shackles on, and as for the vampires, they probably couldn't get through the bars anyway, but they're also starving them."

Nadine scoffs from across the room. "As if wolves are stronger than vampires?"

"Want to go, bitch? When we get out of these cages, I'll take you on, no problem."

"Them?" I ask, trying to keep the squabbling to a minimum. Several other captives are groaning and telling the two of them to shut up. My guess is this is not their first verbal sparring match. "How many vampires do they have?"

"Two. They brought the guy in last night just after you got here."

My stomach drops. "Parker?" When I get no response, I yell again. "Parker!"

"Relax, human," Nadine says, hearing the panic in my voice. "He's all right. He just hasn't woken up from the drugs yet. How do you know Parker?"

I want to spout off some snotty response and surprise myself when I say, "He's a friend of mine. We were working together to find you. But again, Henry's compulsion wouldn't let me call him last night, so I couldn't warn him they were coming for him."

"Compulsion isn't perfect," Nadine whispers more to herself than me. My guess is she cares a great deal for Parker. That's going to endear me to her when Parker wakes up acting all scared for me.

My rage boils up in me at her words, though, and I snap at her. "Well, maybe you bloodsucking assholes shouldn't use it on people. I would have helped Parker if he'd just asked. I was going to. I was already helping Terrance. I didn't need to be compelled. Henry's just a possessive douche, and now we're all going to die."

I hope that isn't true, but I've obviously been here a while, and my cavalry hasn't shown up yet even though I still have my phone. That's not promising.

"I'm sure he was just doing what he thought he needed to find me. Henry cares about his vampires."

"Oh, I know what Henry cares about." Himself.

"If you don't stop disrespecting my master, I'm going to kill you long before the assholes holding us hostage do."

"Why would Henry need your help, anyway?" a new voice asks. It's gravelly and male, but the guy's disdain for me is just as strong as Nadine's. "You're just a human."

"Um, newsflash, they aren't holding us hostage; they plan to sacrifice you all tonight during the blood moon to steal your life force using dark magic. Henry stole me because I'm not without my own gifts. And I would have gotten you all out if not for Henry's damn compulsion. I was close. I'm not your ordinary human."

"No," a cheerful voice interrupts from the other side of the room. The lights flicker on, and Elijah comes to stand in front of my cage. "You aren't just an ordinary human, are you? Though, I'm a bit disappointed to learn you're only human after all. A summer fae, Nora? Royalty, no less?" He shakes his head, tsking, all the while smirking at me. "Someone's been a naughty little liar."

I laugh darkly. "I'm not the only one who's been naughty, am I? Messing with dark magic, Elijah? Stealing underworlders? I'm pretty sure those are bigger no-nos than my pretending to be a full-blooded underworlder."

"You say that like you aren't full human."

"I'm not, asshole. I have underworlder blood in me. How do you think I fooled you with my blood?"

Elijah walks right up to my cage and grips the bars as he

stares at me with a curious expression. "You *are* full human. Underworlders can tell."

"You couldn't," I say. "You must be a pretty weak underworlder. Mid-level sorcerer, my ass."

Rage sparks in Elijah's eyes. I've hit a sore spot. And the truth. He's not as powerful as he claims. Otherwise he would have known I was human, and he would have definitely figured out Nick Gorgeous isn't.

"I doubted your little story all along," he grumbles. "But there *is* something about you that's different, too."

"It's her blood," Nadine says. "I can smell it from here. It doesn't smell like normal human blood. It's much more enticing."

"Gee thanks, Nadine." I shoot Maya a look. "Now I know why you called her a bitch. No sense of fellow inmate loyalty there, huh?"

"I owe you nothing, human."

"I really hope I survive to tell Henry about how you sold me up a river. He'll probably rip your throat out for it. He's more obsessed with me than Elijah."

Elijah laughs. It's totally sinister. "Soon you'll be as devoted to me as I am to you, Nora."

It's my turn to laugh. Mine is obnoxious, not sinister. "Yeah, sure. I've resisted Henry Stadther, Parker Reed, Nick Gorgeous, and Cecile the succubus. But hey. You must be right. I'm totally going to worship at your feet, since you're so much more tempting than any of them."

Elijah narrows his eyes at me and paces the length of my cage. Finally, he stops and looks directly at me. "Perhaps you're right. Maybe I need to think bigger than a mate bond."

I force myself to my feet. I'm already feeling a lot better since having puked out the rest of my magical roofie. "What do you mean?" I ask slowly, making my way to the front of my cage. I stay out of arm's reach but get close enough to feel like I'm having a real conversation.

"It's risky," Elijah mutters more to himself than me. "But it would definitely work, no matter what powers of resistance you might have."

Okay, that doesn't sound good. "Risky how? Just what kind of bond are we talking about? I don't do the Princess Leia/Jabba the Hut love slave relationship."

Elijah frowns at me. "I don't need magic to get my women, Nora. As you may eventually realize. No, the bond I'm thinking about is much more complex than a love spell. I'll make you my familiar."

The word takes me by surprise. I don't know anything about familiars other than that they are a sort of magical companion to a sorcerer or sorceress. "Aren't those just animals? Like cats?"

Elijah chuckles. "Usually. Though, using dark magic, it can be done with humans as well. It's a special relationship, Nora. We would be bonding our life forces, and in return be sharing power."

Yeah, right. *Sharing?* "You'll give me your power?"

"A fraction of it, yes, and you will share your gifts with me."

"So, you'll have control over me for a *fraction* of your power? Doesn't sound like such a great deal to me."

"I won't have control over you," he insists. "But I'll have your loyalty." He meets my gaze again. "And you would have mine. And my protection as well. I am serious about being devoted to you, Nora. I'll make a good mate. I swear."

I don't need his protection or loyalty. I've got Terrance's. And Oliver's. And I sure as hell don't need a mate—good or otherwise. But I do need to get out of this cage, and my best chances of doing that are, sadly, probably trying to seduce him into thinking I'm going along with his dumb plan. "You really like me?" I ask. I make the question wary, but try to push a little hope into it as well. He's egotistical enough that he'll believe I want him, but not if I come on too strong too fast. "This isn't just about my power?"

Elijah stops pacing, surprised by my question. His face actually softens with genuine affection. "We'll be happy together. You'll see."

"I would be tied to just you?" I ask. "Not the rest of those twelve idiots? Because you mentioned sharing my blood with all of them, and I'm not too crazy about that idea."

As I'd hoped, Elijah's eyes fill with jealousy and possessiveness. "Of course not. I brought Parker here so that I wouldn't have to share you." He sucks in a deep breath and steps right up to my bars. "You're mine, Nora. And I'll kill anyone who touches you. You have my word."

He's getting more and more excited now that I'm not fighting him. He wants this union. He wants me. Badly. This is it. Time to use my feminine wiles on this guy. I've never done it before.

When I purposefully try to lure him in, he leans closer to my cage, as if he's literally being drawn to me. Surprise rocks me. Am I doing this? Is this a power of mine? Like Cecile's?

I grip one of the bars and look at him as if I'm falling under his spell instead of the other way around. I chew on my bottom lip, and his gaze falls to my mouth. His eyes glaze over. "Elijah..." I whisper. "Come closer."

He does. Without question. Holy shit! I'm better at this seductress thing than I thought.

I lick my lips and push out my chest until it presses against the bars. I'm in a T-shirt that doesn't show any cleavage, but I've got enough of a shape that the gesture still catches his attention. He gulps and places his hand around mine on the bar. "You can trust me, Nora."

He really believes this. He believes he wants to protect me and take care of me. And he's certain that once we forge our connection, I'll feel so close to him that I'll want to be with him as much as he wants to be with me.

He reaches through the bar to cup my cheeks in his hands. I place my hand around his wrist and allow him to touch me while I prepare to make my move.

"Nora..." he says softly. "I need you. Say you want to be mine."

I know I'll only get this one chance, so I give it everything I've got. I grip his wrists and yank him forward as hard as I can, smashing his face into the bars of my cage. The hit stuns him but doesn't quiet knock him out, so I reach through the bars and grab him from the back of the head. "I'll never be yours, asshole," I say as I smash his head into the bars three more times, until his eyes finally roll back in his head.

CHAPTER TWENTY

A **long, low whistle** sounds and Maya says, "Nice move," when Elijah drops to the ground in front of my cell, knocked out.

"The keys! Get the keys!" the man on my other side shouts. "Quick, girl! He won't be out long!"

"No shit!" I snap. I'm already on the ground, checking his pockets.

Bingo. I get my cell unlocked and hurry to drag him in. He can probably unlock the bars with a magic spell, but I'm hoping it'll slow him down once he wakes up.

I unlock Maya next and then try to unlock her cuffs. It doesn't work. I need a different key. She gives me a pained smile and nods to the other cells. "Free the others. They can go for help."

I was going to do that anyway, but I'm glad she agrees with me. I go to the man on my other side and unlock his door. The man is probably only four feet tall and looks grumpy. He gives me a solemn gaze. "Thank you, girl. The brownies will not forget this," he says, and then runs out of the room before I can even reply.

“Yeah, thanks for your help with the others!” I yell after him.

“Hurry, girl!”

“Do me!”

“Get my door next!”

Though everyone sounds weak, they all seem to have come alive at the possibility of freedom. I quickly get to all of the cages and find one man also in silver cuffs. “The key is with the chains in the cupboards over there,” he says, pointing across the room. He sounds like he’s taken several beatings, or maybe he’s dying of silver poisoning.

“I’ll get it as soon as I get the others free.”

“Maya first,” he says. It’s noble of him, and I nod as I move onto the next cage.

I know the next person is Nadine by the sharp beauty of her and by the deep scowl on her face. “*Hurry*, human!”

Her eyes are red, and her fangs elongate as I near her cage. I hesitate to unlock the door. “Are you going to attack me if I let you out?”

“Unlock me!” she growls.

I don’t think she’s in control of herself, so I move to the next door. Let Parker help her after I wake him up. Nadine rages when I pass her cage and go to unlock Parker’s instead. I ignore the hissy fit and fall to the ground beside Parker. “Parker?” I pat both of his cheeks, then slap him a little harder when that doesn’t work. “Parker, wake up. I can’t carry you out of here.”

“He needs blood,” Nadine shouts. “They drained him to make him weak. He needs to feed.”

Crap. “This is probably going to bite me in the ass,” I grumble as I drag the key across my wrist to scrape it open. It’s not a knife, but it’s the best I can do, and a small line of red bleeds to the surface.

I hold the scrape beneath Parker’s nose. “Come on, Parker.

Wake up. I'm not leaving here without you." I shake him and hold my arm directly to his lips. "Come on. Your one chance to taste me. The buffet closes in three seconds. One. Two—"

Parker's eyes flash open, and he grabs my arm, locking it to his mouth. I gasp as his teeth pierce my skin, and suddenly a warm sensation fills my whole body. I've never felt anything so good in my life. I want to smash my body against Parker. I want him to touch me. I have too many clothes on, and so does he. I just want to rip them all off and make sweet love to him for hours. I let out a moan. I think I'm starting to see dark spots, but I can't tell because my world is overwhelming right now. I've never been so full of ecstasy before. If I'd known getting bitten by a vampire felt like this, I might have let Henry go for it rather than shoving a barstool through him.

The feeling disappears, and suddenly I'm the one being shaken. "Nora? Nora!"

"Holy shit, Parker. Is it always like that?"

"Damn it, Nora, that was dangerous! If I didn't have the control I have, I could have killed you!"

"I trusted you." I giggle, as if I'm completely drunk. "Now help me. We need to get the werewolves out, Nadine wants to eat me, and I can't lift Shandra by myself."

I blink my way back to reality and look around. A soft groan rings out, and Maya shouts, "Hurry, Nora! He's coming to!"

"Shit!" I grab Parker's wrists and jump to my feet.

The second I do, everything goes sideways. Parker catches me with a curse. "Damn it. You shouldn't have fed me after Elijah took too much from you yesterday."

"Whatever. Let's just get the others."

Parker shakes his head as he scoops me into his arms. "I don't think so. The Agency will come back for them. I'm getting you out of here."

"No way." I struggle to get out of his arms and point to the wolves and Shandra. "I'm not leaving without Shandra! I promised Terrance. Get her out of here while I unlock the wolves."

"Not a chance."

"PARKER!" I push away from his chest hard enough that he drops me to my feet. "I'M NOT LEAVING HER!"

His eyes meet mine, and I shake my head. "*Please*, Parker. Just get her first."

Whether he decides I'd just run right back in here—which I would—or he just wants to get on my good side, Parker nods, then runs to Shandra's cage. I head for the cupboard with the keys to the silver cuffs, and by the time I find the key, Shandra and Parker are gone.

I run to Maya, but before I can get her free, Elijah is there. "You shouldn't have done that, Nora," he says, dragging me backward out of her cell by my ponytail.

I fight with everything I've got to escape his grip, but I'm weak from blood loss and he has some kind of inhuman strength. I toss Maya the keys as I'm dragged from the cell, but they don't quite make it to her. "I'm sorry! But Parker will come back, I promise!"

She shakes her head at me, as if her safety doesn't matter. "Be careful!"

"Nora will be fine," Elijah says as he throws me down onto a large table in the middle of the room. "However, Parker won't be back, because no one can get back in through my wards."

When I notice the shackles attached at both ends of the table, I start to think this is less of a table and more of an altar. My heart stops and then starts beating in overdrive. Adrenaline surges though my body, making me come alive with the need to fight back or flee.

I amp up my struggling when he grabs one of my wrists and locks it to the table. I manage to punch him with my free fist, and he falls backward. "Damn it, Nora! Stop it! You already broke my nose on the cell bars!"

"Good!"

I scratch and claw at my locked hand, and I yank at the cuffs so hard my wrist quickly rubs raw and starts to bleed. But I can't break the lock. I'm stuck.

Elijah grabs my feet next, and though I kick and buck so hard I feel like I might dislocate something, he manages to lock both of my feet to the table.

Fear pulses through my veins. Raw terror seizes my lungs. "Please don't do this," I gasp.

I'm so scared my whole body starts shaking. Tears prick the corners of my eyes. Elijah smiles as he grabs my last free limb. I try to pull away from him, but my adrenaline is starting to leave my body, and I'm just plain not strong enough to fight him.

He smiles down at me with some kind of cracked out affection, and something deep within me responds to it. A feeling starts to bubble up in my gut, and my instincts start battling my fear. Something is telling me that I am stronger than this man.

When he holds a chalice to my wrist and lifts his knife as if he means to bleed me, my instincts take over and I call out his name. The word leaves my lips, sounding musical, and Elijah pauses. His eyes lock in mine and his pupils dilate. Satisfaction swells in my chest at his response. Elijah is my prisoner. Not the other way around. "Release me."

Elijah sets his knife and chalice aside and robotically starts to unlock my chains. He frees one of my wrists and then seems to shake himself from his trance. His eyes flash to mine, burning with anger. "What did you do to me, you little vixen?"

The power inside me is starting to slip away, as if retreating back to its hiding place where it will go back to sleep. I reach desperately for it and tug it back to the surface. "Let me go," I command.

Elijah flinches, as if being punched by my power. His eyes widen, but then he narrows them and grits his teeth. His jaw clenches tight, and he refuses to break my stare. "I don't know what you are," he hisses, "but you are not stronger than me."

The tingling sensation of magic washes over me, and I start to feel sleepy. He's putting me under a spell. I steel my resolve and thrust all that power inside me outward. It crashes against Elijah's magic, and for a moment the two of us are locked in a battle of magical wills.

Our concentration is shattered by a huge boom that sounds like an explosion, but nothing has blown up as far as I can tell. The building shakes, though, and Elijah's eyes go wide. "Impossible," he breathes.

"What?"

He blinks at me. "Someone broke through my wards. They were infused with dark magic." He shakes his head. "No one in Detroit is powerful enough to do that."

A goofy grin spreads across my face, and I start screaming my head off. "Oliver! Oliver! I'm in here! Oliver!"

"Oliver *Harrington?*" Elijah gasps. "But he doesn't use his magic!"

"Guess he does now. Oh, and by the way, I'm sure Nick Gorgeous and Terrance Balfrey are with him."

I'm smirking at the stupid sorcerer who knows he's beaten, so I see the exact moment he snaps. "You little bitch!"

He snatches up his knife and tries to stab me in the heart with it. I'm able to throw him off his target with my free hand but not stop him. The knife plunges into my shoulder instead. I cry out as searing white-hot pain rips through me. My scream is echoed by a mighty roar, and then suddenly Elijah is ripped away from me. There's no time to look away from the gruesome sight that follows when Terrance literally rips Elijah apart from limb to limb.

"Terrance!" I scream as tiny droplets of blood splatter across my body. "T-man, I'm all right! You can stop now!"

Terrance whirls around at the sound of my voice, that all-black gaze looking me over from head to toe. My heart skips a beat at the sight of his rage, but I take a breath and will myself to be calm for him. "I'm okay, Terrance," I say softly. "You saved me. You can calm down now."

It's hard to tell exactly where he's looking with his eyes all black like that, but when they narrow, I know he's honed in on the knife in my shoulder. "Nothing a healer can't take care of," I promise him. "Maybe you could calm down and find one for me?"

Terrance stands there, shaking from head to toe, and sucks in a deep breath through his nose. When he lets it out slowly, his rage settles a bit. His eyes are still black, but at least the trembling has stopped. It's something. "Good," I say. "Now, I know you're still worried about me, and I know you're still very pissed off, but do you think you could step out of the way and let someone heal my shoulder? It hurts pretty bad."

Terrance growls, but stomps off. As soon as he's out of the way, Nick and Oliver swoop in. Nick gets to work breaking me free from my chains, and I do mean that literally. He grabs the restraints around my ankles and my wrist and snaps them apart with his bare hands. I guess I can add super strength to the mystery that is Nick Gorgeous. Not that I'm surprised about that.

"Nora?"

I turn my head at the sound of Oliver's voice and smile brightly. "It was you, wasn't it? Who broke Elijah's wards?"

Oliver's face is pained when he nods. Seeing his distress wracks me with guilt. My smile fades, and I have to swallow a lump in my throat before I can speak. "I'm so sorry you had to use your magic for me."

Oliver pinches his eyes shut and releases a sharp breath. He shakes his head. "Nora, I'm so sorry. I—"

"Move," Terrance snaps, pushing Oliver out of the way and shoving Enzo in his place. *"Fix her."*

Enzo bows as if he gets manhandled and ordered around on a regular basis, so I frown at Terrance on his behalf. "Be nice, you big grump. I'm fine now, and I'm safe, so calm down and stop being rude to people."

Terrance growls at me.

"Careful, Nora," Nick warns. "He may be responding now, but he's still very volatile. He might not hurt you if he snaps, but the rest of us aren't safe from him."

"Sorry." I look at Terrance again and force a smile. "Hey, T-man. I promise I'm okay. These guys are just trying to help. Take it easy on them, okay? Please? For me?"

Terrance huffs and crosses his arms over his chest, unwilling to calm down while there's still a knife in my shoulder. Seeing that we're at a standstill, Enzo moves his hands very slowly toward the hilt of the knife. "Nora, be very still," he says. "I'm going to take the knife out now, and I don't want to cause more damage than is already done. I'm afraid it's going to hurt."

"Okay." I'm trying to look and sound brave, but it's bullshit. I'm terrified. It hurt like hell going in, and I don't want to feel that pain again.

"Hang on," Nick says, stopping Enzo as he reaches for the handle of the knife. His eyes meet mine. "You should send your troll outside before he does this, because Terrance will lose his shit again if you start screaming."

I roll my eyes. "Or, you could not be a douche and ask him yourself. He's not *my* troll."

Enzo bites his cheek as if trying not to smile, and Nick smirks. "Actually, he is *your* troll. And you're *his* human. He's claimed you as his, and you're the only one he'll listen to right now, so *you* have to send him away."

My eyes bulge. "He *what?*" I shout so forcefully pain shoots through my shoulder. "You mean like a *mate?*"

Nick smirks again.

Terrance huffs again. "Not mate. Clan."

Terrance seems to be limited in his speech ability right now, so I look to Nick for further explanation. "When you triggered his troll's instincts," he says, "that was his way of claiming you as his own. Him taking you into his home confirmed it. You are his clan."

Whoa. That sounds serious. I glance at Terrance. "We're going to talk about this as soon as you're not ready to kill someone." When he gives me a curt nod, I manage a smile. "Nick's right. You should probably wait outside for a few minutes while Enzo heals me."

He clenches his teeth and glares at me, but I don't back down. "I need Enzo to heal me, and it's not going to be pleasant. You're still worked up. You don't want to hurt Enzo for helping me do you, big guy?"

His teeth grind, so I play the only other card I can think of that might work—I give him someone else to think about. "Why don't you go check on Shandra, and I'll come find you in a few minutes?"

He narrows his eyes and waits a moment just to be stubborn but finally grunts and walks off. Man, my troll is one adorable big lug.

CHAPTER
TWENTY-ONE

Removing **the knife from** my shoulder hurts like a bitch, but I manage to lock my jaw and not scream. Terrance left, but he has excellent hearing and I don't want to risk setting him off again. "Damn, Spitfire," Nick says after the deed is done, and I'm left pale-faced and panting. "You're one tough little woman."

"Years of practice," I say, letting out a breath of relief as the pain in my shoulder is replaced with a pleasant tingling sensation. My entire body relaxes, and I grin at Enzo. "You're my favorite underworlder. Have I told you that?"

Warmth spreads through my shoulder and through Enzo's cheeks as he works. "Thank you, miss."

"You can call me Nora, you know. No more of this *miss* stuff, okay?"

His eyes flicker up to me but quickly drop to my arm again, and he ducks his head once in a nod. "If you'd like." He lets go, and I roll my shoulder. It's a little stiff, but otherwise good as new. Seriously, he's the best.

"Is there anything else, Miss Nora?"

I do a quick internal assessment. "Nothing that a few days'

rest won't fix," I say. I'm stiff and sore from fighting Elijah, and a little queasy from the magic-laced drugs Elijah pumped into me, but other than that, I came out of the ordeal relatively unscathed. "Unless you can do something about extreme blood loss from being a vamp's dinner."

I'm joking, but Enzo's face falls. He shakes his head. "I'm sorry. I wish I could, but that's out of my realm of healing abilities."

"I know. I was only teasing. Sorry." I give his shoulder an awkward pat, feeling bad for my tactless joke. "Thank you for fixing my shoulder. You're seriously the best."

This time, he lets himself grin. "Thank you, Nora." He bows his head slightly. "If you'll excuse me now, I must attend to the others."

"Oh, of course. Go do your thing, rock star."

Enzo walks away from me toward Maya and her werewolf friend, shaking his head and chuckling.

"You're the only person in the world who dares tease him. I think he likes it," Terrance says, joining me again. Thankfully, he seems to be back to his normal self now.

Nobody's ready for me to leave yet, and I'm too weak from blood loss to get up, so I'm still sitting on the table/sacrificial altar. I have to look way up to see Terrance's face, he's so tall. That shiny head and face full of piercings should be frightening, but it's so comforting I reach out and hug the massive troll. Terrance hugs me back and quickly lets me go, knowing I'm not big on touch.

"Why don't people ever tease him?" I ask. "He seems like a sweet guy."

Terrance glances toward the healer. "Respect, mostly. Shamans are revered in the underworld, especially the ones with strong healing abilities."

"Oh. Crap. I hope I didn't insult him."

"No. Like I said, I think he likes it. Enzo isn't a typical shaman. He's not so stuffy. He prefers working for the Agency to sitting around in a temple all day. I think he would rather people treat him as a normal person, but he can't quite shake the title."

I watch Enzo heal Maya. The woman who was all sarcasm and spunk with me is being very demure with Enzo. "Huh." I pull my attention back to Terrance. His face and hands are clean now, but the red stains on his shirt remind me I had a question for him. "So...Elijah's dead, but what about the rest of his brotherhood?"

Terrance grimaces and lets out a sigh. "When Oliver called, I sort of lost it. He was wise to wait until he knew your location, or I may have rampaged through the entire city. The Agency kept me contained for the most part, but while we were trying to figure out how to get past the dark magic surrounding this place, three people exited the warehouse headed for that hideous yellow car. No one could hold me back from actual targets. To be honest, I'm not sure they wanted to hold me back."

He's not saying it, but I know he killed whoever the unlucky bastards were. I wonder if I should feel bad about that, but I just can't seem to muster up any moral conscience over the fact that my kidnappers—who were seriously evil psychotics about to murder a dozen innocent people—are dead. The underworld is a dangerous place with a different set of rules. I'm not sure what it says about me that I seem to fit into this darker new world better than I ever fit into my own, but I'll save that thought for another day. "And the rest?"

Terrance shakes his head. "I came straight here, so they live. The Agency raided their house and have all of them in custody." He frowns. "Their futures look pretty grim. The Agency doesn't take kindly to dark magic or humans who threaten our world.

Some of those guys may end up wishing I'd gotten to them first."

I shiver. Note to self: don't get on the Agency's bad side. Or a troll's. Terrance misinterprets my shudder. "Nora...I know I don't always have control of my temper, but you will *always* be safe with me."

I pat his big shoulder. "I know, T-man."

This conversation reminds me that we still have something to talk about. "So what's this claiming business Nick mentioned?"

Terrance sighs. "It's not what you're thinking. I have accepted you. I've taken you in as clan."

When I wait for more, he shrugs awkwardly. "Trolls can't control who they claim—as clan or as mates. When our protective instincts kick in, the way mine have with you, it's for life. My instincts have forced me to claim you as my clan. I will always consider you mine to protect and care for; however, *you* don't have to accept me." He glances away and rubs the back of his flaming neck, as if nervous that I'll refuse him.

"What does it mean?" I ask. "To be clan?"

He pierces me with a sure gaze. "Family." Something warm lances my heart. I've never had real family before. "You are mine now," Terrance says. "Here in Detroit, I have my own territory. It makes me head of my own clan. I've been alone for a long time. You're the first I've taken in. You are my first family. You have my support and protection for life." He swallows. "But again, you do not have to accept."

My throat closes up. Every foster kid dreams of finding that perfect family where they fit in. We all dream of getting adopted. It never happened for me. And, in fact, because I was such a strange and troubled child, I bounced around to more homes than normal. I gave up on the dream of having a real family a long time ago. Terrance has no idea how much what he's offering means to me. "Terrance..." I choke out the word. "Of course I'll accept. You're my first family, too. I'm honored to be part of your clan."

We hug again and are interrupted by a loud, giddy squeal. I look toward the noise and notice four trolls. Two of them I recognize. Shandra looks groggy and like she might be in need of a puke bucket, but it's good to see her conscious. She's standing with two men who make Terrance look like a runt. They look like a grumpy lot, but I have a feeling that's just how trolls always look. Terrance's sister, however, has a wide smile plastered on her face. The squeal had come from her, and when we make eye contact, she can no longer contain herself. She bounds across the room toward us. The entire place thumps with each of her footsteps. Terrance blocks her before she can tackle me. "Little sister, she is *human*. Do not break her."

The affection in his voice makes me smile, as does Nell's enthusiasm. Once she calms down enough, Terrance steps out of the way and allows her to wrap her arms around me. She's almost as big as Terrance, and her hug engulfs me just as much. "I'm so excited!" she cries, letting me go to grin at me. "We've all wanted Terrance to start his clan for years. Surprising that it's a human, but my brother's never been much of a rule follower."

Terrance and I both snort. "Well, I've definitely found the right family, then," I say, making Terrance unleash his booming laugh.

"Nora, meet my little sister Nell. Nell...this is Trouble. And trust me, she lives up to the name."

My grin only widens at his stern look. I look around the room and shrug. "I won't deny it."

Nell squeaks. "Oh, you guys are just perfect for each other! I'm so glad my big brother isn't alone anymore. Now if we can only find him a mate..."

Terrance sighs, exasperated, but I can't help casting a glance toward Shandra. She and the two other trolls are headed our way. "I thought..."

Nell follows my gaze, and her face falls. "Nope. They didn't bond. Shandra isn't the one."

"It happens right away?" I ask, startled. I'm not much of a fan of the love at first sight theory.

Nell and Terrance both shake their heads. "No," Nell explains, "but if it was going to happen, it would have kicked into place when she went missing. Or, at the very least, when Parker brought her out of the warehouse unconscious. A male troll's instincts for his mate are even stronger than for those in his clan. He was concerned for Shandra, but his instincts didn't take over like they did for you."

I blush and shoot Terrance a look. He understands what I'm asking. "No. You are not my mate. My instincts for you are clan only. I promise."

I huff out a breath of relief that has Nell snorting. "So you're as afraid of commitment as he is?"

I laugh. "Something like that. Told you we're a good fit for each other."

I hold up my fist to Terrance, and he smashes his meaty knuckles against mine just as his friends reach us. Shandra is the first to speak. "I heard you're the one who found me. Thank you for saving my life."

"It was no problem. Happy I could help."

She blinks, seeming stunned by my response. I hold back the urge to sigh. This is the part I hate—the gratitude. The awkwardness of feeling like they owe me something. I'd tell her she doesn't, but if she's anything like Terrance, I know it won't matter.

One of the men clears his throat. He's frowning at me, but I think it's just his normal expression, because he doesn't seem angry when he speaks. "Miss Jacobs, you are in favor with the Mackinac Clan. If there is ever anything we can do to repay you for your service to us and to Shandra, please let us know."

"I will," I agree, because, yeah, this guy definitely won't accept a *not necessary* answer. "But honestly, I've got Terrance now. Seems like a fair trade to me."

Terrance chuckles.

The two male trolls exchange wary looks. "It is...unconventional for a troll to claim a human as clan," the first one says.

The second shakes his head. I can recognize his bewilderment through his permafrown. "It has never been done in the history of trolls."

"But there is no denying that Terrance's instincts have kicked in where you're concerned. He is a good man, and you have proven yourself worthy, so we will honor the claim."

He holds out his hand, which is a third of the size bigger than Terrance's giant one. I place mine in it, and my entire hand fits in his palm, so he covers my hand to shake it instead of gripping it. "Welcome to the family, Miss Jacobs."

"Thanks."

With that, both men bow to Terrance and me and then tell the girls it's time to leave. They need to get Shandra home, the poor, traumatized girl. I don't blame her for wanting to get away from here as quickly as possible. Detroit isn't a city for just anyone. It takes a special kind of psycho—or someone with no other choice—to stay here.

"We should get you home, too," Terrance tells me after they walk away. "You should rest for at least a week."

I'm so weak I can't really stand on my own. Terrance has to hold an arm around my waist. He offers to carry me, but I'm determined to walk out of here on my own two feet. If it were just us, I'd let him, but I don't want to look weak in this room full of underworlders. Thankfully, Terrance understands this and lets me walk even though he's struggling with his instincts to take care of me.

On our way out, Director West stops us. Parker and Nick both follow her over. "Hang on a minute, Nora." She flashes me that small, stern smile that seems forced even though I don't think it is. I think she's just naturally a little prickly. "We still need to get your statement before you go."

I try not to be rude, but I'm starting to get a headache, and I'm tired as hell. "Can it wait? Elijah took too much of my blood the other day, and then I had to feed Parker in order to wake him up and get him out. I'm really feeling the blood loss."

Director West shoots me a startled look. I try to make her feel better by saying, "Come over to Terrance's place after all this is cleaned up, and I'll tell you everything, I swear. I just need to sleep for a while, and maybe eat an entire cow."

Terrance laughs at that. Parker looks green with guilt, and Nick is glaring at me for some reason. I'm not sure what crawled up his ass, but I know there's a lecture he wants to give me about something. That should be fun.

"Talk to Maya," I say, meeting Nick's scowl with a frown before turning back to Director West. "Maya, Nadine, and that other werewolf guy know everything that happened here since I woke up. Maya will tell you. She was in the cell next to mine."

Director West narrows her eyes in thought, then nods once. "Very well." She gives me another curt smile. "Go get some rest, and we will come to visit you soon."

"Thanks."

"Just one thing before you go," Nick says, stepping forward, his glare as severe as ever. "What the hell were you thinking, Nora? We were supposed to be partners on this. You promised if I let you help me, you wouldn't go off on your own. Why the hell didn't you call me?"

I'm surprised that I detect as much hurt as anger in his

voice. It makes it impossible to jump on his case back. My anger has to find a different target. Good thing Henry is standing across the room with Nadine. Two of my least favorite people in the world. "You can blame Henry for that," I tell Nick.

Everyone looks in Henry's direction. And thanks to Henry's super vampire hearing, he hears me say his name and returns my gaze. I glower at him. "It was his compulsion that forced me into this mess. I was just out having a burger when Elijah and Mark tracked me down. Once I learned they wanted to kidnap me and bring me to the sanctuary, I had no choice but to let them. Henry compelled me to do everything I could to find Nadine. Coming to the sanctuary, even kidnapped, would accomplish that. I guess the compulsion didn't know the difference between me finding her and being in a position to rescue her."

In a flash, Henry is standing in front of me, face crumpled with regret. He isn't going to find forgiveness from me anytime soon. I glare at him before ignoring him completely, and turn back to Nick. "I wanted to bolt. I *tried* to call all of you for help, but the compulsion wouldn't let me. Somehow, the magic knew that if I called you guys, you'd come rescue me, stop the kidnapping, and I might not get to the sanctuary to find Shandra. My fingers literally couldn't dial the numbers to call for help. The only thing I could do was leave that message for Oliver, because he wasn't online at the time. I knew he wouldn't get the message right away. I'd have time to go to the sanctuary and find Nadine first before you all could come rescue us."

Henry makes several choking noises throughout my speech, and when I'm done, opens his mouth, trying to find the right words for an apology. I hold up a hand. "Nope. Don't want to hear it. I'm too raging pissed for an apology right now. Just get out of my face before I ask Terrance to hulk out on you."

He looks like he wants to argue, but Terrance's low growl

scares him enough that he snaps his mouth closed, gives me a sad nod, and goes back to Nadine. I turn my attention back to Nick. This time, I do find the will to scowl at him. "I didn't ditch you. We made a deal to work together. First of all, I'm not stupid. Second, I don't break my promises, and third, promise or not, I don't punk out on the people who trust me."

Nick narrows his eyes at me, but then breaks into a smile. "Acceptable explanation, Spitfire. And all things considered, you made a hell of a partner."

I chuckle. "You weren't so bad yourself, Cowboy."

He laughs. It seems playful banter is sort of becoming our thing.

"All right." His gaze shifts to Terrance. "Get her home and in bed."

Terrance puffs out his chest proudly at the order. I get the feeling he likes being in charge of my care. I won't admit it out loud, but I like it, too. "We're going," I say. "I just have to say good-bye to Oliver first." I glance around but don't see him. "Where is he, anyway?"

Everyone's faces fall, making my heart kick up into a panic. "What? What happened? *Where's Oliver?*"

Director West sighs. "Oliver's fine. He's outside."

"Pouting," Nick adds.

"Pouting? Why?"

Nick rolls his eyes. "He's blaming himself for Elijah stabbing you. For not using his magic sooner to get into the warehouse as soon as the location was discovered."

"What? That's ridiculous. He's a hero for breaking the shields on this place at all." I somehow find the energy to stomp outside. "Oliver!"

I find him sitting on the curb in front of the parking lot, looking completely forlorn. "Ollie. Stop it right now. No blaming yourself."

He looks up with pain-filled eyes. "I stood by for three hours, Nora, watching those sorcerers try to break the wards on the sanctuary. *Three* hours. You were hurt because I was too scared to use my magic. He could have killed you."

"Oh, hush." I sit down on the curb beside him and bump my shoulder against his. "I got hurt because of *Elijah*. And because Henry compelled me. Blame them from now on. That's what I'm doing. It's much more satisfying, I promise."

When Oliver still can't manage to nod or smile, I drop the play from my voice. "Why were you too scared to use your magic?"

His face becomes desperate, as if he's pleading with me for understanding and forgiveness. "I knew I was powerful enough to break the wards, but I haven't used my magic in years. I'm not trained. I was afraid I wouldn't be able control my power, just like the night I killed those guys in the park. I was worried I'd blow up the entire building with you inside it. It wasn't until Parker came running out, with Shandra in his arms, unconscious, and said Elijah was still in there but you refused to come out without the werewolves, that I panicked enough to help."

"So you were protecting me," I insist. "You didn't want to use your magic because you didn't want to risk hurting me. There's nothing shameful in that. And then you did break those wards when no one else could. You got everyone inside to help me. Who knows what else Elijah would have done if you hadn't come when you had."

"Yeah, but—"

"Plus, it was you who tracked my phone, wasn't it? After you got my message, you tracked my phone and found the sanctuary, didn't you?"

Oliver flinches in surprise and finally smiles a little. Grinning back, I pull him into a hug. I've hugged more people in the last day than I have my entire life. Oliver squeezes me back and is blushing slightly when I let him go. "You *found* me," I tell him. "Then you broke the wards. You're as much the big damn hero of the day as I am. I couldn't have done it without you."

Some of the stress seems to melt out of him. "Thanks, Nora."

"No. Thank *you* for coming along on this crazy adventure with me. No more moping, okay?"

The light finally returns to his eyes, and he bumps my shoulder the way I'd bumped his. "All done. Promise."

There's my bestie. "Thanks, Ollie. Now let's get me home before I pass out."

Oliver helps me to my feet and puts my arm over his shoulders to help me walk to Terrance's car. Terrance hovers behind us the entire way and actually buckles my seat belt for me like I'm a child. *"Terrance."*

He graces me with one of his ever so eloquent grunts.

Before he can close my door, Director West stops him. "One last thing, Nora."

"Yeah?"

"I know you mentioned planning to leave town after you found Shandra," she begins reluctantly. "Before, I agreed it might be best for you, but now I would advise against it."

"How come? What's changed?"

Director West blinks at me. "What hasn't?"

"Word is already spreading about you," Nick says. "The strange little human girl who saved a dozen underworlders out of the goodness of her heart."

"You're a personal hero to half the underworlders in this city, and a puzzle to all of them," Director West says. "The rumors and curiosity will follow you if you leave town. The underworld will not stay away from you any longer, I'm afraid. Here, we can keep an eye on you, and you have friends to protect you."

Director West and Nick both stare me down, almost daring me to say I'll stay, while neither Terrance or Oliver will meet my gaze. I clear my throat and put as much confidence into my next words as possible. "Then I guess it's a good thing I've decided to stick around."

Both Oliver and Terrance whip their heads up to gape at me. "You have?" Terrance asks.

I shrug. "If you're sure you don't mind a permanent roommate."

Terrance glares at me. "You are *clan*, Nora. I don't just not mind having you; I *want* you to stay."

That's exactly what I need to hear. My smile stretches to reach my eyes. "That's just what I was hoping you'd say. After all, I finally have a real family. I'm going to need you to keep me out of trouble." I wink at Oliver and add, "Especially now that I have my best friend to help me get into more of it."

Also by Jackie May

Nora Jacobs Series

Don't Rush Me

Don't Cheat Me

Don't Bait Me

Don't Tempt Me

Shayne Davies Series

The Devil to Pay

Magic in Those Eyes

Heart and Soul

Just Dare Me

Novellas

My Soul to Keep

Urban Fantasies

ABOUT THE AUTHOR

Jackie May is a husband and wife writing team. Josh and Kelly share a love of things that go bump in the night. Josh brings the horror, Kelly brings the romance, and they both bring the snark. They live in Phoenix, Arizona with their four children and a million gaming consoles.

Jackie May is their only daughter. (And she keeps asking for her cut of the profits since we're using her name).

Sign up for my NEWSLETTER or follow me online for upcoming releases and promotions!